WAL   Walters, A. Meredith.
         Seductive chaos

2014   FRA

Seductive CHAOS

D1526935

ST. MARY PARISH LIBRARY
FRANKLIN, LOUISIANA

Seductive CHAOS

A. MEREDITH WALTERS

All rights reserved. No part of this publication may be reproduced, distributed or transmitted in any form or by any means including photocopying, recording, or other electronic or mechanical methods without express permission from the author.

This is a work of fiction. Names, characters, places, and incidents are either the product of the author's imagination or are used factiously. Any similarities to persons, living or dead, is coincidental and not intended by the author.

Trademarks: This book identifies product names and services known to be trademarks, registered trademarks, or service marks of their respective holders. The author acknowledges the trademarked status and trademark owners of all products referenced in this work of fiction.

Copyright © 2014 by A. Meredith Walters
Cover design © 2013 Sarah Hansen, Okay Creations
Photography © Regina Wamba, Mae I Designs
Editing Services by Tanya Keetch/ The Word Maid
Interior book design by E.M. Tippetts Book Designs

ISBN-13: 978-1499335668
ISBN-10: 1499335660

For Matt.
Because you always knew I could.

Chapter 1
COLE

"**M**MM." the deep throaty moan almost made me chuckle. But that would have been the wrong reaction to have when a girl had her tongue shoved down my throat and my hands were gripping her ass.

This chick was embarrassingly loud and I hadn't even grabbed a boob yet. She was practically riding my thigh, rubbing herself all over me like a cat in heat.

I chanced a peek under lowered lids and couldn't help but snort. She was throwing herself into it; I'd give her that. Her exaggerated hip thrusting would make porn stars stop and pay attention.

I really wished she would shut up. It made hearing what was going on out in the hallway difficult. Because I was waiting anxiously for what I knew was about to happen.

The impending explosion. The nuclear meltdown.

The possibilities of what would go down when the dressing room door flew open had me grinning like a damn fool.

And that was what was turning me on.

The impending shit storm had me really, really excited.

"Oh, yeah!" the girl groaned. I tore my mouth away from hers

1

and glared down at her.

"Can you keep it down?" I suggested, annoyed.

She gave me, what I guessed was meant to be a sexy smile. "Shh," she whispered, putting her finger over my mouth. Was she on something?

Then she was attacking me again.

Damn, she was aggressive.

Her name was Karly. Spelled with a "K." She made sure to point that out after she had shown security her tits to get backstage after my band's show. I wasn't a stranger to randoms doing all sorts of crazy shit to see me.

It was the price you paid for rising fame and notoriety.

And I was Cole Brandt. Lead singer for the buzz worthy up and coming band, Generation Rejects. Even before our name started being thrown around as the next big thing, I had been playing the part of psychotic rock star for years. I partied. I did stupid stuff like run naked down a busy street or start a fistfight with a room full of bikers. I got so drunk I felt it into next week.

My bandmates laughed it off. The fans expected it. The women loved it. I had a reputation to uphold. I gloried in all of the hedonistic bullshit that came with playing rock and roll for a living.

The biggest perk was the women. And there were a lot of them. I wasn't shy about it. I didn't blush and make excuses.

I fucked.

A lot.

I was a slut. I embraced that. I slept with whomever I wanted, whenever I wanted.

My dick spent more time out of my pants then inside them.

So why was Karly (spelled with a K) and her double D chest and an ass I could set a cup on not doing anything for me?

Karly was the type of girl I usually couldn't wait to drop my pants for. She had long blonde hair and a pretty enough face. Though honestly, her looks wasn't what would have grabbed my attention. It was the body. It was curved in all the right places. And it was currently Velcroed to mine.

I knew what she wanted. It was the same thing I usually

wanted. Quick, dirty sex.

And six months ago, I would have instantly taken her up on her blatant offer. I would have had my hands up her skirt before she told me her name.

But that wasn't the purpose of this round of lick and grope. I had no intentions of letting Cole junior anywhere near this girl.

My ears pricked up. There was yelling out in the hallway. My heart started to thud loudly in my chest. My lips moved mechanically against Karly's. She was shoving her tongue so deep into my mouth I could taste the burrito she must have had for dinner.

If I weren't already completely turned off, that would have done it.

"I want to bang you so bad!" she moaned into my mouth. Bang? Really? Who said crap like that?

She reached down between us and cupped my flaccid junk in her palm.

She might as well give up if she thought that would get any sort of reaction. Russell the Love Muscle wasn't interested in her. I wasn't interested in her.

So why was I letting her tongue fuck my face you ask?

Something smashed against the wall outside my dressing room. There was more shouting and I couldn't help but grin.

I heard a familiar voice yelling just beyond the shut door.

And finally, my dick started to rise to attention.

More shouting.

Someone was angry.

And my cock was really happy about that.

Karly was mid-thrust against my leg when the door slammed open, bouncing off the wall behind it.

"What the hell?" a shrill scream echoed around the tiny room and just like that, as if on cue, I developed a full-fledged hard-on in less than two seconds.

I pulled my mouth away from the writhing female in my arms and prepared myself for what awaited me.

And damned if it didn't have me quivering like a virgin on prom night.

My erection strained against my pants and I couldn't help but stare at the beautiful woman standing there, ready to take my head off.

"You asshole!" Vivian Baily yelled, reaching down to pull off her shoe. She quickly chucked it in my direction. I was used to her temper tantrums and had the sense to duck when I saw the four inch spiked heel hurling towards me.

Unfortunately for Karly, she didn't possess the necessary reflexes to avoid it. Vivian's shoe hit her square in the face.

"Ouch!" the girl shrieked, her hands coming up to cover her nose. "I'm bleeding!" she screamed, her words muffled.

Vivian was pissed. I could practically see the wheels spinning in that gorgeous head of hers as she plotted a million and one ways to dispose of my body.

My head on the other hand, was thinking of the million and one ways I could get her clothes off and my cock inside her.

"Baby, I had no idea you'd be here," I excused half-heartedly. It was a lie. I knew Vivian had planned to be here for the show tonight. I knew Maysie had gone to meet her at the airport while the guys and I were setting up for the concert.

I had known exactly where she stood in the audience. I screamed every lyric just for her.

So what the hell was I doing with Karly with a K?

"You fucking asshole!" Vivian yelled again, just in case I hadn't heard her the first time. She ran across the room and slapped me hard across the face, her nails scrapping down my skin.

Her chest was heaving. Her see-through top had slipped down so now I was getting a nice eyeful of creamy, round breasts. Her neck and cheeks were flushed and her strawberry-blonde hair had come down and fanned out wildly around her shoulders.

Jesus, she was hot.

Her green eyes flashed and she slapped me again. I pressed a hand to my stinging cheek and started to feel the telltale signs of my own anger. It fueled my lust to an almost unbearable degree. They were all mixed up. Rage and hate and dick twisting desire.

"Fucking hell, Viv!" I roared, grabbing her wrists as she flailed

4

about.

"Let go of me! I'll rip your nuts off and then shove them down this bitch's throat!" Vivian hollered, yanking her hands free of my grip.

Before I could figure out what she had planned, Vivian launched herself at Karly. I almost felt bad for the poor girl who was still covering her nose from the shoe assault.

Karly screamed and tried to run from the room. Vivian wasn't a small girl. She was taller than average and she worked out. She had the body of a woman who liked to kick ass and take names later.

And unfortunately for Karly, she was about to learn that firsthand.

This was getting out of hand fast. I grabbed Vivian from behind, my arms wrapping around her waist. Her hands were curved into claws as she tried to grab chunks of Karly's hair.

"Calm the fuck down!" I yelled into Vivian's ear, my anger and my need making my lower body throb painfully.

"I'm sick and tired of it, Cole!" Vivian wailed, her hands waving wildly.

My eyes glazed over and she started sounding a lot like the teacher from Charlie Brown.

Blah, blah, blah.

But every time she jerked her hands, her shirt slipped down a little further off her shoulders.

It was official. I saw boobs!

I was like Pavlov's fucking dogs!

A tiny flash of cleavage and my mouth hung open and drool dripped down my chin.

"Are you listening to me?" Vivian asked shrilly.

I nodded, even as I was shaking my head on the inside.

Dude, I could see boobs! Don't judge me.

And Vivian's tits were amazing. I loved them. I worshipped them. I thought about starting a religion around them. People would come from far away to bow before the altar of her awesome breasts.

Nothing made me happier than burying my face between

their curves and motor boating the fuck out of them.

Mmm. Motor boating. . .

Something hard hit me on the side of my head.

"What the hell?" I yelled, leaning down to pick up the black piece of weaponry Vivian had hurled in my direction while keeping a firm grip on her wrist. It was her other freaking shoe!

"I was talking, you dick!" she screeched. I rubbed my temples, feeling a headache coming on.

"I know you were baby. I'm sorry." I tried to placate her. It had always worked in the past. But honestly, I loved when she was mad at me.

She was hot when she was furious and it usually led to the best sex of my life.

Viv shook her head.

"Vivian! What are you doing?" I heard someone call out. I tried to keep Vivian from squirming out of my grasp. But she was strong. Almost stronger than me. And she was filled with a murderous rage. That gave her super human strength. Her nails dug into my arms and I knew that would leave a mark.

Maysie Ardin, the girlfriend of Jordan Levitt, my band's drummer, and Vivian's best friend, came running into the room. She took one look at the chaos around her and knew instantly what was going on.

She gave me a disgusted look, as though this were all my fault (which yeah, it sort of was) and then turned her attention to a cowering Karly, who was in the corner with a look of shock on her face. Some of her makeup had started to smear down her face unattractively. Damn, I was glad things hadn't progressed any further. The chick was a total double bagger.

"Get out of here. Now!" she said harshly, pointing to the door.

Karly grabbed her purse and hurried out like her round, pert ass was on fire.

Vivian elbowed me in the gut and I instantly loosened my grip on her arm. She whirled around and shoved her finger into my chest.

"You are a complete and total jerk! Why do I do bother with you at all? And why can't you keep it in your pants for one freaking night?" Vivian seethed.

I should have corrected her. I should have let her know that I had no intentions of screwing Karly or any other girl. Perhaps I should fill her in on the fact that I hadn't had sex with anyone but her in the last six months. That even when I kissed another girl, it was for one reason only.

To get this crazy, psychotic girl to lose her shit all over me.

Because an angry Vivian was addictive. It was the stuff of every one of my fantasies.

I was fucked up. I was an asshole. I never pretended to be anything else.

But this hot piece of woman wanted me because of it.

"If I kept it in my pants, then you couldn't play with it," I murmured, wrapping her long hair around my hand and pulling her head back.

"I hate you!" Vivian hissed, her eyes heated. She licked her lips and I knew from experience that she was soaking wet.

"No you don't, baby. You just wish you did," I grinned. I slid my other hand up the inside of her thigh, pushing her skirt higher as I felt the edge of her panties.

Vivian's breathing became erratic as I pushed her underwear to the side and teased her with my finger.

"You want this?" I growled.

"No!" Vivian glowered at me. She bit down on her bottom lip as I pushed the tip of my finger inside her, my thumb rubbing lightly against her clit.

"You sure? Because, baby, I can feel how much you want it. You want it so bad, it's dripping down your legs," I whispered, licking the curve of her ear and shoving my finger up inside her perfect warmth.

I thought I had died and gone to heaven. Her silken heat enveloped my finger and I wished it were my dick.

And I knew by her body's reaction and the way Vivian was starting to relax into me, it would be soon enough.

Someone cleared her throat behind us. I didn't pull my hand out from between Vivian's legs, but I did loosen my grip on her hair.

7

I had forgotten Maysie was there.

"Are you serious, Viv? There was another girl in here only thirty seconds ago!"

Maysie wasn't my biggest fan. We had clashed a lot over the last few years. When Jordan had suggested we take Maysie on as our band manager, I hadn't been particularly thrilled with the idea.

Girls on the road were a bad idea. We were going to be practically living out of Garrett's van and having to deal with female shit on top of that seemed like a nightmare.

Plus when Maysie was around, Jordan wasn't focused on the band. He was focused on his chick and making her happy. That didn't seem very rock and roll to me.

We were building an image. We were hardcore dudes with a reputation for awesome music. Having a clingy girlfriend around 24/7 would only cramp our style.

And I hadn't been entirely wrong. With Maysie around, none of us felt like we could fart and burp and jerk off the way we wanted to. We had to eat regular meals and stop at Walmart for tampons.

It drove me freaking nuts. And anytime I had voiced my opinion, Jordan had gone all 'roid rage. There had been a lot of fights. A lot of threats. I walked out of the band more than once.

There were times I thought we were destined for a VH1 Behind the Music special before we had even started.

But then we had started making some cash and could afford to sleep in shitty motels and that gave us all some much needed space. Jordan and Maysie could go do their mushy couple crap and the rest of us wouldn't feel the need to throw up every time Jordan called Maysie sweet cheeks.

Obnoxious nicknames aside, I couldn't completely ignore how it was Maysie who had created our website and maintained our social media. She was the one that started a mailing list and found cheap advertisement for our earlier shows.

And whether I wanted to admit it or not, I was pretty sure her dedication to Jordan and our band helped get us to where we were now.

Which was playing bigger shows with a bigger band to bigger crowds.

The perks were better, the hotels were cleaner, and the women were hotter.

I was on my way to my own debauched version of happily ever after.

And always on the side, just where I needed her to be, was Vivian Baily.

She wasn't my girlfriend. She wasn't even my friend really.

Most days I was convinced we could barely stand each other. She was a whiny, self-involved drama queen. She spent entirely too much time getting ready and freaked out if her hair got messed up.

She was vain and overly emotional. She spent ninety percent of her life angry. At me.

But I couldn't get enough of her.

She was, without a doubt, the best lay I had ever had.

And from me, that's saying something. I was a boy with a super fantastic toy. And that toy was between Vivian's smooth thighs.

I was addicted. I couldn't get enough. Even if we had to do this song and dance to get there in the end, I'd do it. Because the reward was so damn sweet.

And it was only getting worse. I had never given up regular pussy. If I hadn't been able to get it from Vivian, I'd get it somewhere else. I was a connoisseur of the ladies. I liked them in all shapes and sizes. Though a pretty face was mandatory. I had experienced my fair share of beer goggles. No one liked a morning after consisting of showing a fugly bed partner to the door.

Vivian was without a doubt the most gorgeous woman I have ever been with. So I put up with her psychotic tendencies because it was a small price to pay for what I got out of our arrangement.

Insane, swing from the rafters, go all night sex.

And I could have it without being expected to call her the next day. Who wouldn't jump at the chance for such an arrangement?

It's a horny man's dream.

And goody too shoes Maysie Ardin definitely didn't get it. She thought I was using Vivian. She thought I took what I wanted and tossed her aside until I wanted her again.

She didn't see that we were using each other. That Vivian didn't want to stick around anymore than I wanted her to stay.

Vivian got exactly what she wanted when we were together. She was as sex crazed as I was. And if I was the guy she wanted to have stick it to her, then who was I to say no? Just call me a philanthropist. I was doing my part to help out the hot chicks of the world.

And Vivian Baily was one super hot chick.

And I had convinced myself it was due to her extreme contortionist abilities that had me abstaining from sex with anyone but Vivian.

Why settle for a less than adequate substitute when I could hold out for the real thing?

So let's go back to why I allowed Karly with a K to smear her whore red lipstick all over my mouth. Why, if I wanted Vivian, did I kiss and grope another chick when I knew she'd be looking for me?

Did you see Vivian's reaction? She went nuts!

Do you see where I currently have my fingers?

Get the picture?

And now we were going to head back to the hotel and she was going to work all of that anger out on my all too eager body.

It was a messed up pattern. But it worked well for me.

It was exciting. I was aroused. I dug Viv's extreme bursts of rage.

So our drama wasn't really any of Maysie's business.

"Back off, Mays," I warned, feeling my anger spike. And this time it wasn't mixed with anything but annoyance.

Vivian pushed on my chest, causing me to stumble. My finger pulled out of her with an audible pop. I grit my teeth in irritation.

I knew that look on Vivian's face. She was pissed. And not in the good, I'm-so-angry-I'm-going-to-screw-your-brains-out kind of way.

It was more of the I'm-about-to-end-up-with-a-serious-case-of-blue-balls sort of angry.

"Come on, Viv. Let's find Gracie and Riley. We'll go get a drink," Maysie prompted. I could feel the daggers she was glaring my way dig into my back, but I didn't give a crap.

"Vivian. Come on. You know it didn't mean anything. You're here. Let's hang out." And yeah, "hang out" was a euphemism for squeeze my face between her thighs.

I tried to reach for her again. My plans for the night had taken a shitty turn.

Vivian let me grab her and I felt a twinge of relief. Maybe she wasn't that upset. I didn't entirely understand why she was getting so worked up.

It wasn't like we were a couple or anything.

It's not like she didn't know what happened when I was on the road and she wasn't around.

And it's not like she didn't get that when she was here, there was no one else.

I heard Maysie's frustrated sigh and it was seriously messing with my vibe.

"Come on, Viv. Let's go back to the hotel. Let me make it up to you. You know you're the only girl I want to be with tonight," I said softly, kissing the skin on the side of her neck.

I felt her shudder and knew I had her.

I pulled her flush against my front. I wanted her. That had always been enough.

"Vivian, come on," Maysie urged and I pressed myself tighter against Vivian.

"Baby, please. I want to spend time with you," I pleaded, meaning it. I wasn't a complete heartless jerk. I really did want to be with Vivian.

Vivian closed her eyes, her brows furrowing. I didn't like the look on her face. It confused me. I didn't like to be confused. I liked to live my life with minimal thinking.

I slept. I woke up. I ate. I sang. I fucked.

That was my life.

And Vivian provided just enough complication to keep things interesting.

I didn't want anything more than that.

I certainly didn't want to examine why Vivian looked like that.

Or why I felt suddenly panicked.

"Vivian?" I said her name like a question. I ran my hands up and down her back, trying like hell to ignore Maysie's crusty attitude that was funking up the room.

"I'll catch up with you later," Vivian said to Maysie over her shoulder, after what felt like an incredibly long time.

"Vivian," Maysie started and I knew an epic scolding was on its way. If she started on Vivian, I would be forced to intervene. I wouldn't let her make Viv feel bad for spending time with me.

I didn't care if it would cause more tension between Jordan and me. I didn't care if I would be labeled the bad guy. What else was new? But I'd be damned if I'd let Maysie or anybody else make this woman in my arms feel badly about anything.

Where did this sudden protectiveness come from?

Vivian beat me to the punch.

"Just go, Mays. I'll call you later," Vivian said shortly and I could tell she was annoyed. I just didn't know if it was with Maysie or me.

Maysie didn't say anything else. And I didn't give a shit what she thought. I was just happy when I heard the dressing room door slam shut.

Vivian shook her head. "I'm such an idiot."

I turned her around so that we were chest to chest. I leaned down and took her bottom lip between my teeth, sucking it into my mouth and moaned when I heard her sharp intake of breath. She was just tall enough that I didn't have to bend too much to taste her mouth.

Her curves fit against my body perfectly. I loved knowing what this girl felt like inside and out. It made me feel territorial and proprietary.

Vivian Baily was mine.

"Shut up," I told her, biting down on her lip with a bit more strength.

Vivian slithered her fingers up into my hair and gave it a

vicious yank. I winced.

"Don't ever tell me to shut up," she warned, her fingers digging into the back of my skull painfully. Her eyes flashed with a heat I recognized and brought my flagging erection back to life.

"I'll say whatever the hell I want to," I volleyed back, tearing my mouth from hers and attacking the side of her neck. I sucked and licked and bit hard enough to break the skin.

Vivian pulled on my hair again. "Fuck you, Cole!" she seethed.

I lifted my head from the curve of her neck and grinned. My hands hastily pushed up her skirt and I ripped her panties off in one of those macho, romance novel moves. I was pretty proud of myself. I dangled the shredded white lace off the edge of my finger, twirling them in a circle before tossing them onto the floor.

Without preamble I dropped to my knees and spread her legs so I fit between them. I looked up at her from my spot between her thighs.

"I plan to, sweetheart," I promised before helping her use all that rage to make us both very, very happy.

Chapter 2
VIVIAN

I FELL out of the bed.

I hadn't done that since I was six years old. But here I was, sprawled out on the carpet and dazed from being pulled out of a deep sleep.

"Ouch!" I whined, rubbing my elbow where it had collided with the bedside table. I got up on my knees and squinted in the poor lighting. The blackout curtains were drawn over the windows so it was hard to see. Sunlight filtered around the edges and the clock said it was already eleven in the morning.

I braced myself on the edge of the king sized bed and hoisted myself up. It was no wonder I had fallen off. Cole was taking up the entire space. His legs and arms were spread out as he lay like a starfish across the mattress.

The covers had been kicked off at some point between passing out after our marathon sex-capade and falling out of bed. His naked ass was on proud display, his lean back, covered in black tribal ink, demanding that I ogle him.

I ran a hand through my tangled hair and let out a sigh.

I sort of hated myself right now.

I got to my feet and stood on top of a mountain of condom

wrappers. I grimaced as I saw five empty packets littering the floor.

When would I ever learn?

I slowly headed to the bathroom and closed the door quietly behind me, so as to not wake up Cole. Though honestly, a nuclear blast wouldn't wake him up after a night of sex and drinking.

I turned on the bathroom light and tried not to run screaming from my reflection. I looked like a war victim. My long hair, normally a pretty and perfectly styled strawberry-blonde, hung in a gnarled mess down my back. I tried to smooth it out but it would require a deep condition and a good amount of time with the hair straightener.

I tilted my head to the side and gingerly touched the red and purple skin. I looked like one giant hickey!

Upon further inspection I could see several, very obvious bite marks on my boobs and one on my inner thigh.

I turned on the shower and cringed as I stepped inside. I was sore. My muscles ached and my vagina felt as though a tractor-trailer had driven through it.

Marathon sex with Cole Brandt was rough on the body.

And the self-respect.

I lathered the hotel shampoo in my hair and thought about what had happened yesterday.

I had flown into Dallas, Texas from Virginia to see the Generation Rejects show. The venue had been their biggest yet. After almost a year of touring around the country and playing in small bars and nightclubs, they had finally gotten a break.

A huge, change-their-lives-forever break.

Their manager, Jose, who had taken over duties from Maysie six months ago, had gotten them on as an opening act for Primal Terror, an indie rock band with a very radio friendly sound out of Portland, Oregon. Primal Terror had just been signed with a huge label and was on their first official nationwide tour.

Jose had connections. And it was lucky for Cole and the guys that he had seen something in them he liked. Because since he had come on board, their visibility and success had started to skyrocket.

What had once been nothing more than a bar band with sex appeal, was becoming something so much more.

And I was excited to see it.

I loved Generation Rejects. I had been friends with Jordan Levitt, Maysie's fiancé and drummer in the band, since we were freshmen at Rinard College and he was dating his then girlfriend, my former Chi Delta sorority sister, Olivia Peer.

I remembered the first time I heard the Rejects play at Barton's Bar and Grill, the local watering hole in Bakersville, Virginia, where we went to school.

I had been there with Olivia and a few other girls in Chi Delta. I didn't know the other guys in the band. Olivia had said, with quite a bit of disdain if I remembered correctly, that they were townies, aka guys not in college and thus not worth our time.

Whoever they were, they had kicked ass. They didn't play my normal style of music. I was typically the queen of bubblegum pop. And Generation Rejects played music meant to make your eardrums bleed and your brain turn to mush.

But they had stage presence. Their songs were good and the lyrics, when you could understand them, were amazing. I hadn't been able to take my eyes off them.

And that had mostly everything to do with the man in the front. The lead singer, with a voice made of razor blades and liquid sex.

Cole Brandt.

In the early days of our acquaintance, when Jordan and Olivia were still together, our interactions were minimal. A hello here and there when I saw him in Barton's. A beer passed when I had gone with Olivia to Garrett's house after a show.

He had always been with a girl. He was good-looking but he was a townie. And our social circles rarely ever intersected.

I was the happy sorority girl more interested in frat mixers and planning rush events.

Of course I had liked to party as much as the next slightly rebellious college girl. As I went through school I started to develop a bit of a reputation for being a crazy drunk. My wild side became the total antithesis of who I was the rest of the time.

Because somewhere along the way, the prissy pretty girl who liked to match her lip-gloss with her handbag started to become notorious for getting wasted and making scenes. For dancing on top of bars and showing the room her crotch.

I made out with my girlfriends just to turn guys on. I reveled in the attention.

I couldn't help myself. I loved people looking at me. I loved knowing I had the eyes of everyone in the room. It felt good. It felt powerful.

And it spelled disaster when my world crashed into the narcissistic Cole Brandt.

He liked to be the center of attention as well. He led his life as though he were always on stage. He was loud; he was funny; and he made sure everyone around him had a good time. He was utterly enticing.

I was attracted to him instantly.

He was molten hot.

Listening to him sing was something close to a religious experience. He was talented and amazing.

And he knew it.

People loved him.

Particularly women.

And I had been no exception.

We slept together not long after Jordan and Maysie got together. I had gone with Maysie to a party at Garrett's. She had gone off with Jordan. I had proceeded to get drunk. And get loud. And Cole was drunk. And loud.

And we found each other irresistible.

After an evening of flirting and barely veiled innuendos, Cole had pulled me into the pantry off the kitchen and pushed my pants down.

There had been no foreplay. It was me, with my legs wrapped around his waist, my back pressed painfully against a shelf, boxes of crackers and pasta falling around us as he pounded into me.

And when we were finished, Cole had kissed the top of my head, said "Thanks," and went back to the party.

I had been mortified. I wanted to crawl home with my dignity in tatters around me.

I had sworn never to let him touch me again. I had my pride. I wasn't the type of girl a guy fucked and forgot.

I had gone home angry and vowing the worst kind of revenge. And I had gotten it.

During the next Generation Rejects show, I announced to the packed room at Barton's that Cole Brandt was the worst lay I had ever had. I grabbed the mic away from a fuming Cole and told them all that his dick was tiny and he could barely keep it up.

Maysie and her roommate, Riley Walker, had tried to pull me from the stage, but I wouldn't leave. I knew I had pissed him off. He had been clenching his teeth so tightly it surprised me that they didn't break.

But I hadn't cared. This man had humiliated me. He had used me and thrown me away. I didn't take that stuff lying down.

What had resulted was a very loud round of screaming and yelling. Cole had called me a crazy bitch. I had called him a self-centered jackass.

And somehow in the middle of hurling insults, we had ended up in the storage room at the back of the restaurant, our clothes on the floor and going at it for round two.

That had become our routine.

Cole did something douchey. I got pissed off and threw a fit. He got angry at my reaction. We screwed.

And any time we attempted to talk or engage in an interaction not defined by sex he ended up saying something rude and condescending. I would become infuriated and we would be back to where we started.

Naked.

The truth was Cole needed to stop using his mouth for anything other than kissing and singing. They were the only two things he was good at. Talking or, god forbid, trying to have a conversation with him, only got him into trouble.

And I was growing sick and tired of trouble.

But I could never get enough of the kissing.

And that was becoming my biggest problem.

Cole was like a drug that I couldn't stay away from. And no

matter how many times he upset me. No matter how much he made me hate and despise him, the moment he touched me, it became dangerously easy to lose good sense.

My best friends, Maysie, Riley, and Gracie, didn't understand why I put up with Cole. They argued that he was a womanizing ass. He wasn't faithful. He would never even pretend to be.

But I knew better than to expect that.

Not once in all of the times our bodies had been joined intimately did we ever kid ourselves that this was something more.

Cole Brandt was NOT my boyfriend. Hell, he was someone I barely liked on a good day.

There were no delusional thoughts of forever and undying love. I didn't dare expect more from him then what he was currently giving me.

Cole was good for sex and nothing else.

But I was starting to feel the strain of having no strings attached. I was exhausted and tired. And it had nothing to do with the fact that I had less than five hours of sleep.

But this is what I had signed up for. And the thought of not having this, whatever it was, made me sort of panicky. My body craved Cole's.

And I was okay with our friends with benefits scenario. I had to be. Because the alternative wasn't something my demanding vagina would be happy with.

My face was covered with soap when I heard the door to the bathroom open and shut and then the shower curtain moved as Cole got in behind me.

I tilted my face under the warm spray and leaned back as he wrapped his arms around me. He gently kissed between my shoulder blades and ran his nose upwards to the base of my skull.

"I missed you," he murmured into my skin.

Just when I was okay with resigning myself to what we were, to being just fine with the lack of real emotional connection, Cole had to go and do things like that.

He peppered me with soft kisses, hugging me tightly.

"I really love you being here when I wake up. I wish you

could be here every morning." I could feel him smiling against my back and I wanted to bash his head in.

He really needed to shut the hell up.

Emo mushy crap was taking things too far. I didn't need to engage my heart in this already sticky situation.

But this was Cole. He could be this amazing, beautiful person when he wanted to be. In the aftermath of sex he said things that sent me reeling. And I couldn't help but allow my mind to wander to possibilities.

I hated him for it.

"You smell and taste unbelievable. There needs to be an AA program for this. Vivian Anonymous. Sign me up because I can't get enough of touching you." Cole ran his tongue along my wet skin and I couldn't help but moan.

"Stay with me another night. Please," he begged.

I wanted to give in. God, did I want to. When he was like this it was hard to deny him anything. But I couldn't pretend that what we had was something else. That the two of us were ever destined for more than a temporary physical relationship.

If I started thinking like that, I was setting myself up for a hell of a fall. And I wasn't sure I'd survive the impact.

Cole was an egotistical manwhore. That was what I needed to remember right now. If I didn't stay, he'd have someone else ready and willing to take my place.

He may ask me to stay but he'd be just fine if I didn't. Our hearts were not involved here.

I snorted inelegantly. "What would all the groupies say if I was here again tonight? I don't want to cramp your style," I scoffed, leaning my head back on his shoulder.

Cole's hands came up to cup my breasts, kneading and rubbing in a way that made me weak in the knees. He played my body against me each and every time.

"Why do you have to say stuff like that, Viv? You know when you're around, there's no one else. I don't want anyone but you," he admonished, his teeth scraping along the side of my neck, making me shiver, despite the warmth of the shower.

Enough with the syrupy compliments however messed up

they really were. I pulled away, putting some physical distance between us. Cole's hand dropped from my body.

"Say that to the girl last night," I muttered, scrubbing the rest of the soap from my face. I was quickly turned around, my back shoved against the cold tile wall.

Cole's mouth was set into a firm line, his dark brown eyes narrowed. My heart started beating faster. I got such a sick, sadistic joy out of pissing him off. I enjoyed the look of fury that shadowed his face and the way he poured that frustration into making me feel oh so good.

God, what was wrong with me?

I wasn't some sad, little girl with daddy issues. I didn't have an abusive family that made me look for affection wherever I could get it. I wasn't a stereotypical broken woman with no self-respect.

I was raised in a loving home, with two doting parents. I had a good relationship with my older sister and brother. I had been happy and popular in school and had gotten good grades.

There was absolutely nothing in my life that would make it easy to understand how I so willingly entered into this messed up situation. Why I engaged in this dysfunctional tug of war with a man who wasn't remotely interested in committing to me.

There was nothing in my past that would make you understand why I loved every minute of it so damn much.

All I could say is that my inner drama queen was drawn self-destructively to the only person who could give me the excitement I craved. A man who was just as dramatic and headstrong as I was.

"Stop saying shit like that, Vivian! I'm sick of hearing about it! Karly doesn't matter…"

"Her name was Karly? Seriously? Well I suppose I should be impressed you took the time to learn her name at all," I snarked. I couldn't help it. Cole brought out the ugly jealousy, whether I had a right to feel that way or not.

"Dial the bitch knob down a bit. Or I won't do this," he warned, his hand disappearing between my thighs.

My legs buckled instantly and Cole brought his arm around

my waist to support me.

I threw my head back, the orgasm brought on by his skilled fingers hitting me with the force of a freight train.

He made me so angry.

And he made me feel so damn good.

I really hated him.

"YOU'RE late," Maysie remarked as I pulled the chair out from the table and sat down. Her lips were pursed and she was wearing, her best I totally disapprove of everything you are doing expression.

I rolled my eyes. "Yeah, I know."

Riley Walker, who had flown down to visit her boyfriend, Garrett, the lead guitarist for Generation Rejects, raised her eyebrows.

"What's with the cattiness, Mays?" she asked, breaking off a bread roll and dunking it in her soup.

I opened the menu and made a show of reading over the items, purposefully ignoring Maysie's huffiness and Gracie and Riley's confusion.

"She's pissed I spent the night with Cole," I explained blandly.

"He was kissing another girl last night!" Maysie exclaimed. I closed the menu and put it down on the table, folding my hands over it.

Everyone was staying at the Holiday Inn, which was less than a mile from the Granada Theater, where Generation Rejects and Primal Terror had played last night.

The restaurant in the hotel was pretty busy, even for a Sunday afternoon in the middle of February. Though, I noticed none of the guys had made it down from their rooms yet.

They had another show tonight, this one at the House of Blues. I had planned to leave with Gracie before the show to catch our flight back to Dulles Airport in Washington, D.C.

Though Cole had worked really hard at changing my mind during the course of the last couple of hours. I still wasn't sure if staying was a good idea. I never liked to push things with Cole.

Being together in small doses seemed the best idea if we wanted to maintain our sanity and Cole wanted to keep his appendages.

And I wasn't sure I could handle more of Maysie's increasingly verbal displeasure. I loved my best friend. Really, I did. I understood she was looking out for me. That she was worried I'd get hurt.

How could I possibly explain the warped, convoluted insanity of my questionable relationship so I wouldn't look like a total moron?

I didn't think it was possible. So it was best to keep my mouth shut.

The light glinted off Maysie's diamond ring. She rubbed it mindlessly, not realizing she was drawing attention to the gleaming rock on her left hand. That obvious piece of jewelry is why she would never understand what I had with Cole.

She and Jordan were the perfect, enviable couple, even though they began under less than ideal circumstances. Maysie had spent a period of time as the other woman. She had been vilified and ridiculed for breaking Jordan and his ex, Olivia up. I would have thought out of anyone, Maysie would understand twisted and complicated relationships.

But despite their less than savory start, Jordan's love for Maysie was epic. He would never even think of looking at another girl. She was his entire world. His reason for getting up in the morning. And when Jordan proposed at Christmas, no one was in the least bit shocked. It had been inevitable.

I knew she wanted all of her friends to have what she had. Riley had found it with Garrett. That just left Gracie and me. And I wasn't going to get anything resembling a fairytale ending as long as I was spreading my legs for Cole; I sleep with tons of women-Brandt.

Riley, however, didn't seem as concerned as Maysie. She swallowed her mouthful of bread and shook her head.

"Cole's always kissing another girl and Vivian is always screaming at him about it. If she is okay with the situation, no matter how messed up you and I think it is, it's really none of our business. But that doesn't mean we can't dish out a gigantic helping of I told you so, when she wakes up and realizes she's so much better off without him," Riley reasoned in her perfectly succinct, no-nonsense way.

"Can we talk about something else, please?" I pleaded, not wanting to lose my cool with my friends, particularly when they were only looking out for me. But I was already edgy today. Cole and his honey sweet words and pleas for me to stay had really done a number on my head.

A peculiar warmth had started in my chest and it worried me. A lot.

"How's school, Ri?" I asked, looking at the dark haired girl who stared back levelly.

"Just peachy, Viv. Thanks for asking," she replied sardonically. Having effectively shut down my efforts to change the subject, Riley turned back to her food.

I smiled at Gracie who smiled back. She wasn't eating much, which wasn't unusual for her. She barely ate enough to keep a bird alive. She had lost a considerable amount of weight she couldn't afford to lose since being released from rehab last year. No one realized she had a drinking problem until she collapsed and her heart stopped beating. After being released from hospitalization she had started regular addictions and mental health treatment.

She admitted to me a while ago that on top of her addictions issues she had also suffered from Anorexia since she was a little girl. I had always thought her minimal eating habits odd, but yet again I had not realized how serious things were for her. Gracie Cook was very adept at showing the world what she wanted them to see. And even her close friends had no clue as to what was really going on inside her.

She and I had lived together for the last two years. Before that we had lived down the hall from each other at the sorority house. Out of our group of friends, I had liked to think I knew her best. It was a smack in the face to realize you didn't know your friend as well as you thought you did. But I hadn't been completely ignorant. I had known something was up when Gracie had started drinking like a fish and acting like a psychopath. She had gotten it in her head that she was in love with Garrett and had flipped her lid when it came out that Riley had slept with him. I had been extremely worried about her. And rightfully so.

I had spoken to her family, expressing my concerns about her erratic behavior. They had seemed supportive but I wasn't entirely sure whether they had helped or hurt the situation. Gracie had a lot of secrets. Ones that I knew she held close to the chest.

"Did you tell them about your new job?" Gracie prompted and I wanted to hug her. Whereas Riley had left me floundering in the awkward tension, Gracie had galloped in to the rescue.

Maysie perked up and looked at me. "You got a job?" she asked and I scowled at her.

"Yes, I got a job," I said, not bothering to hide my annoyance at her incredulous response.

Okay, so I had been less than successful since graduating from Rinard College over two years ago. I had decided to stay in Bakersville as opposed to returning to Pennsylvania, where my family lived.

Gracie and I had gotten an apartment and I had then gone on to work a string of low paying, mind numbing occupations while I still struggled to figure out what I wanted to do with my life.

I had graduated with a major in Business. But I hated business. I hated numbers. I hated anything and everything to do with sitting behind a desk and click clacking at a computer all day, every day.

I had worked as a teller at a bank for a few months. But again the whole numbers thing had been against me. I had walked out after a lady yelled at me for messing up her deposit. Screw that!

Then I had worked as a dog groomer for a while. But I couldn't handle scrubbing the smell of wet canine off my skin at night.

I had gone on to be employed as a secretary for an overly touchy attorney and a hostess at the local country club. Neither had worked out and I had been job free for almost three months.

My parents graciously covered my expenses and they did so with minimal scolding. Though I knew I was disappointing them. It was a feeling I wasn't overly familiar with. In their eyes I had always been able to do no wrong. I was smart and popular and had an uncanny ability to always get what I wanted.

My siblings had always joked that I was the favorite. And maybe they were right. I had always been treated a little differently just for being awesome.

But as the years passed I found that I could no longer rest on the laurels of my youth. My sister and brother had amazing jobs and now my parents were starting to look at me, wondering what had gone wrong with their perfect little girl.

Because here I was, twenty-four years old, screwing a wannabe rock star with serious commitment issues, and a resume that could only include questionable skills such as beer pong champion and an impressive ability to experience multiple orgasms.

There was more to me than that.

I hadn't expected much when I applied on a whim for an Events Coordinator position at The Claremont Center for the Performing Arts. It seemed like the perfect blend of respectable employment and throwing outrageous parties. It was almost too perfect. I hadn't believed I had a chance in hell at landing it.

So when I was called in for an interview and then a second interview, I had been shocked. And I had almost keeled over when the Assistant Director of Marketing had phoned to offer me the job.

I was due to start on Tuesday. Which is why I had planned to fly back tonight. I wanted Monday to prepare myself for what lay ahead. This was my official launch into adulthood. Sure, I had been hanging out in the deep end for a few years but I had kept one foot firmly in the kiddie pool.

This was my chance to show my parents that I didn't suck. I wanted to feel like I was at least trying to accomplish something with my life.

Yet here I was, planning to stay in Dallas another night, all because my fuck buddy wanted me to.

Way to have your priorities straight, Vivian.

"I didn't mean it like that," Maysie said sheepishly and I tried to rein in my bristling temper.

"So what will you be doing?" Riley asked.

Before I could answer, I noticed a group of so hot it should be illegal men walking into the restaurant. The boys of Generation Rejects had arrived.

Jordan was talking to Riley's boyfriend, Garrett who was his usual grungtastic self. He would be gorgeous if not for that stringy blond hair and no sense of style. But seeing the way Riley's face lit up when she saw him, I knew that his ability to coordinate outfits wasn't even a factor.

Jordan and Garrett bee-lined for our table. I tried not to feel a twinge of jealousy as Garrett leaned down and kissed the top of Riley's head. She smiled; a genuine, full-lipped smile that was so dazzling it took me aback.

They were such an unlikely couple. But now, watching them, and despite how different they were, you could see how much they loved each other. It was times like this, when I was face to face with the fabulousness of my friends' love lives that I felt like I was missing something. Most of the time I was okay with things.

But I was a woman damn it! And I wanted to feel loved and adored as much as the next girl.

I can't get enough. I'm addicted to you.

Cole's words from that morning rang in my ears. When he was sweet and caring it made me think that maybe one day. . .

It was official. I was an idiot.

My eyes flitted over to Cole, who was standing with Mitch at the entryway to the restaurant. Cole was chatting up the cute and overly flirtatious hostess. I recognized the sexy smirk all too well.

The hostess, a pretty little thing with dark red hair and pert little breasts, brushed her fingers over Cole's arm and his grin grew wider. The two walked a few steps away from Mitch and I could see they were engaged in a very private conversation.

I felt my face go hot and my temper start to flare.

Maybe one day my ass!

I hated how easily he made me look like a fool.

I hated that Cole humiliated me without a second thought.

I hated that he made me feel as though I didn't matter, despite all of his protests to the contrary just hours before.

'I'm addicted to you' apparently didn't equate to I won't make you look like the world's biggest moron.

Mitch seemed to get bored with waiting for Cole, so he came over to join our table. He sat down beside Gracie, who blushed strangely. They gave each other a shy smile, their heads bowed in close together.

Normally I would have paid a bit more attention to that. But right now I was trying to control my need for blood.

I caught Maysie looking at me with that mixture of sympathy and frustration that was becoming all too familiar.

I purposefully turned away from my friend and thought about how best to react.

I watched as the hostess wrote something down on a piece of paper and Cole tucked it into his pocket.

I wanted to scream.

I wanted to flip over the table.

I wanted to rip the trampy hostess' hair out.

Then I caught Cole's less than subtle glance my way. Our eyes clashed and I knew instantly that he was more than aware of what he was doing.

He was silently daring me to act.

He wanted me to.

I could almost smell his excitement from here.

The red head hostess touched his arm again, but his attention stayed on me. I knew what he wanted from me. What he expected.

I thought back to the hundreds of times before when I would do exactly what he was waiting for me to do right now.

I looked back to my friends, each of them were staring at me, wondering what I was planning. The guys were less obvious but I knew they too were poised and ready to intervene should it come to that.

When had I become such a joke?

I swallowed thickly and picked up my purse from the floor.

I gave Gracie a thin, fake smile. "Can I have your room key? I think I'll wait up there until it's time for us to catch our flight," I said tightly.

I couldn't help but notice the way everyone around the table sagged in obvious relief. No sideshow today folks.

Gracie handed me the key card and I got to my feet, noticing that Cole was heading my way. I didn't want to talk to him. I didn't want to hear anything he had to say. I was just really, really tired all of a sudden.

I turned on my heel and left the restaurant.

"Viv!"

I kept walking, knowing what would happen if I stopped.

"Vivian! Hold up!" Cole called out.

And for the first time, I didn't wait for him to catch up. I didn't give him the chance to dance his way out of trouble and into my pants.

This time I kept on walking.

Chapter 3
VIVIAN

"**H**OW'S this skirt?" I asked Gracie as I modeled the fifth outfit I had tried on that morning. I was getting ready for my first day at my new job and I was having a near coronary as I tried to figure out what I was going to wear.

Clothing was essential. It could either make or break a first impression. And I was looking for competent yet sassy. But I was having a difficult time finding the right outfit to showcase my personality.

Everything seemed to say trying too hard or gettin' my club on.

"It's a little working the corner don't you think?" Gracie asked, screwing her face up. I pivoted around, looking at my reflection.

"Really? I love this skirt," I complained. I had really hoped this one would work. But Gracie was right. Flashing my hoo-hah when I bent over would not project the professional image I was going for.

I unzipped and slithered out of the confining fabric. I stood in my garters and thong, not embarrassed in the least. Gracie had seen me in less. Modesty was not my thing anyway.

"I wish we were the same size, G. Your blue skirt and white, lace blouse would be perfect," I muttered, rooting through my considerable wardrobe to look for a suitable ensemble.

My phone chirped from where it lay on the dresser. Before I could reach for it, Gracie snatched it up and tapped the screen.

"Ahh!" she shrieked, tossing the phone onto the bed.

I grabbed it, wondering what had elicited such a response from her. I swiped the screen and started laughing. Because staring back at me, was an up close and personal picture of Cole's junk. I'd recognize that vine tattoo and slight bend to the left anywhere.

And I swear to God it was winking at me!

Trying to stop giggling, I quickly deleted it and turned off the phone with a roll of my eyes.

Gracie looked mortified. "I could have gone my whole life without seeing that!" she groaned, making me laugh harder.

"Glad you find my disgust and horror so amusing," she snipped.

I shook my head. What could I say? Disgust and horror went hand in hand with Cole. As well as frustration, irritation, annoyance, knee trembling, palm sweating, dissolving into a pile of pent up sexual frustration…

"Does he do that a lot? Send you pictures of his penis?" Gracie asked primly.

"This is Cole we're talking about here," I said. And she nodded. That was all the explanation she needed.

After I had locked myself into Gracie's room on Sunday, I had spent the next hour ignoring my ringing cell phone. Cole had bombarded me with texts and calls.

I didn't answer right away. I was feeling touchy and upset and I couldn't pin down the exact reason.

Was I mad at Cole? Hell yeah. Though to be fair, he hadn't been doing anything unusual. He had just been behaving in typical Cole Brandt fashion. But that had been the problem.

The typical was getting old.

Because this time, instead of being angrily aroused, I had felt painfully empty.

Gracie had finally returned to the room and being the great

friend that she was, she didn't ask about Cole or mention what had happened after I had left the restaurant. We had gotten our things together and taken a cab to the airport. And then we had flown back to home.

I had spent Monday trying to get my head straight. Maysie had called and said the show was great. She mentioned that several local newspapers and online blogs had covered the concert and the boys had gotten some great press. The indie label they were signed with was already pushing for a bigger album release than they had originally planned given the increase in media attention the Rejects were getting.

Great things were coming. We all knew that.

I was really proud of the boys I had known for years. I was proud of Cole most of all, stupid bastard that he was. I knew how much this meant to him.

So when he called me the next time I had answered. We spent the first ten minutes going through the customary banter

"What the hell is your problem?" Cole had demanded.

"You're my problem, dickhead!" I had responded.

Insults were hurled, frustrations were voiced. And then when our anger had finally abated and when we normally would have run out of things to say to one another and hung up, we actually began to talk.

Cole started telling me about the concert. He began to share with me what it was like to sing up on stage in front of a crowd that wanted to own him. It was as though he were desperate to share this important part of his life with me.

His excitement was infectious. It filled me and spilled over. I was happy for him. And that felt so much better than the anger.

And we had, just like that, fallen into something better than our usual. Because for the first time in the history of our relationship, we were talking to one another. Or Cole was talking and I was listening without wanting to tell him to shut up.

It was disconcerting how easily it happened. And by the end of the phone call I was in a good mood and more than willing to engage in a boisterous round of phone sex.

I should be annoyed with how quickly I was turned around

by Cole. That despite all of my strong resolve, it was no match for a sexy laugh and a great set of pipes.

Why did Cole have to make it so damn easy to forget that I wanted to hate him? Why didn't I have any sort of self-control? Yes, ladies and gentlemen, I was the cutest doormat in Bakersville, Virginia.

Gracie nudged me out of the way and started rummaging through my walk in closet. I loved our apartment. It sat on the bottom floor of an old Victorian house in the heart of historic Bakersville. It had been completely renovated before we had moved in and was open, light, and airy.

My room was painted a soft, pale yellow and had French doors that led out onto a small, stone patio. My large four-poster bed that sat in the middle of the room had been a gift from my parents when I started high school. They had loaded it up with the rest of my bedroom furniture and driven it over four hundred miles from Pennsylvania the weekend Gracie and I had moved in.

My mother helped me to arrange my room and even had a hand in choosing the tastefully framed artwork that adorned the walls.

My parents really were wonderful.

This room screamed Vivian Baily. You only needed to walk through the door to know everything about me. My personality, my passions- they were all there.

I realized looking at my cream comforter and bright orange throw pillows that Cole had not once in the two years we had been sleeping together been to my apartment. He had never spent the night in my bed, wrapped in the blanket I had purchased for myself when Gracie and I had moved in.

I had never shown him the pictures of my family and friends from back home. Hell, I don't think he even knew whether I had siblings.

And again, just like that, and despite Cole's funny yet crude text that had made me laugh, I felt hollow.

"Wear this. You'll look gorgeous," Gracie said, holding out a classic grey pencil skirt and blue silk blouse.

"Wow, I didn't realize I owned something like this," I said, taking the clothes from her.

"They're Maysie's. You borrowed them for the wine tasting we went to last year," Gracie remarked dryly.

"Oh, well that makes sense," I said, quickly changing.

"You really need to do some shopping. Halter tops and hooker shoes won't cut it at The Claremont Center," Gracie advised.

"Maybe we can go after work! Oh, goodie! Retail therapy!" I enthused, clapping my hands together.

Gracie smiled and nodded. "Sounds great!" she said, just as excited by the idea of shopping as I was.

"Thanks again, G," I said with a smile before shooing her out so I could sort out my makeup. It required my total and complete concentration. The perfect blending of foundation and blush was a work of art.

My phone buzzed again and I saw Cole's name flash across the screen. It was eight fifteen on a Monday morning. This had to be a record for him. Normally he'd sleep until the early afternoon.

"Hello," I said as I wiggled into my skirt. I smoothed the material down and looked in the mirror. Gracie was right. It fit me perfectly.

"Did you like it?" he asked immediately.

I smirked, knowing exactly what he was referring to, but I decided to play coy.

"Excuse me?"

"The picture, Viv. I knew you'd enjoy an eyeful of my tackle. What better way to start your day," Cole stated with enough arrogance that it tiptoed between attractive and obnoxious.

"Well, I couldn't really see anything. It was so small," I responded, trying not to laugh.

Cole growled in my ear. "Don't play that game with me, baby girl. Size has never been a problem. I've got more than enough package to keep you happy."

I laughed. "Yeah, me and every other girl out there." I just couldn't help myself. The jealous shrew seemed to be rearing her head already and we had only just started talking.

"Don't start that shit again, Viv," he warned and I knew my

remark had annoyed him.

I could almost hear Cole grinding his teeth.

"Just stating facts," I said.

"Always about the other chicks! Look, I love your possessive shtick. It's hot and all. But not so much when I'm trying to have a little conversation."

Was he serious?

"Well, I sent you a picture of my boys, you need to send me a picture of your boobs," he said, bringing us back to more important topics apparently.

"What?" I asked incredulously.

I could hear Cole sighing. "Your boobs, Vivian. I want a picture of your magnificent tits."

I laughed. I couldn't help it. He was so unbelievable sometimes that it was hard to take him seriously.

"I am not, and I repeat, not texting you a picture of my boobs. So get that thought out of your head right now," I said firmly.

"Aww, come on, baby! I need something to whack off to this morning," he whined.

"I'm sure there's a magazine or two under your pillow as we speak. I'm sure you can find more than enough wank material," I assured him, applying some mascara. It was getting late. I was going to have to leave soon.

"But it's not the same. I know what yours feel like. It makes the fantasy so much more real."

I wasn't sure if I should be flattered or repulsed. I settled on a strange mixture of both.

"Sorry, Cole. I can't help you out. I've got to get to work. I start a new job this morning, so I can't waste time texting you pornographic pictures."

"This is bullshit," Cole muttered.

"Stop being such a baby."

"Stop being such a prude!"

"Fuck you," I lobbed back.

"I would if I were there," he countered.

I found myself laughing again. Sometimes we were just too ludicrous.

"That right there is my favorite sound in the entire world," Cole said suddenly and my giggles subsided immediately.

I cleared my throat. "I have to go, Cole," I said, not liking the tightness in my throat at his careless, throwaway compliment.

"You got a new job?" he asked, surprising me. Cole wasn't one to take much interest in anything that didn't have a direct correlation to him.

"Yeah. I'm pretty excited about it," I answered.

"Tell me about it," he urged, shocking me again.

I was silent for a heartbeat too long.

"You still there?" Cole asked, snapping me out of my dumbfounded stupor.

"What's this about, Cole? Why the sudden interest in what's going on with me?" I asked shortly.

I was met with stunned silence.

"I'm a dick," Cole said suddenly.

Then I was laughing again. Side splitting, snort out my nose laughing.

"Well, I'm not going to argue with that," I told him when I was able to settle down.

"I am interested in what's going on with you, Viv. I know I don't act like I care, but I do. When you left on Sunday, that hurt. I didn't like thinking that you were upset. I wanted to talk to you. Make you feel better," he admitted and I had to sit down on my bed so my legs wouldn't give out from underneath me.

My mind tried to process what he had just said. Me leaving on Sunday had hurt him. I found that so incredibly hard to believe. Yet Cole wasn't one to say things he didn't mean.

I had hurt him. He cared about me.

Those shiny possibilities danced in front of my eyes again. Damn him!

Cole cleared his throat. "Uh, so tell me about your job. Please tell me it involves you in some high heels and a pole." His voice became husky and I had to chuckle, relieved that he had taken some of the edge off the serious turn of our conversation.

"No, Cole. There's no stripping involved," I said. It was amazing how seamlessly we could move from being angry to teasing and comfortable. This had always been the ease of being with Cole. While he didn't profess to be the love poetry and watch The Notebook with you kind of guy, you knew what to expect from him.

Most of the time.

Though the tender comments and personal admissions left me totally unbalanced and I found that I needed this side of Cole that I was familiar with. I didn't have time to think about the other side he was starting to show me in bits and pieces.

"Damn. Because I would have flown back just so I could be your most devoted customer," he quipped.

"Well, I think I'd like more out of my life then to dangle off a pole while guys shoved bills down my G-string."

"Yeah, you're too smart for that shit. Besides the only stripping you'll be doing is for me," Cole announced firmly. And here was that odd subtext again.

"I'm going to be the Events Coordinator at The Claremont Center," I added quickly, brushing off my discomfort.

"That place that has the opera and shit?" Cole asked.

"Yep, that's the place."

"So you'll be an opera singer?" he asked and I could hear the grin in his voice.

"Ha, ha. No, dumbass. People hire the hall out for special events. I'll help coordinate those. As well as charity events and fundraisers." I buttoned up my blouse and did a quick turn in the mirror. I looked good. Professional but classy. I hit the speaker button and set my phone down on my dresser so I could wrap my hair into a bun at the back of my head.

"That sounds awesome, Viv," Cole said sincerely. Was that genuine interest I detected? No, couldn't be.

"Uh, yeah," was all I could say.

"You'll kick ass, Viv. You always do." Since when did Cole designate himself my personal cheerleader?

It was disconcerting to say the least.

"Thanks," I replied shortly.

"I should let you go. I'm sure you've got all of that girlie crap to do. I just wanted to call and hear your voice and to say, I uh, I hope I see you soon. Maybe you could fly out for another show. I could pay for your ticket. It's just better when you're around."

It sounded as though the admission were strangling him.

I leaned my forehead against the mirror and closed my eyes. He made it so easy to forget the ugly stuff he did. He made it so easy to want to be with him for real. For keeps.

"Cole," I began and then I heard something that brought the reality of who he was and who we were to each other crashing into my chest.

"Hurry up, Cole! I need to go to the bathroom!" a female voice whined in the background.

"You asshole," I couldn't stop myself from saying.

"What?" he asked, sounding bewildered.

"It sounds like you need to go and I have to get to work." I tried to control my temper. I needed to. I was tired of giving him the reaction he was looking for.

"It's not what you think, Viv. Don't start being a bitch before you know what's going on," he snarled.

He did not just call me a bitch!

"Look, some of us have commitments to keep. Not that you'd know anything about that!" I spat out.

"Is that what all of this has been about? Commitment? Because we've talked about this, Vivian, you know how I feel about you. About us. But maybe we need to talk about it again. Because I don't like feeling like I'm fucking up all the time," he retorted angrily.

I didn't have time to get into this with him. And I didn't want to. My head couldn't be wrapped up in him when I had to get to work.

"I've got to go," I stated.

"Fine, if that's what you've got to do," Cole shot back.

My mood had done a one-eighty. Cole could make me giddy like a schoolgirl one minute and so unbelievably angry the next. Why did I subject myself to this over and over again?

"Can I call you later?" he asked gruffly.

"Why?" I demanded, slamming my brush down. I didn't have time to do my hair now. Cole was going to make me late on my first day. He had an uncanny ability in screwing everything up royally.

"Because, I don't know, I just want to talk to you. We've got a conference call with the label later. They've been talking about some new opportunities for the band. I'd like to tell you about them, I guess. But if you're too busy being pissed at me, maybe not." No apology for talking to me with another girl in his room. No contrition for playing the slut once again. Just blanket acceptance of what he was and what we were to each other.

"I don't know," was all I could say.

"Well, I hope you answer when I call," Cole said before I could hang up. I didn't say anything, the silence stretching between us.

"I'll let you go then. Good luck today. Not that you'll need it. You'll be amazing," he said softly.

"Thanks. Bye, Cole," I said before I could succumb to his charm.

"Bye, Viv," he said, my name a whisper in my ear.

I quickly disconnected the call.

I gripped my phone in my hand and stared hard at my reflection in the mirror. Why was I so weak? Why had I settled for this, whatever it was?

I stared hard into the eyes of the tired girl looking back at me and knew one thing for sure.

I was stuck.

And I was ready to make a jail break.

THE Claremont Center sat on the edge of town on six acres that spread along the river. At one time it had been a working plantation. The three-hundred acre estate had been broken up and sold off over the years and in 1986, Gregory Claremont, a local textile tycoon and his wife Jillian had bought the decaying manor house and surrounding property and pumped millions into fixing it up.

Jillian had been some sort of Broadway star in the 1970s and a well-known champion of the performing arts. At that time the closest playhouse was an hour and a half away. So with their considerable fortune they had turned the stately home into one of the most illustrious performance halls on the east coast.

I parked my car and started walking toward the front of the building. The lawn was impeccably manicured and the large windows twinkled in the early morning sun. The frost still clung to the grass, making it crunch beneath my feet.

I had tried to shake my early morning conversation with Cole on the drive over. Sitting in traffic listening to angry chick music had gone a long way in soothing my jangled emotions.

I refused to fixate on the thousand meanings to our phone call. I couldn't let myself dissect and tear apart everything he had said to me.

And I sure as hell wouldn't think too long about the girl's voice I had heard in the background. Because if I did, my professional first impression would go right out the window.

I was proud of myself when I was able to simmer down and change the radio station to something more upbeat. By the time I pulled into the parking lot out front of my new place of employment, I was feeling much better.

And now my emotions took a nosedive again. Anger being replaced by plain ole nerves.

I was still in a bit of shock that I had gotten the job. I was totally underqualified but obviously I had made someone think I was competent. I really wish I knew how I had achieved that particular feat. I just hoped this job lasted longer than the others.

I desperately needed to get my act together. I couldn't expect my parents to give me money for the rest of my life. Even if mooching came naturally, I'd still like to have something to show for the four years I spent at college. Believe it or not, I did have some pride.

I walked through the large, oak doors and stood in the middle of the grand foyer, trying to figure out where I was supposed to go. One entire wall was made of glass and overlooked the river. A baby grand piano stood off in the corner. A wide staircase led to the second floor balcony.

A door opened and shut and I turned to see a petite woman with beautifully coiffed grey hair walking toward me. I recognized her from my second interview as Marion Vandy, the Director of Events and Programs for The Claremont Center.

"Vivian! Hello!" she said, holding out her hand for me to shake. Her palm was warm and dry and she gave me a calm and collected smile. She needed to share some of that composure because I was starting to quake in my fantastic pumps.

"Nice to see you! And five minutes early as well! Great start!" she complimented, releasing my hand and gesturing toward the hallway she had come from. I didn't feel the need to explain that I had broken several traffic laws in getting here.

"I like to make a good first impression," I said demurely, hiding my trembling hands behind my back and trying to choke the fluttering butterflies in my stomach.

"Impression is everything," Marion said with a nod, leading me into a spacious office. "Have a seat." She indicated a comfortable looking chair as she took her place behind a massive desk made from dark, shiny wood.

"There's a lot to go over. Normally you'd have at least a week to settle into your position. There's orientation and paperwork. However, some extenuating circumstances are going to change the course of your probationary period."

"Extenuating circumstances?" I asked, not liking the sound of that at all.

Marion gave me a pained smile. "I'm going to be throwing you into the deep end I'm afraid. We are horribly short staffed right now so unfortunately you're going to be getting your hands-on training a lot faster than normal." God, did she have to sound so ominous about it?

Marion folded her hands and leaned back in her chair. "I know from looking over your resume that you have some event planning experience. But I'm sure nothing to this scale." She didn't say it condescendingly. It was just the facts. And the truth. I nodded in agreement.

"I planned most of my sorority's functions and I was involved in event planning at the country club back home in high school. But no, nothing like this. Though I'm a quick learner and I'm more than ready to jump in with both feet," I told her with more confidence than I actually felt. The team player cliché seemed to do the trick.

Marion gave me a smile full of relief.

"I'm so glad to hear that. Our last Event Coordinator left us in a bit of a lurch. She decided running off with her boyfriend to Europe was more important than giving notice at her job. I am pretty easygoing, Vivian. But I don't tolerate unprofessional behavior and lack of courtesy. And most of all I expect respect and consideration," she stated firmly, sizing me up.

I found myself nodding again. "Absolutely. These things are essential. It's important not to burn bridges," I babbled. I was going to be responsible. I was going to be competent. I was going to nail this job if it killed me!

Vivian reached across the great expanse of her desk and patted the top of my hand like a kindly grandmother. "You and I are going to get along just fine." My relief made me sag.

Marion passed me a folder of paperwork to fill out before taking me on a tour of the center.

She showed me the beautiful concert hall decorated in red velvet and dark wood. The acoustics were amazing and I wanted to yell at the top of my lungs to see what it would sound like. But I didn't think prim and proper Marion would approve.

The Opera House was slightly larger and more ostentatious. The marble etchings on the wall were almost overwhelming and standing in the back of the grand room made me wonder what it would be like to attend an event there. To get dressed up and socialize in a setting that didn't involve mosh pits.

The much smaller Wheat Theater was a complete contradiction to the rest of the building. It was almost modern with straight, clean lines and an almost non-descript stage area.

When we were finished with the tour, we returned to the foyer to find a small group of four people waiting.

Marion turned to me and gave me a smile. "I told you that you'd be thrown into the deep end today." She gestured toward the group who were talking amongst themselves. "This is your deep end."

I felt myself go pale. "What do you mean?" I asked, trying not to panic.

"They are from the Kimble Greenhouse Project. They are planning a large gala to benefit their charity. This will be the gala's third year. You will be managing this event."

"Me?" I squeaked, trying to resist the urge to run screaming from the building. The likelihood of crashing and burning became increasingly more likely. I thought I was ready for responsibility and all that other crap but I was beginning to think I was very wrong.

I didn't like pressure. It gave me hives. I preferred the whole, no expectations and you won't get hurt thing. Huh. Maybe Cole and I were more a like than I thought.

Marion patted my back. "I'll go and get the files from the previous years so you can see what was done before. Just talk with them. Find out their ideas, what they want. Take some notes. Then we can sit down and go through everything. I'll help you as much as I can, but given how few of us are here right now, I can't walk you through it the way I normally would. This is your trial by fire, Vivian." Marion inclined her head toward the group.

"Theo Anderson is the public relations chair at KGP. He'll be your point of contact. Now let's head over there so I can introduce you. You'll be fine." I was glad Marion had such faith in my abilities. But then again, she didn't know me yet. Sure, I was no dummy, but I wasn't sure a whole lot of credence could be given to my ability to not fall on my ass.

I plastered a smile on my face. The same smile I wore during each and every rush event. I figured I could imagine that I was getting ready to chat up a bunch of vapid freshmen hoping to get into my sorority. And if that didn't work, I'd just picture them in their underwear.

I quickly learned that picturing one particular person in the group would be a very bad idea.

"Mr. Anderson, I'd like to introduce you to our new Events Coordinator, Vivian Baily," Marion announced, placing a hand on the arm of a very attractive man.

Theo Anderson turned to Marion and blessed her with a smile that was absolutely swoony. He had a mouth full of blinding white teeth. There was no way he achieved that sort of perfection without years of braces and bleaching.

He wore a tailored suit that fit snuggly over broad shoulders. His face smooth and fair and classically handsome. He looked almost boyish with thick brown hair that fell over his forehead and an adorable dimple in his cheek.

He didn't look to be much older than I was and when he turned his eyes to mine, the deep blue twinkled warmly, putting me instantly at ease. I couldn't help but smile stupidly at him.

He held out his hand and I took it without hesitation. "I hear we're going to be spending a lot of time together," he said and I laughed nervously.

"You heard right," I replied quickly. I pulled my hand away hastily and tucked it into the pocket of my skirt. Theo Anderson was really pretty. Almost too pretty. His appeal was obvious. And my interest was instantaneous.

Uh oh.

Theo Anderson turned to the other people in his group and quickly introduced them, though his eyes never left my face.

Marion excused herself a short time later, leaving me to my doom, err, job.

"So, Mr. Anderson, why don't we start with having you tell me what ideas you have for the event. We can brainstorm and narrow down concepts," I suggested, proud of myself for sounding like I knew what the hell I was talking about. I waved the group toward a small table by the open bar and concession area.

"Please, call me Theo. Mr. Anderson makes me feel so old," he quipped and it was on the tip of my tongue to ask him exactly how old he was. And normally I would have. But the personality quirks of every day Vivian Baily wouldn't fly in my new nine to five.

"Okay, Theo," I acquiesced. I sat down with Theo and the rest of his team. A woman, he had introduced as Shelly, opened a file folder and began to hand me printouts and project schemes.

I was trying not to get overwhelmed. But the scope of this event was huge. It was way beyond anything I had ever coordinated before and I was silently cursing Marion and whole "time to throw you in the deep end" pep talk.

After thirty minutes of making illegible notes and shuffling piles of papers as they were shoved my way, my head felt like it was going to explode. Theo Anderson's eyes spent most of the time fixed to my face in a way that both exhilarated me and left me uncomfortable.

"Okay, I think that's enough for today. I'm getting the feeling that you've taken in about all that you can," Theo laughed and I didn't know whether to be insulted or relieved.

His team gave their thanks and left, leaving me alone with Theo. I held up the pile of papers I had been given. "I'll look these over and come up with a project plan and email it to you for approval. If there's anything you need or if you have any questions, don't hesitate to call," I said, wishing he'd hurry up and leave so I could have a few minutes to breathe.

Theo put a heavy hand on my shoulder, surprising me. "Marion had mentioned this was your first day. If I were you I would have run out of here by now," he chuckled and I found myself relaxing.

"I definitely thought about it," I teased. Theo's hand remained on my shoulder, his palm hot through my blouse.

"You're doing great. You have some amazing ideas. I know this gala is in the right hands," he reassured me, squeezing his fingers slightly. I cleared my throat, the awkwardness of his hand on my skin becoming pronounced. Perhaps picking up on my tension, he finally dropped his hand back to his side. He flushed slightly and looked away almost bashfully.

"It was nice meeting you, Vivian. I look forward to talking to you soon," he said, giving me a sweet smile before leaving.

I had officially survived my first two hours on the job. And not too shabbily either. I watched as Theo got into the passenger side of a blue Honda. He really was a good-looking man. And what had been that odd hand on the shoulder move before he left? I chewed on my bottom lip, trying to work it out. Suddenly he turned to face the building again and even though I was almost sure he couldn't see me staring, I looked away quickly.

My phone buzzed in my pocket. I pulled it out and was greeted with another picture from Cole. Though, thankfully this one wasn't so risqué. I looked down at a snapshot of the marquee at the theater in Houston where the band would be playing tonight. Generation Rejects stood out in bright red letters.

Missing my favorite reject.

I didn't bother to respond. I wasn't sure what I was supposed to say.

Instead I turned off my phone.

Chapter 4
COLE

I **TRIED** to roll over but smashed my elbow into the wall. I let out a barely audible grunt and rubbed at the throbbing flesh. With my other good hand I felt around for the cell phone I vaguely remember tucking under my pillow before I went to sleep last night.

You know, just in case.

I found it and flicked my finger on the screen, turning it on. There were a few text messages from random acquaintances. A few tit shots from chicks I had screwed at some point in my shady past.

But nothing from the only person I had secretly hoped to hear from.

Not that I'd ever admit that crap out loud. I wasn't cockless for fuck's sake. There was no way I had sat around last night, staring at my phone willing it to ring.

That shit was for bitches and dudes with their nuts tied up in a bow. Definitely not for me.

So what if Vivian hadn't answered when I called. I didn't need to talk to her every single night, for Christ's sake.

So what if she never sent a text after the few dozen I had sent her. If that's the game she wanted to play, then so be it. I shouldn't have to explain myself to her.

Even though I knew she had the total wrong idea about the girl she heard when we last spoke.

I hadn't been given a chance to explain that the girl had been with Mitch and the two of them had passed out drunk on the floor of my hotel room. I hadn't been able to tell Vivian that I had gone into the bathroom for privacy so I could call her because I couldn't stop thinking about her. Even though I wouldn't have dared admit that, it was the truth.

She had jumped to the obvious conclusion. Not that I blamed her. But it still irritated me that she had chewed me a new asshole when for once, I hadn't done anything wrong. The need to defend myself made me cranky.

I had wanted to tell her about the conference call with the label. They were sinking some serious money into promoting us. There was going to be a major photo shoot and press release for our upcoming album.

I really wanted to talk about it to someone. No, I wanted to talk about it with Vivian. But it was obvious she was going to play the pissed off card for a while longer.

Before I could think twice about it, I tapped out a quick message and hit send. Then I waited for a few minutes. Not because I was waiting to see if I'd get a response.

Hell no!

And that wasn't disappointment that I felt when my phone stayed silent. That was just hunger. Because I hadn't eaten anything last night. That had to explain the aching in my gut. That was the only thing that made any sense.

I swung my legs over the side of my cramped bunk and slid out to the floor. Damn, it was freezing! I reached back in behind the curtain and felt around for my shirt. I hurriedly put it on and stumbled my way back to the bathroom so I could take a leak.

I pushed open the folding door that led to the toilet and instantly started gagging. Living on a bus with eight other dudes was disgusting. Even for my sorry bachelor ass. I wasn't a clean freak by any means, but at least I tried to hit the bowl when I was taking a piss.

Maysie had claimed the tiny bathroom at the back of the bus, which was smart on her part. Guys were freaking barbarians.

I held my breath as I whipped out my junk and took the quickest pee on record. I thought about taking a shower, but didn't think I could stomach the smell for that long.

God, I missed having my own space.

It was easy to get sick of being on the road. It sucked cramming into a bunk the size of a dog's asshole in order to sleep. And there was always some dipshit who decided to be a dick and eat all of your Ding Dongs.

Even though I was getting tired of tripping over empty beer cans and dirty boxer shorts, it was still pretty amazing.

Somehow, someway, Generation Rejects was on an actual, totally legit tour. We were living it up on an actual tour bus, sharing a space with one of the coolest bands out there.

This was actually my life.

It was still pretty hard to believe.

Particularly for a former jock who had been expected to go into the military in order to make his dad happy.

I hadn't been Generation Reject's first singer. Garrett, Mitch and I had been friends in high school but I used to laugh at their lame attempts at music. I was too busy playing basketball and screwing my way through the cheerleading squad.

Garrett had been the guy you went to if you needed to buy drugs. Mitch was the slow kid that sat in the back of the classroom and made stupid comments that had the rest of the class laughing at him more than with him. And even though I was their friend, I hadn't taken them too seriously.

No one had.

After we graduated, none of us had gone on to college. Big shocker. Garrett's parents had just died and Mitch certainly didn't have the grades to do much more than pick up garbage and shovel horseshit at a local farm.

I was by no means an idiot. I had been offered a couple of scholarships to play ball. But I hadn't wanted the responsibility. I hadn't wanted the pressure. I was sick of school. I was sick of doing what my parents wanted me to do. I was ready to go my own way.

My dad was former military and he had told me when I turned eighteen that I had the choice of going into the Navy like he had done or I could get the fuck out.

I had gotten the fuck out.

And I hadn't talked to my old man since.

Not that I hadn't tried. They lived ten minutes away from my apartment in Bakersville. Hell, I ran into my mom in the grocery store from time to time. And I learned pretty damn quickly that I was persona non grata in my own family.

I had finally stood up to my father and refused to let him tell me what I was going to do with my life. As a consequence for growing some fuzz on my balls I had been forced out of the house I had grown up in. It had sucked at the time but I was glad I had done it.

But that didn't mean it didn't hurt to be ignored by my mother when I called her name when I saw her on the street. Or to hear the click of a disconnected call when I tried to phone to wish my father a Merry Christmas.

"You're a fucking loser, Cole. You'll never be anything, never do anything. You're a fucking waste of skin." My dad's final words to me still buzzed around in my head all these years later.

And I was still trying to prove him wrong.

And maybe this time, I would.

So after I left school I had rented a crappy studio apartment and had gotten a shit job at the local poultry plant. And Garrett and Mitch had started a band.

Garrett had met Jordan, who was going to Rinard College and was working at Barton's. Jordan played drums and soon their laughable pastime became a legitimate thing. They had asked another friend of ours from high school, Fred Rhodes, to sing for them.

They sucked. Mitch could barely play bass and while Garrett and Jordan had talent, Fred sounded like a tortured cat when he sang into a mic. They were booed off every stage that would have them.

Until I came along.

I'm not saying that to be a jackass. It's just the honest to god truth.

Because I could sing. I always could. When I was little, my mom would dress me up for church where I had to suffer through hours of god shit just so I could belt out the hymns. The old ladies loved me.

As I grew older, my musical ability wasn't something I broadcasted around. I was a jock, plain and simple. I didn't have the time or inclination to jam or whatever the hell you call it.

But when Garrett had finally wised up and kicked Freddo out of the band, he approached me. We had gone out one night and gotten plastered. Mitch spent most of the evening worshipping the porcelain god. And I, in a moment of weakness, agreed to front their sad, pathetic band. Who knew that it would one day be the best decision I had ever made.

We were called the Headless Chickens at first. In homage to my dismal day job. I had a morbid sense of humor.

But the name didn't quite roll off the tongue and it looked crappy on T-Shirts. We weren't feeling particularly optimistic about our future as a band when the name Generation Rejects had been born. Because that's what we had felt we were.

A bunch of rejects.

Things had been pretty bleak in the early days.

Jordan and I had clashed almost immediately. I hated the college kids who came into Barton's. Townies and Rinard students fought on a regular basis. And Jordan was just another obnoxious frat guy with his pretty boy looks and talent that came entirely too easily.

I hated him. Like really hated him. The chicks loved him and I hated him even more. I had always been the big fish in the little pond until Jordan fucking Levitt came into the picture. And the feelings were definitely mutual.

Yeah, so I had gotten to second base with this bitch he had been dating for a few months at the time. She was some sorority chick named Olivia who had an attitude. She had always looked down her nose at the rest of us.

But it had been easy enough to get my hand up her shirt and my tongue down her throat. That hadn't gone over too well with Levitt. And maybe I felt crappy afterwards. And maybe I didn't really fight back when he punched me in the face and broke my nose.

And just maybe I had taken things a step too far. But that didn't mean that Jordan wasn't a dick. Because he was. But over the years my animosity had cooled some and Jordan and I now almost tolerated each other.

We'd never be friends the way I was with the other guys, but he wasn't all that bad.

And the dude could really play. And even if I didn't like him all the time, I had mad respect for his talent and his contribution to the band.

Because Generation Rejects and the guys in it were my life. They were my family. And when push came to shove, despite our differences, despite any history of bad blood, I knew those fuckers had my back.

And I didn't have anyone else in my life I could say that about.

Certainly not my family.

Just my band.

But maybe there was someone else.

Even if she wasn't currently returning my calls.

I walked out to the small kitchen on the bus and turned on the coffee maker. It was ridiculously early. Way earlier than I was normally awake for. Usually I didn't bother putting my feet on the ground until the afternoon.

But my silent phone had kept me awake.

And then there was the day ahead of us. It was going to be a big one.

We had our first radio interview at a midsized station in St. Louis, where we would be playing tonight. Then later we had some principal photography that the label had set up for our upcoming album release.

Constant Static was set to go live in a couple of weeks. Now that our tour with Primal Terror was doing so well, Pirate Records told us that they were planning on pumping more and more money into our release.

We were all pretty excited about it. But for me this was my chance to prove that I wasn't a waste of space. That I could do something with my life without going into the military or going to college.

That I hadn't made a huge mistake by walking out of my parents' house all those years ago. That I was going to make it with or without their support.

It was kind of pathetic that here I was, a twenty-four year old man and still hung up on his mommy and daddy issues. It was so cliché.

"Pour me a cup, will ya?" I looked over my shoulder to find Jose Suarez, our new manager, sitting down at the table and pulling out his laptop.

"Sure, man. Cream or sugar?" I asked.

"Black," he said shortly.

Of course. That didn't surprise me. Jose Suarez wasn't the type to mess up perfectly good coffee with bullshit.

We had been on the road for a little over four months, sleeping out of Garrett's van or in crappy Motel 6s when Jose approached us after a show.

We had been playing steady gigs with the help of Dougie, Mitch's club promoter cousin.

At first, the whole thing had been embarrassing. Hardly anyone showed up and we were playing to crowds of twenty to thirty people. We were living off fifty bucks a show and were close to calling it a day and heading home.

But then, something changed. I still don't know exactly know what did it. What that magic moment was when we went from being third-rate garage band to up and coming stars.

Suddenly people were talking about us. And people started showing up to watch us play. What had begun as a pipe dream slowly became a reality.

And when Dougie hooked us up with a marketing manager with a rising indie rock label, Pirate Records, we jumped at the chance to record a single to sling out to radio stations.

And then Jose Suarez had entered the picture. He had heard

about us and decided to check us out. He had liked what he had seen. He wanted to manage us. He was positive he could take us to the next level. He had been working in the industry for over fifteen years. He had connections. He had experience. He was exactly what Generation Rejects needed.

Jordan was adamantly against it. He hadn't wanted to screw over his girlfriend. That had pissed me off. And that had led to one of our worst fights. When all was said in done, we had forty stitches between us and had signed Jose as our manager.

Maysie had been fine with it after I had gotten tired of Jordan's shit and gone behind his back to talk to her about it. She had understood that working with Jose was a once in a lifetime opportunity. She hadn't been as blind and emotional about it as her pussy-whipped boyfriend.

But I still got the feeling that Jordan resented me for strong-arming the decision. Whatever. The one thing you could never accuse me of is not having the best interests of the band at heart.

I wanted us to rock the world. I wanted us to be a success. I wasn't going to let Jordan and his pink, fluffy relationship get in the way of that.

And once we had signed on with Jose, things took off pretty quickly. Using his connections he got us bigger and better venues. He got our single, Perfect Regret, airplay on a bunch of college radio stations.

Slowly and surely, we were building a fan base that consisted of more than just the drunks that hung out at Barton's Bar and Grill on a Saturday night.

And then he had gotten us the prime gig as the opening act on Primal Terror's first nationwide tour.

Now here we were, six months later, getting ready to release our first album, playing to sold out venues and preparing for our first radio interview.

Shit couldn't get any better than that.

I wanted to fist pump the air like a Rocky. I wanted to click my heels Fred Astaire style.

Life was good.

And it would be just about perfect if my stupid phone would

just freaking ring.

"Here ya go," I said, sliding the mug to Jose and sitting down across from him. He barely looked up but he nodded his thanks.

I had learned that Jose wasn't one for niceties or manners. It was one of the things I appreciated about him.

"The interview has been rescheduled for two so you aren't so crunched for time. You have to be back for sound check at four," Jose explained in his cut the BS delivery.

"Yeah, okay," I responded.

Jose looked over the rims of his dark framed glasses and seemed to be studying me. I hated when he did that. It was as though he were trying to steal my soul or something.

Jose wasn't your stereotypical manager. He didn't prescribe to the school of khakis and pressed shirts. Jose Suarez was covered, head to toe, in crazy looking tats. His face was full of piercings. It must be a pain in the ass for him to go through a metal detector.

He looked more the part of rock star than most of the actual rock stars I had seen.

He was one badass motherfucker.

It was rumored he had been a gang banger when he was younger and it was on the streets that he gotten to know some dudes who went on to become some of the biggest musicians out there right now.

It was through those connections that he built his business and he had established himself as a reputable manager. He had personally catapulted at least two other bands into the stratosphere. Blind Susan and Catch 'Em Cal were two of the biggest rock acts on the scene. The latter of which had just gone on to win the Grammy for Best New Artist.

He was rumored to have the magic touch. He understood the industry and knew how to turn shit into gold. And he was committed to doing the same for Generation Rejects.

The whole thing was still so unbelievable.

"You nervous?" Jose asked arching what should have been eyebrow if he had any. I had seen him shave them off meticulously every other day. It was fucking weird.

I scoffed at his question. "Hell no," I snorted.

Jose stared at me again.

"Good. That's the attitude I like to see," he said shortly.

I picked at the black nail polish on my pinkie finger. Vivian had thought it would be cute. And she had been naked with her tits in my face so I had let her paint my nails. Now I could admit it looked ridiculous.

What can I say; I was weak when it came to Vivian's boobs. And the rest of her.

"So what sort of questions will there be?" I asked, flicking the black flakes onto the floor.

Jose shrugged. "The standard stuff I'm sure. How do you write your music? Stuff about your upcoming album. What are some crazy stories from the road? But fair warning, you're being interviewed by some female DJ who originally only wanted you there. So don't be surprised if she asks you if you have a girlfriend or some trite shit."

That shocked me.

"She only wanted me there?" I asked incredulously, feeling extremely flattered by that. Not that I would have ever done an interview without the other guys, but my ego needed the little boost. Particularly since the fact that Vivian still hadn't returned my text was making it all to obvious she was ignoring me.

Jose was doing that staring thing again. He shut his laptop, crossed his arms over top of it, and leaned forward.

"I think you've come to realize in the last few months that I don't bullshit people. Am I right, Cole?" he asked.

"Well, yeah," I agreed. Because it was the truth. Jose chewed up bullshit and spit it out.

"Then listen to me when I tell you that while Generation Rejects is a good band and your music is catchy, you are the one who will be selling records. It's your image as the bad boy rocker that will have chicks clamoring to your shows. And their boyfriends will tag along because aside from being a pretty face you can fucking sing."

Jose pointed at me. "You are the face of Generation Rejects. Not Garrett. Not Mitch. Not even Jordan, though he has his own appeal. But he's not at the front fucking the crowd every night.

He's not the one bleeding his soul as he sings. That's you, Cole. And that's what will send you to the top."

Not you guys.

Just you.

I instantly picked up on that subtle difference.

I didn't know what to say. Part of me wanted to squeal like a little bitch. This was the validation I had always wanted. Sure, I played the part of egomaniac, but I still liked to know that I was fucking awesome.

And even though Jose was saying some pretty fantastic stuff, it seemed as though he was about to drop a hammer on my unsuspecting head.

"Which is why you should think about going out on your own. You'd kill it as a solo act. The record companies would be all over you." And there it was, the big ole hammer. Jose dropped his words nonchalantly and then opened up his laptop again like he hadn't just blown my world up.

"What did you just say?" I asked, my mouth dropping open.

Jose shrugged, not bothering to look at me. "Don't play dumbass with me, Cole. Because you aren't stupid. You had to have thought about it."

"Actually, no I haven't," I said angrily and truthfully. I never in a million years ever contemplated a musical future without my bandmates. But even still, the suggestion was traitorously appealing.

"Then you are an idiot. Because you're great as a frontman, but you'd be even greater with only your name up on the marquee. You don't need to share the limelight with anyone. You should let me help you be great, Cole. Otherwise you'll be floundering around in a mid-level band until you become a joke."

I was starting to get pissed.

"What the fuck are you doing as our manager if you think the Rejects are just a 'mid-level band?" I air quoted him. Yeah, I had just fucking used air quotes.

Jose's eyes flashed and for a second I felt intimidated. And that didn't happen often. No one intimidated me. . .ever. But Jose wasn't just anyone.

"Look, the band is good. Garrett and Jordan write decent songs. But I've been in this game long enough to know where the real money lies. And while Generation Rejects will achieve some success, you Cole, have the potential to go all the way. And you can take it or leave it. But if you want to talk about your options, I'd be happy to do that."

I opened my mouth to say something. What it was, I wasn't entirely sure. A part of me wanted to tell him where to shove it. That I came as a package deal. That there wasn't a way in hell I'd ever leave Generation Rejects.

But his words stoked my ego in just the right way. Come on, who doesn't like being told how great they are? Who wouldn't be slightly swayed by the prospect of fame and fortune? Who wouldn't, even slightly, be tempted to shit all over their friends for the chance to show the world how incredible they could be?

And if you say that you wouldn't do it, that you wouldn't even think about it, then you are completely delusional. And a big, fat liar.

Because it was tempting.

Way too tempting.

I didn't know whether to be disgusted or proud of myself.

Before anything else could be said, I started to hear people stirring around at the back of the bus. A few of the guys from Primal Terror came out and started rooting through the fridge. Jose's attention was now completely focused on his computer and it was like he hadn't just suggested, moment ago, to leave my friends and go on this journey by myself.

Bastard.

"Mornin'," Geoff Finley, the lead singer for Primal Terror said, sitting down beside me. I only nodded; still trying to digest the lump of fat Jose tossed my way.

"Just think about it," Jose said suddenly before getting to his feet, his laptop tucked under his arm, heading to the front of the bus, presumably to talk to the driver.

"You want one?" Nads Mason, Primal Terror's bassist asked, indicating a box of donuts. I shook my head, feeling slightly nauseous.

I got up and headed back to my bunk.

Jose thought I should leave Generation Rejects and be a solo artist. He thought Generation Rejects was a mid-level band. But me, well he thought I could be a star.

I was flattered.

I wanted it. So badly. I wanted to reach out and grab fame by its scrawny, fickle neck and make it my bitch. I wanted to set the world on fire and smoke the ashes.

I wanted the money. I wanted the recognition. I wanted the mansion and cars.

I wanted it all.

I wanted to look at my dad's sanctimonious face and give him the goddamned middle finger. I wanted to look at my judgmental mother and tell her to fuck off. That I didn't need their approval; that I had done this all on my own.

That I could own the universe.

"You okay, dude?" Garrett waved his hand in front of my face and I realized I had been standing, unmoving, staring into space.

Looking at the guy I considered my brother I felt like shit for even contemplating leaving him and the other guys behind.

I wouldn't be anywhere if it weren't for Garrett Bellows and our band.

"Yeah, sorry. Didn't sleep much," I said with a wry smile.

Garrett clasped his hand on my shoulder. "You need to get laid. It's been what? Two weeks? Three? You'll get gangrene if you don't use it, man," he joked and I tried to laugh. It didn't really work.

Garrett frowned and peered into my face. I really wasn't in the mood for his look into your soul and talk about your problems stuff.

"You sure you're all right?"

I pushed passed him and angrily threw the curtain back on my bunk, climbing in.

"I'm fucking fine," I said harshly, shutting out Garrett and my guilt.

"**F**INALLY,**"** I said with a relieved chuckle when Vivian answered the phone.

The tour bus had just gotten to St. Louis an hour and half ago. We had all checked into the hotel and I was enjoying some much needed alone time.

I had spent the remaining time on the bus hiding out in my bunk. Mitch and Jordan had tried to get me to jam with them for a bit but I said I had a headache. That I wasn't in the mood.

Yes, I had officially grown a vagina.

I had practically run from the bus when we pulled up at the Best Western. And now I was in my room, alone, clinging to my phone and entirely too happy just because I finally got a girl to talk to me.

"Sorry. I went out last night. I had one hell of a hangover this morning," Vivian laughed and then groaned.

I smiled, knowing what her morning must have been like. Vivian didn't wear hung-over very well. She was mean. And she had no qualms about making everyone within a ten-mile radius as miserable as she was.

But what I wouldn't give to be in Bakersville with her right now. I didn't like this crazy confusion swirling around in my head. I liked cut and dry, black and white. I didn't feel comfortable with the temptation I had been given.

"Sorry, baby. I wish I were there to take care of you," I said huskily, thinking graphically about exactly how I would take care of her.

I wasn't sure when things had changed for me where Vivian was concerned. We had been fucking for almost two years now. We weren't dating. And we most certainly didn't have a commitment.

Up until six months ago, I routinely screwed who ever I wanted, not thinking twice about how Vivian felt or what she would say about it. I didn't particularly care. Sure, that was messed up, but it was the truth.

I knew Vivian didn't like it. She made her feelings pretty clear on a number of occasions. But I also knew that she got off on feeling jealous. That she enjoyed getting mad and taking it out on me. That it gave her the same sick sense of satisfaction that it gave me. That despite all that when she was around, she was the only one I wanted.

She was spiteful. She was retaliatory. I knew that if I made her angry, I'd get it back in the worst way possible. She'd make me feel it.

And I dug that about her. She wasn't like most girls I knew who said what they thought you wanted to hear. She was mouthy. She was loud. She flew off the handle at the slightest provocation.

And she drove me fucking crazy.

She pushed my buttons like nobody else. She pissed me off. She frustrated me to all hell. And she turned me on like no girl had ever known before. She just had to flip that gorgeous hair of hers and I was rock hard.

The sex had always been amazing. Viv was a tiger. She scratched, she bit, she pulled chunks of hair out of my head. And she took it as good as she gave it. She loved it when I bent her over a chair or laid her out on a pool table.

She loved it loud and public. Vivian was a total exhibitionist. She thought nothing of riding me in a bathroom at Barton's or sucking me off in a darkened corner at the back of a club.

She was exciting. And sexy as hell.

And she had never been anything more than that. I hadn't wanted her to be.

She was the girl I could call in the middle of the night when I needed to get my rocks off. She was the girl I knew was waiting to warm my bed when I came home in between shows. And she was the girl who would fly half across the country just to see me naked.

And she was the girl who would lose her fucking shit if she found me with anyone else. She'd scream and throw a scene. She'd turn me on in an instant. And then we would fuck all night long.

It was who we were together. I didn't expect anyone to understand it. There were times when even I couldn't wrap my head around what we were to each other. So I didn't expect anyone to approve or comprehend.

It was what it was.

And there was a nice simplicity in that.

But at some point along the way, I had found it easier and easier to talk to Vivian in between bouts of marathon sex. When my dick wasn't inside her, I would tell her about my parents. Or about the crazy shit going on with the band.

And she'd listen. She always did.

And I liked it.

Almost as much as I liked her magnificent breasts.

"Shut up, Cole. I can't laugh right now. It hurts too much," Vivian moaned, low and deep and I felt my cock stir at the sound. It's what this girl did to me. Just the sound of her voice had me hard as a rock.

"Sorry, babe," I said sincerely.

"So what's going on? Why the million and one texts and phone calls? If I didn't know better I'd think you missed me, Cole Brandt," Vivian teased tiredly. I knew she felt like crap and if I were a nicer guy I'd let her go so she could rest.

But I needed to talk to her.

I was a selfish prick.

"You weren't answering. I thought you were pissed at me again," I said jokingly, though it was 100% true.

Vivian sighed. "So that warranted stalking?" she asked, sounding perturbed.

"I don't like it when you're pissed at me," I told her, coating my words in warm honey. I knew how hard it was for her to resist me when I was sweet. And damned if I didn't like being sweet to her.

"Yes, you do," Vivian mocked.

I chuckled. "Yeah, you're right. You're hot when you're mad. I like it when your claws come out," I admitted.

"So how are things out there in the land of rock and roll?" she asked, changing the subject.

I lay back on the bed and tucked the hand not holding the phone under my head. I stared at the ceiling. "It's going," I sighed.

"You don't sound too happy about that. Is the rock and roll lifestyle losing its luster," she teased. Shit, if she only knew.

I wanted to tell her about my conversation with Jose. I needed to get this great big pile of guilt off my chest. Ever since Jose had mentioned the possibilities for me this morning, I couldn't stop thinking about it. I was obsessing.

But I couldn't tell Vivian. Because I wasn't ready to admit out loud how much I wanted to take Jose up on his offer. That would be to admit how much of a traitorous ass I really was.

I played the part of dickhead really well. I fucked chicks; I started fights. I spoke out of my ass and pretended not to give a shit about consequences.

But it was just that. . .pretending.

I had learned a long time ago that being a jerk was easier than being someone people walked all over. That it was better to hurt someone before they had the chance to hurt me.

It was fucked up. It was wrong. I knew this. But I didn't do heartache and pain very well. I was big pussy about it actually.

And the thought of screwing over the three people closest to me, while repulsive, was also entirely too appealing.

And if I verbalized it, the asshole thing wouldn't be an act anymore.

It would be who I was. I would feel it deep in my bones.

It would be all I knew.

"It's just overwhelming sometimes," I said, feeling safe to admit that small truth.

Vivian's sigh filled my ears and made me feel better than I had all day.

"I'm sure. I can't even imagine. But you'll be fine. You're Cole Brandt. This is what you do. You'll get up on that stage tonight and you'll become everyone's fantasy and you'll love it."

"Am I your fantasy?" I chuckled, hoping to god she said yes.

Vivian's soft laughter was like a kick to the gut. I seriously loved her laugh.

"Some days," she muttered.

"Only some days? What about today?" I asked, grinning from ear to ear. I don't think I had ever smiled this wide in my entire life.

"I don't know. There's still time for you to piss me off."

Then we were both laughing and life felt good again.

Chapter 5
VIVIAN

"THE guys will be playing in Raleigh next week. You wanna drive down with me and stay over?" Gracie asked, getting into the refrigerator and taking out a bottle of tomato juice. I cringed as she poured herself a cup and drank it.

"How can you drink that stuff?" I gagged, handing her a piece of toast. Gracie shrugged and took a bite of bread, crumbs falling to the floor.

"So, what do you think? Will you come with me?" she asked, following me into the living room. I turned on the morning news and sat down on the couch to eat my meager breakfast of toast and grapefruit before I headed into work.

"I don't know. It really all depends on what's going on with work," I said lamely. And while that was true, it wasn't my biggest reason for not wanting to trek down to North Carolina.

I also wasn't entirely sure I was up for a weekend of crazy with Cole.

While things had been pretty nice between us lately, I knew it was only a matter of time before he screwed it all up. Or more specifically screwed someone.

We had spoken on the phone almost every night since last

week and he had tried his hand at phone stalking. I hadn't purposefully avoided his calls, but Gracie and I had gone out and gotten wasted and I had left my phone at home.

I had purposefully left it behind mostly because I somehow knew a certain buzzkill lead singer would call when I was trying my hardest to forget about him for one night.

And it had been working for a while.

We had met some guys at Barton's and they had come back to our apartment. They were a few years younger, both seniors at Rinard. I had felt a bit like a cougar when the one named Lambert had started putting the moves on me. He was a fresh-faced twenty who obviously hadn't ventured far from the family farm. He seemed awestruck when I gave him my attention, which was good for the ego.

So I had gone along with it for a while. We had kissed and there had been some mild groping but then Cole happened. Or more like the memory of his mouth and his hands ruined any chance for poor Lambert.

I had shut it down. I had sent poor country boy home with nothing to show for it but a raging case of disappointment. And I had spent the rest of my evening eating ice cream and watching Mob Wives.

It wouldn't have been such a bad night actually, if I hadn't had to suffer through the sounds of Gracie enjoying herself with Lambert's roommate Nathan, on the other side of our all too thin walls.

I had woken up in the afternoon the next day to the incessant dinging of my cellphone. I had been shocked as hell to see the number of texts and missed calls I had from Cole.

It was like he knew or something. I was beginning to think he had hookup ESP. He was able to psychically know when I was trying to have a good time without him.

For a brief moment I thought something had happened to Maysie. That she had been hurt. So I had called him back immediately. When he had asked where I had been in that sexy, husky way of his, I realized that his manic calling had to do with something else entirely.

If I hadn't known any better, I would have thought Cole had been missing me. And when I asked him as much, he had blown it off just as I had expected him to. But there was a note to his voice that was confusing. He seemed almost sad. And a lot vulnerable.

We ended up talking for over an hour. Up until he had to leave for his radio interview. And then he called me again after his show and we ended up staying on the phone until the early hours of the morning.

And there hadn't been any women in his hotel room. I could tell by the silence in the background that he had been completely alone. That alone was a reason to believe in miracles. Cole Brandt without a girl in his room had me almost believing in unicorns and fairies.

Then I started to wonder what he wanted. It was like when a husband buys his wife flowers out of the blue. The first thought the woman has is, "What did he do wrong?" Or "What is he up to, the bastard?"

And if it involved handcuffs and dressing like a nun again so I could smack him with a ruler for a being a "naughty boy" I'd tell him where to shove it.

Several months ago I had spent four hours, in a nun habit, handcuffed to a hotel bed because Cole couldn't remember where he had left the keys. In the end he had to call a locksmith to pick the lock.

Imagine my total mortification when a complete stranger took in my odd get up, bound to a bed. And Cole hadn't even bothered to put away the obscenely large, neon blue vibrator that sat proudly on the bedside table, announcing to the world that we liked it kinky.

The locksmith didn't say anything, thank god, but I think he was enjoying himself a little too much as he took an inordinately long time to free me.

After Cole had paid him, he thought we could launch back into his quirky sex game. I had let him know, in no uncertain terms, that the only sex game he would be indulging in would involve his hand and his balls.

He had tried to butter me up with his patented version of

sweet-talking. Though being told my tits made him want to bust a load in his pants didn't make my heart skip a beat.

This was definitely different. He was different. This strange, tender man who called me every night and spoke about things other than his band or wanting me to rub his Long Dong Silver was disconcerting.

Something was changing between Cole and me and I wasn't sure how to handle it. I wasn't sure I was ready to accept a side of him that wasn't cocky and arrogant. I could admit that throughout the duration of our less than conventional acquaintance, I got off on the crazy, insanity inducing tirades he incited as much as he did. There was something predictably unpredictable about wanting to rip his pit hair out and making him eat it. Even though I hated with a fiery passion finding him with other women, it's what I expected from him.

It made it easier to not dream of more with him. Cole wasn't boyfriend material. I couldn't be delusional about that if he was screwing around the second I wasn't in sight. My heart couldn't engage and in turn be broken into a million tiny pieces.

But perhaps I was deluded. Because whether I wanted to or not, I did care about him. My stomach flipped and turned over when I saw him. I was at times reduced to a squealy teenage girl around her crush.

Because when the asshole touched me, my entire body ignited. For the last two years, Cole had been slowly ruining me for any guy that would ever come after him.

Poor, pitiful Lambert learned that lesson the hard way.

And now Cole was playing Mr. I'm-So-Sensitive-Don't-You-Want-To-Hug-Me. The man I had always been able to count on for delicious, sometimes boundary pushing, toe-curling sex, was appealing to my emotional side.

Damn him!

So, no I wasn't jumping at the chance to see him. He was terrifying me. He was making me question everything about the way things between us operated.

He was making keeping my distance increasingly difficult. And I was more than a little worried that once I saw him I'd launch myself at him and confess my undying love.

And that was a humiliation I was not signing up for, thank you very much.

"Well, I'm going. It's Mitch's birthday that weekend and I'd like to see him." I raised my eyebrows at my friend. Gracie stared blandly back, not giving me anything.

I almost snorted. It was on the tip of my tongue to start singing "Mitch and Gracie sittin' in a tree." But given my friend's carefully neutral expression, I figured that taunting her about her tip toeing the line between friends and fucking his brains out relationship with Mitch Delany would not be greeted with laughter.

I wanted to smack Gracie. I thought she was being deliberately obtuse and more than a little cruel when it came to the Rejects' bassist. He was a nice guy. Probably one of the straight up sweetest people I had ever met.

He adored Gracie. He worshipped at the altar of her awesomeness. He'd give her a kidney if she needed one.

And she was keeping him securely in the friend zone. Even though she tossed him just enough line to make him either hopeful for an actual relationship or to strangle himself with.

I honestly didn't understand what Gracie was thinking. Personally I suspected that there were more than friendly feelings beneath her staunch denial. I knew they had never hooked up. No kissing. No questionable touching. But I knew she thought about it. I saw the green eyed monster rearing its nasty head when girls flirted with him.

Mitch, like Cole, was no saint. He slept around like any self-respecting up and coming rock star. He sampled his way through the tang buffet.

And it pissed Gracie off, though she would never say so.

She only had herself to blame though. So it was hard to feel sorry for her when her face took on the green pallor of imminent upchuck as she watched girls slip Mitch their telephone numbers.

Then Gracie would go and screw the first guy she came in contact with.

Their pattern was about as destructive as my own.

But Mitch would still be there to call her every day. He'd send her packages from the road full of thoughtful presents just to let her know he was thinking about her.

She was always the girl at the front of his mind.

But I worried that the day would come when Mitch would no longer be content to play the part of Gracie's pet. He wouldn't coast along forever in the ambiguous state of limbo they existed in. One day one of those random girls would catch his eye and his heart and he would move on.

And I knew, whether Gracie could admit it to herself, she would be devastated.

"Isn't that sweet? It's almost like you love him or something." I couldn't help it. My maturity level was questionable at the best of times.

Gracie's eyes narrowed and I smirked.

"I'm not even dignifying that with a response," she sniffed.

"But you just did," I pointed out, giggling.

"So are you going to come with me or not? Isn't it time for your drama fix? Aren't you in withdrawal from not having a reason to throw something?" Gracie asked, grinning.

I stuck my tongue out at her. "Touché, bitch," I conceded.

"We'll see. I'm pretty slammed with this gala I'm planning. I'm not sure I can afford to go gallivanting off to North Carolina for the weekend. I'm pretending to be a productive member of society, darn it."

Gracie rolled her eyes. "Whatever. You live for gallivanting. And I think your emerging alter ego can take a rest for two days. I've been getting the feeling that Maysie could use our company. I get the impression that things are getting tense on the road," she said, surprising me.

"Really? What has she said?" I asked. Cole hadn't mentioned anything about tension or problems on the tour. But maybe that explained his sudden clingy need to call every day.

Gracie shrugged. "She hasn't said much, just that the guys have been at each others' throats a bit more than normal. Apparently the radio interview didn't go that well."

That shocked me. I had gotten the impression from Cole that

it had been really good. Their airplay and visibility was rising considerable.

"Really?"

Gracie nodded. "Yeah, this DJ chick only wanted to ask Cole questions. She pretty much ignored the rest of the guys. And you know that went down like a lead balloon with Jordan particularly. They had a huge fight and Maysie thought security at the radio station was going to call the cops."

I was in total recoil. Not that some DJ lady wanted to focus on Cole but the fact that Maysie was picking up on so much bad blood. I knew Cole and Jordan had a contentious relationship. You couldn't necessarily call them "friends" but they got on well enough when it came to their music. And both of them put their feelings aside for their music. This was not good at all.

"Maysie said this is becoming more and more of the norm. Their publicity photo shoot ended up being a Cole Brandt wank fest. They took some shots of the band but I guess the record label had asked for a bunch of pictures with just Cole. Seems they're pushing him as the face of the band. This time it wasn't just Jordan that had the problem. Apparently Mitch wasn't too happy with it either. I asked him about it but he didn't seem to want to talk about it. Maysie says that it's causing a huge division in the group. Jose, their manager keeps suggesting that they beef up Cole's vocals; he wants Jordan to cut his drum solos. They've even changed the sets and have cut all the songs where anyone else sings. And Cole doesn't see what the big deal is. Maysie is spending all of her time trying to convince Jordan not to quit."

I wasn't entirely surprised that the label would want to push Cole forward for increasing publicity. He was hot. He was sexy. He made girls drop their panties in less time it took for him to get their names.

He was a hell of singer. He was talented. He was a bad boy. He was the entire freaking package.

And those very things are what made me want to simultaneously kiss him senseless and bash his brains in.

Cole's ego, when unchecked, was a dangerous thing. I had seen it firsthand. I was often on the receiving end of his insensitivity.

But I never thought he'd allow anything to mess up his band.

Cole clearly needed a hard smack in the face.

"Yeah, okay, I'll go. I'll make sure things are square at work. Figure out the hotel details and I'll give you the money," I said, knowing my earlier excuses had been feeble at best.

Of course I'd go.

Cutest doormat in Bakersville, remember?

"Okay, I'll let you know." Gracie looked at her watch. "Shouldn't Miss-Productive-Member-Of-Society be getting to work?" she asked.

I checked the time on my cell phone and almost freaked. I had ten minutes to get to work.

"Crap, crap, crap!" I jumped to my feet and grabbed my purse, barely saying goodbye as I ran out the door.

Why is it when you're running late, that it is the perfect time for everything to go spectacularly and splendidly wrong?

Chapter 6
VIVIAN

MY car wouldn't start.

I sat in the driver's seat, turning the key, hoping the clicking noise was only in my imagination and that my engine would magically turn over.

Nope. It was dead as a doornail.

I got out of my car and screamed at the top of my lungs. A woman getting into her perfectly working car gave me a strange look and I gave her the middle finger. Bitch with her shiny Acura that started so damn easily. I bet she was on time for work.

I pulled out my phone and called a cab. They said they'd be there in ten minutes.

It took them fifteen.

I gave the driver my best stink eye as I climbed into the back.

Then we hit roadwork then there was an accident on the highway.

By the time I got to work, I was forty-five minutes late and in a really bad mood.

I ran to the entrance of The Claremont Center just as the heavy wooden door swung open and hit me right in the face.

My purse flew into the air, my cellphone fell to the ground, smashing into a thousand pieces while my nose started hemorrhaging blood all over my adorable pink sweater.

"Fucking hell!" I screeched, covering my nose as blood dripped through my fingers.

"Oh my god, I'm so sorry!" a voice said, shoving tissues into my hand. I didn't look up as I snatched the tissues and pressed them to my bloody nose.

"What sort of moron swings open a door like that? It's not that heavy! Are you stupid as well as an asshole?" I seethed. My nose was throbbing. I gingerly touched it, hoping it wasn't broken.

"You should get that looked at."

"No shit, Sherlock," I hissed, finally looking up into the face of my one and only client.

Theo Anderson.

Because of course he would be the moron to smash me with a door.

Theo's gorgeous face was contrite and concerned and I vainly started to freak out about what I must look like. I looked down at my blood-splattered sweater and would have cringed if only it didn't hurt so badly.

"Uh, sorry about the verbal assault. You're not a moron," I apologized.

"I deserved it. It's fine," Theo smiled, his pretty eyes crinkling at the edges. He really was nice to look at. I would have enjoyed it more if I weren't in total agony.

Busted nose aside, I really wish I could dig myself a hole and climb into it.

"I'll go get Marion. You should come in and sit down. Pinch the bridge of your nose and lean forward. We need to get you to the hospital. It may be broken." Theo in all of his hot efficiency went to locate my boss and also found ice in the employee break room. He brought both Marion and an ice pack back in less than three minutes.

Marion agreed with Theo in that I should go and have my nose checked out. She offered to drive me but Theo was insistent he take me.

"It's my fault after all," he said and I nodded because hell yeah it was his fault.

While Theo grabbed his coat and briefcase, I pulled my compact out of my purse and tried to straighten my hair.

I may have a possible broken nose, but I had my priorities after all and damned if I wouldn't try to look my best given the situation.

Theo ushered me out to his car, a black beast of thing that I needed help to climb into. And I totally caught him checking out my ass as he lifted me into his Hummer.

I gave it an extra little shake, just for good measure, before depositing myself into the passenger seat. I was never one to waste an opportunity to be ogled.

Theo went around to the driver's side and soon we were headed toward Bakersville General.

"I'm really sorry! I should have pushed the door open with a little less enthusiasm," Theo apologized for the millionth time.

"I'm sure my face will be just fine," I offered, still a little annoyed. But it was hard to hold anything against someone who was so sincere in their regret. Theo Anderson was a seriously nice guy.

He looked at me briefly, a soft smile on his face. He really was too pretty to be real. Cole was good-looking in a savage, rough and tumble sort of way. He was the kind of hot that made you fearful for your sanity.

Theo was good-looking in a way that was both safe and reassuring. He was the sort of gorgeous that made the perfect arm candy and looked great on Christmas cards. His was the kind of face that made you think about merging your DNA because you just knew your children would be unbelievable.

"I sure hope so. I'd never forgive myself if I did anything to mess up that beautiful face."

Oh he was good. He was smooth without being obvious about it. He gave the compliment with just enough reserve that you'd never know he was flirting with you.

He cast a quick glance in my direction and I found myself preening, despite the wads of bloodied tissue I held against my nose.

I fluffed my hair a bit and stuck out my chest. I smoothed the lines of my skirt over my thighs and I noticed Theo's eyes flickering to my legs. He swallowed and I knew he appreciated what he saw.

I was a woman who knew when a man thought her attractive. I was by no means oblivious and I didn't like to pretend I didn't know when I was being given the full body perusal.

I was also a firm believer in coquettishness and eye batting. My low cut blouses, tight fitting sweaters, and short skirts were the fiercest weapons in my arsenal.

I liked the attention and I enjoyed being the center of anyone's interest.

Theo's shy interest was more fulfilling than a seven layer chocolate cake.

The air in the car was thick and I could taste the delicious tension. It had been a long time since I felt a sexual spark with anyone that wasn't a certain tattooed lead singer. After my fizzling disaster with Lambert, I was beginning to think that Cole had broken me. That he had taken my desire and kept it all for himself like the greedy bastard he was.

I felt myself blush under Theo's gaze and thought to myself, Maybe not…

"I think at the very least, I need to buy you a new phone," he said, indicating the shattered pieces of my iPhone in my lap, killing the moment.

"That's okay, Theo. It's on warranty," I said, waving off his offer.

Theo shook his head. "No, I'm the reason it's busted. It's the least I can do."

"Who am I to argue with such chivalry?" I murmured, maneuvering my body so that it angled toward him, distracting him with my curves.

He gripped the steering wheel and swallowed again.

Being desired was a heady feeling. It was addictive. And with everything going on with Cole recently, I could use a new sort of rush. I needed something to distract me from my uncomfortably evolving emotions.

"I don't think smashing your nose with a door is an example of chivalry. Bad timing perhaps, but definitely not chivalry." Theo's self-deprecating comment was remarkably endearing.

He chanced a glance at my legs again, his eyes lingering. Until a horn blasted and he had to swerve back into his lane. I tried to hide my self-satisfied grin as Theo kept his eyes resolutely on the road after that.

Taking pity on the poor guy, I turned toward the window and pulled my jacket around my chest. It was the least I could do to ensure we got to the hospital in one piece.

"What were you doing at The Center so early? Did we have a meeting?" I asked, hoping I hadn't forgotten to write it down. Given the morning I had been having, it wouldn't surprise me. And my flakiness wouldn't go far in helping me project that whole responsible vibe I was really going for.

Theo shook his head. "No, I was just thinking about you last night and had some ideas I wanted to toss your way about the gala. I wanted to get your opinion."

I grinned again and then wished I hadn't. My nose throbbed. But I couldn't help but teasing him anyway.

"You were thinking about me last night? Why Mr. Anderson, I'm not sure that's entirely appropriate. You're my client after all," I remarked, affecting a thick southern drawl.

I was rewarded by the noticeable flush that quickly rose to Theo's cheeks.

He cleared his throat and gave me a shaky smile. "I just meant that I was thinking of things to tell you. I didn't mean, I'm sorry, I just. . ." he was fumbling. It was ridiculously adorable. And I let him stumble around for a bit before I came to his rescue.

"I was just giving you a hard time, Theo. I knew what you meant," I reassured him and he relaxed a bit. For being such a fantastic example of the male species, Theo Anderson lacked a lot of confidence.

Theo relaxed and gave me a much easier smile. "You're a bit of a ball buster aren't you?" he asked, taking his turn to tease.

"I was voted Most Likely to Squeeze a Man's Nuts in school," I joked.

Theo laughed and the sexual tension eased somewhat.

We pulled into the Emergency Room parking lot and Theo hurried around to my side of the car and let me out. He started walking me toward the entrance when I put my hand on his sleeve.

"You don't need to go in with me. I'm a big girl."

Theo's eyes were warm as he looked down at me. "I have no doubt, Vivian. But I want to wait with you," he said.

Before I could argue, he was already walking me toward the hospital.

And true to his word, Theo waited with me for the two and half hours it took for me to be seen. I kept telling him to leave. I felt guilty he was giving up his morning to hang out in a waiting room.

Theo pulled a manila folder out of his briefcase and handed it to me. My nose had finally stopped bleeding so I wasn't in danger of dripping blood all over the place.

"Well, let's do some work then," he suggested, pulling out some printouts for me to look at.

"This is beautiful," I said, looking at the picture of a ballroom decorated in rich blues and greens in a rendition of a sea scene.

"We always go for something that has to do with our charity. Last year the theme was Our Endangered Environment. The girl who had the job before you had decorated the place like an Amazon jungle. It was horrible. It looked like a kid's birthday party. We almost didn't come back to The Claremont for this year's gala," Theo shared, cringing.

He pulled out pictures of last year's party and he was right, it was laughable. Green vines and fake flowers had been everywhere. It was hard to be taken seriously when your main fundraiser looked as though it had been organized by a six year old. What had this girl been thinking?

Theo pointed to the printouts he had handed me. "Now something like that could be cool, don't you think?" he asked and I looked up at him and smiled as much as my aching face would allow. I was still all too aware of how repulsive I looked, but it didn't seem to bother him. His grin was contagious.

"I think it could be amazing. In keeping in line with these ideas and the mission of your charity, what if the theme was Our Fading Blue? With an emphasis on rising sea levels and melting icecaps," I suggested. I pulled a pencil out of my purse and started drawing over top the printout.

"The color scheme would be blues and whites and silvers. Lights and crystals hanging from the ceiling. Winter flowers in tasteful vases with prisms throwing rainbows on the tables and walls. Something like this." I doodled some rough ideas and showed them to him.

Theo pondered over it for a minute before his lips turned upward into a pleased smile. "This is perfect. These ideas are incredible! Do you think this can be pulled off?" he asked and I gave him my best bitch, please look.

"If there's one thing I know how to do, Theo, it's throw a damn good party," I told him.

"You're pretty amazing, you know that?" he said, his smile never wavering and my stomach flipped over.

It was on the tip of my tongue to say "Damn straight," in order to lighten the moment. To give it levity so it didn't have the power to make me feel all bubbly inside. But the sincerity in his eyes gave me pause.

I couldn't remember the last time I had been assessed with such blatant appreciation, not only for my face and my body, but also for my mind.

Certainly Cole had never cared much for my ideas and thoughts. He was too busy chasing me around with his penis.

Even with his recent interest in things outside of our rampant sex life, he had never looked at me like that.

Like I was incredible.

Like I was capable.

Like I held the answers to every question he could ever possibly ask.

And I realized that no matter how nice it was Theo wasn't the man I wanted to look at me that way.

Another example of the Cole Brandt vag block.

"Thanks," I said, with a lot more modesty that was normal

for me.

"Vivian Baily," a nurse finally called out.

I gathered my purse and jacket and got to my feet. "Thanks for waiting with me Theo, I'll give you a call when I get back to the office and we can set up a time to go over some more details," I said.

Theo got to his feet as well. "I'm not going anywhere, Vivian. I'll be here when you're done. You'll need a ride back to work won't you?" he asked and shook his head before I could argue with him.

I wasn't used to Prince Charmings saving my day. It would have been awesome.

Except I was all too aware that Prince Charming wasn't my style.

I preferred the bad guy, which would only end up destroying me in the end.

Because that's how those stories tended to end up.

With the damsel in distress tied to the train track.

Chapter 7
COLE

"**Y**OU broke your nose?" I asked, stretching my legs out in my bunk. We were back on the road after our show in Detroit. We were heading to Cincinnati next. And then next week we'd be on the east coast again. I couldn't wait to be closer to home. Even though we didn't have any gigs slated for Virginia for several months.

"Am I gonna have to brown bag you the next time we fuck?" I asked crudely. I know you're probably thinking I was being an asshole. That I deserved a kick to the dick for such a rude comment. But I could say shit like that to Viv because she wouldn't take it seriously. She knew I didn't mean it. It was how we rolled.

Or maybe not.

"That's a really messed up thing to say, Cole," she said quietly and I instantly felt like a jerk.

"I didn't mean it, baby. You know I think you're beautiful. Junked up nose or not," I promised.

"You are such a fuck face," Vivian said with venom. I thought I'd been pretty nice. What was her problem?

"And I didn't break it. It's just bruised. A little swollen. No brown bag necessary." She sounded pissed, which wasn't new.

83

And normally I'd goad her a little, just to get the explosion I liked so much. But something felt off about her.

And call it an ingrained survival instinct, but I thought better than to pour more fuel on a smoldering fire right now.

"Does it hurt?" I asked, trying to smooth things over.

Shit with Vivian had gotten complicated lately. Or maybe it was just me. I was a fucking mess.

Things with the band weren't the greatest. The radio interview had been a disaster. Jose had been right, Molly, the DJ, had been more interested in whether I had a girlfriend, than the tour we were on. And after we were done, she offered to take me into the break room so she could suck my cock.

I didn't take her up on it, just so we're all straight. I hadn't even been tempted. There was something really unappealing about a girl with a Miss Piggy tattoo on her neck who offered to let you spooge on her back. So I had respectfully declined.

While we waited in the lobby for Jose, Jordan had turned on me. He claimed I had hogged the interview time. Was he not in the same room as I had been in? How could he miss Molly's blatant come-ons? I couldn't be the only one who had caught the innuendo behind the question: "Do you like it in the dark or with the lights on? Performing that is."

"You think you're the fucking star of the show, Cole! You need a reality check! This is a band! There are four of us! We're all equal here! If you can't remember that then maybe I need to remind you," Jordan had snarled and I felt myself getting pissed.

"I can't help it if she was more interested in my cock then our music! Why the fuck is that my fault?" I had yelled.

Jordan had tried to punch me then and being the ninja that I am, I had dodged it. But I hadn't expected the sucker punch when I bent to pick up my phone that had fallen out of my pocket.

Next thing I knew Jordan and I were both bleeding and the frightened little receptionist was threatening to call the police if we didn't leave.

Maysie and Jose had separated us before it escalated further. And when Jose had me cordoned off in the back of the bus, he took his opportunity to remind me of my "options."

"They don't understand that you're the one the public cares about, Cole. This will only get worse. Jordan already resents you. The bigger you get, the more those three guys are going to try to hold you back. You need to think about the big picture here and what's best for you long-term," Jose had said and I didn't want to hear it.

Jose and his "go out on your own" pep talks were fucking with my head. And Jordan's negative attitude was making the possibility look pretty damn appealing.

Despite the testosterone overload Jordan and I had made peace and we entered into an uneasy truce. That is until our publicity photo shoot the next day. And then shit hit the fan all over again.

Yeah, so a bunch of the pictures were of me. Yeah, the guys had felt slighted and felt like crap about it. But what was I supposed to do? Tell them no? Why didn't they see that if people liked me, they liked the band?

It resulted in me getting the silent treatment from Jordan and Mitch, who was starting to piss me off as much as Jordan was. Garrett didn't seem happy either, but at least he wasn't pulling the whiny little girl act like the others.

And Jose kept giving me the See, I was right looks every time I glanced his damn way.

I was a mess.

And then there was Vivian.

Because in all this craziness, the only person I wanted to talk to, the only person I wanted to see, was Vivian. Vivian who drove me mental. Vivian who seemed to look for any chance to be angry with me.

I was really losing my shit.

"I'll live," Vivian said shortly, obviously still irritated with my less than sensitive remark.

"When you come to see me in Raleigh next weekend, I'll take care of you," I said, sleazing it up.

"Who says I'm going to see you next weekend?" Vivian asked snidely.

I grinned, feeling comfortable and back on familiar ground.

I loved Vivian's bitchy attitude. Even if she hated that I loved it.

"Because Mitch said you were coming down with Gracie. Why? Was it supposed to be a surprise?" I teased.

"No. I just wasn't sure it would be a big deal if I was there or not," Vivian said flippantly but I knew she meant it.

She really had no idea how fucking excited I was that she was coming to Raleigh. How excited I got each and every time I knew I would see her.

"It's a big deal, Viv. You know intimately just how big a deal it is." I chuckled as I shoved my hand in my pants, stroking myself as I thought about all the things I wanted to do to the beautiful girl on the other end of the phone.

"I know that voice, Cole. You're jacking off, aren't you?" Vivian laughed. A deep, throaty sound, that sent blood rushing straight to my dick. I pumped my hand harder.

"Fuck yeah, I am. Talk dirty to me, baby," I pleaded, already feeling the tingles in my belly. I was about to come like a thirteen year old.

Hard and quick.

"How about I tell you all the things I'm going to do with my mouth."

And it was all over.

AFTER my phone call with Vivian, I cleaned up and joined Garrett at the front of the bus. Mitch was hanging out with the dudes from Primal Terror, Jose was working on his computer, and Maysie and Jordan were noticeably absent. I guess I wasn't the only one blowing a load.

"Whatcha workin' on?" I asked, listening while Garrett tinkered with a new song.

"Just something that's been buzzing around in my head for a while. Though it's not clicking the way I want it to," he said, strumming the worn strings of his guitar.

I started to tap my hands on my knees in an upbeat rhythm in time to Garrett's playing. "What if Jordan took a solo here?" I suggested, smacking my knees frantically.

Garrett grinned. "Yeah, I like that."

I ended up finding Jordan's beat up acoustic and jamming with Garrett for a little while, helping him polish the song he had been messing with. Mitch joined us a bit later and bobbed his head in time to our playing.

Jordan and Maysie came wondering out from the bunks and sat down with the rest of us. Jordan didn't say anything about me playing his guitar. Instead he grabbed a pair of drumsticks and started stringing together a beat on the table.

Garrett started singing and the lyrics began to flow. We all worked together and the music was effortless. There wasn't any tension; egos were checked. This was just the four of us doing what we always did. Creating stuff we were proud of.

For all of our arguments and bullshit, when it came to our music, we just got each other. In a totally non-pussy way, of course.

A couple of the guys from Primal Terror ended up jumping in and it became one gigantic musical orgy. Musical masturbation at its finest.

And when we pulled into a diner off the interstate to eat dinner, everyone was in a pretty good mood.

"That song is going to be pretty awesome," Jordan said as we sat down at the table. Maysie handed out menus. Jose nodded his agreement.

"Definitely. I think it just needs more of a vocal presence and it will be tight." Jordan's mouth tightened and I could see Mitch's fists clenching. I didn't say a damn thing. Though I agreed with Jose totally. A little more singing and it would be the best song we had ever written.

But then I would be accused of hogging the limelight. Why didn't they just get me a T-shirt that read: Generation Reject punching bag?

"The label would love it. It's got a great edge with enough radio appeal to make it work in the mainstream market. And with Cole's vocals all over it, it will be fucking perfect." Jose nodded his head.

"Hmm," Jordan grunted and Garrett shrugged.

The good mood we had all been in sort of fizzled out and died and now we were left sitting together awkwardly.

"Maybe I could have another verse between the drum solo and the last guitar riff," I suggested, figuring I had as much a right to be heard as the others.

Mitch snorted. "I think there's more than enough vocals in the song as it is," he said and I wanted to punch the smirk off his face. I also noticed the look he exchanged with Garrett.

I got the feeling I had missed out on a lot of meetings lately.

"What's the problem with putting another verse in there at the end? I think it would be cool to end the song on the vocals rather than a fade out on the guitar. It would be more dramatic and shit," I said.

"Yeah, cause we need more of your dramatic shit, Cole," Jordan sneered.

"What's that supposed to mean, man?" I asked, trying to keep my temper in check. This was not the place to put my fist in Jordan's smug face. Maysie was already talking to her boyfriend under her breath. Probably trying to get him to settle down. I didn't need the intervention.

"Nothing. Forget it," Jordan backed off, though I knew he had a lot more he wanted to say.

I looked around at the rest of my band and none of them had the balls to look me in the eyes. These guys were supposed to be my friends. So why did it feel like I was the ugly redheaded stepchild in the group?

Jose was pointedly looking at the menu. He had stirred up this hornet's nest and now he was backing up and letting the destruction go down.

"So let me get this straight, it's cool for Jordan to get an overindulged drum solo. Garrett can riff away even if it sounds like shit. And Mitch can have all the input that he wants, but when I make a suggestion, there's a fucking problem?" I slammed my fist down on the table, causing the glasses to rattle.

"I think you get more than enough glory for the rest of us, Cole. So don't play poor, pitiful bitch," Jordan's voice rose to meet mine.

"So that's the problem. The fact that some stupid chick played twenty questions about Cole. And I had a few pictures taken that didn't include you guys. So that's a reason for you to play poor, pitiful me and get your panties in a bunch. Are you not getting enough attention, Jordan? I thought you were done with the strange now that you're a one-woman man. But if you need me to toss some your way, I'm happy to do it," I laughed hatefully.

Maysie looked like she was just as ready to punch me as her fiancé. But I just didn't give a fuck. I was sick and tired of feeling like the bad guy because I was doing my job. I was the lead singer. I was supposed to be front and center. So why was it a problem all of a sudden?

"You need to be taken down a peg or two," Jordan growled and I laughed again.

"I dare you to try," I taunted him.

"Enough you two. This is ridiculous!" Garrett barked, leveling both of us with a shut- the-hell-up-before-I-make-you-choke-on-your-teeth look.

"He started it," I said, sounding like a two year old. But I didn't care, because it was true.

"You're both asses, so shut the fuck up and eat your goddamned dinner," Mitch piped up.

"Mitch is right. This isn't the place. If you guys need to talk your shit out, do it on the bus without an audience," Jose reprimanded and Jordan finally settled backed down in his seat.

Maysie had been quiet and I knew I had overstepped by making the comment I had about Jordan. Even though she annoyed the shit out of me, she was still a decent chick and didn't deserve that.

"Sorry, Mays," I said under my breath and only for her ears. She nodded and gave me a tight smile, though I knew, despite my apology, it would be held against me for a while.

There were no attempts at further conversation. We all sat like the uncomfortable fuckers that we were, eating our dinner while my "friends" tried not to look at me.

When we finished, Maysie and Jordan went to the convenience store next door to load up on supplies, Mitch went to have a cigarette and I was ready to get back on the bus and head to my bunk.

"Cole," Garrett called out from behind me.

I slowed down and let him catch up. Out of all the guys, Garrett was my closest friend. He had given me a place to stay when my dad kicked me out of the house. I had been with him when he found out his parents died. We had been through some stuff. I had thought we were tight.

But he never once disagreed with the shit Jordan said. That led me to believe he agreed with him.

That he thought I was a limelight stealing fame slut just like the rest of them.

Maybe we weren't as tight as I once thought.

"What?"

"That shit back there was fucked up. You and Jordan need to deal with your beef before it starts impacting the band," Garrett said and I got immediately defensive. I felt as though, once again, I were being blamed for everything.

"I think Jordan needs to get a handle on his own insecurities and low self-esteem. It's got nothin' to do with me." I started walking toward the bus.

"That's BS and you know it. You're not helping things. We're called Generation Rejects. Not The Cole Brandt Experience. We're not your back-up band, you know."

I turned on my friend and got into his face.

"I'm sick and fucking tired of defending myself. But let me remind you, I'm the lead singer. I'm the one who sings every fucking night and gets the audience off. I'm the one who interacts with the crowd while you hide behind your instruments. You guys need to realize that I make this band what it is. I bring those bitches in the door. Fucking accept it or go back to playing Barton's. I don't give a shit."

"Do you hear yourself, man? I think you actually believe that line of junk coming out of your mouth," Garrett said with a shake of his head.

"You guys would be nothing without me. Let's remember until I came along you were getting booed off every stage. You would still be playing dime shows at Barton's for the drunk and ugly. Be thankful I'm here. Show some fucking gratitude," I growled.

And then Garrett punched me!

The motherfucker punched me!

I couldn't remember the last time Garrett had been in a fight. I was so in shock that I couldn't do anything but stand there and stare at him, my hand cupping my jaw.

Garrett shoved me hard in the shoulder and I stumbled backwards, catching myself before I fell on my butt.

"That's what I'm talking about! Your ego has always been something to laugh about. You're a dick, we get it. You're the slutty lead singer. Way to go for being a stereotype. But I think you need to remember where you came from, dude."

I rubbed my skin and grimaced.

Garrett had hit me. I still couldn't wrap my head around it.

"You all right? Did I knock your brains out of your ass or something?" Garrett asked, not looking so angry anymore.

"I'm just still trying to figure out how you landed a punch," I said.

Garrett chuckled. "Cole, I can kick your ass any day. Do I need to remind you of the tenth grade?"

"I tripped. It had nothing to do with you hitting me," I argued, remembering all too well what he was talking about.

I had kissed Carmen Jenkins, the girl Garrett had been drooling over for months. I had been young. Carmen was cute and had a thing for basketball players. Garrett had caught us underneath the stairwell at the back of the high school.

He punched me. A lot like he had just done.

And that time I had fallen on my ass. Though I swore it had more to do with the book bag at my feet than his fist.

"Sure, you keep telling yourself that," Garrett smirked and I knew we were cool again.

For the moment.

Chapter 8
VIVIAN

MARION had agreed to let me take Friday off so I could travel to Raleigh. Provided that I have the outline for the gala plans on her desk for approval by end of business Thursday, which was in less than five hours.

I was almost finished and was just putting the last touches to the proposal and budget plan. Theo and his team had already approved most of my suggestions. I was only finalizing the minute details. The event was less than a month away and I was already flustered with trying to keep everything straight.

The gala was going to be amazing though. I had even impressed myself in how easily everything had come together. Once I had the idea for The Fading Blue theme, it was like a dam had burst and my creative juices wouldn't stop flowing. Everything from ice sculptures to a silent auction that would include an Alaskan cruise through the glaciers.

I would have a big projection screen with images of the ocean and ice caps and placards on the table with facts and figures about global warming and rising sea levels.

The colors were simple yet classic. The decorations bold yet not overwhelming. It was meant to give the attendees the feelings of being underwater. Of being surrounded by a great open expanse.

Personally, I thought it was going to be incredible. And Theo seemed to think so too. Every suggestion I made was the best thing since sliced bread. His enthusiasm was sweet and flattering.

I had been working my ass off for weeks and I think even Marion was stunned.

The phone on my desk rang, startling me out of my single-minded focus on facts and figures. Who would have thought Vivian Baily would find numbers so consuming?

"Vivian Bailey, Events Coordinator. How can I help you?" I asked, loving how cool and professional I sounded. I still got a thrill out of saying my title.

"Hi, Vivian. It's Theo," his rich, warm voice said through the phone.

"I know," I said, smiling. I had come to recognize his voice instantly, considering how often he called me during the week. I had come to look forward to it. What usually began as a conversation about work, typically devolved into a discussion about anything and everything else. And he was interested in absolutely everything I had to say!

Theo chuckled nervously. No matter how much we spoke, he continued to stumble over himself. It was refreshing to talk to someone who didn't think the sun shone out of their own ass. I had learned that a lack of ego wasn't a bad thing and that arrogance was sexy, modesty was too.

"What can I do for you, Theo?" I asked, lingering over his name.

I could hear him clear his throat. "I'm glad I caught you. I know you're planning to be out of the office for the rest of the week. You never did say where you were going," he said, blatantly fishing for information.

"No, I didn't," I agreed, not giving him anything. A girl had to keep some mystery. And there was no way I was explaining that I was headed for a weekend with my fuck friend.

It wasn't the first time I felt a sharp flash of shame at the way I rushed to Cole every chance I got.

"Won't give me any clues will you? I'm starting to think you're involved in a secret cult with plans for global domination."

It was my turn to laugh. "Not even close. So tell me why it's so important that you caught me before I left?" I asked, changing the subject.

"Well, I was wondering, if you're not too busy, if you'd like to grab some lunch today. We could look over the proposed budget and I could go ahead and approve it for you. You know so it wouldn't delay things for you next week when you got back," Theo suggested and I couldn't help but smile at his less than subtle offer.

"Is that the only reason you want to have lunch with me? To see the budget? Sounds pretty boring to me," I baited.

I was horrible.

I knew flirting with Theo was a bad idea. But it felt really nice to have the attention of such a hot guy who was genuinely interested in me.

Theo thought I was smart. Theo thought I was capable. He liked to tell me how incredible I was. He cloaked it in professionalism, of course. After all he was a client. But I knew he meant it as so much more than that.

I knew a hot and bothered male when I saw one.

Theo was the man you'd take home to Mom. He was the perfect guy for my slowly evolving lifestyle change.

Yet I was going with Gracie this weekend to Raleigh to see the other man in my life. The one Mom would never, ever know about.

The one I had no doubt would ruin me in the worst possible way.

Theo's answering laugh was predictably uneasy but happy. He liked my flirting. But I made him nervous. He didn't quite know if I was joking or being serious.

That made two of us.

"Well, I. . .I'd like your company as well, of course," Theo stuttered adorably. Knowing I kept him off-balance was such a powerful feeling. With Cole I was always the one off kilter. I couldn't think of a time he ever stumbled over his words when he spoke to me.

But what more could I expect from a man who gave me orgasms and little else?

"I'm not really worried about delays. We're way ahead of schedule," I stated, dialing back the flirting a bit, feeling somewhat deflated by my guilt and Cole based shame.

I had been steeling myself all week for what I expected to find when I got down to Raleigh. Who I would have to fend off and how much damage I would have to inflict.

And I was excited about it. I knew exactly what that said about me. I knew what sort of person that made me.

I had no delusions. I was addicted to the rush only Cole could give me. But it exhausted me as well.

I was torn and conflicted and oh so ashamed to feel anything at all.

Cole turned me upside down and inside out.

I loved it.

But I hated him for it.

"Vivian? Did you hear what I just said?" Theo asked and I shook my head and pressed the receiver to my ear. Fixating on Cole in any way shape or form was not conducive to getting my job done.

"I'm sorry," I apologized.

Theo chuckled good-naturedly. "I said the budget was just my excuse. I'd really like to take you to lunch and not talk about work at all. What do you think?" he asked in a rush.

And there it was. I had been anticipating it. I knew it was only a matter of time. I had practically forced this to happen.

So why did I feel suddenly apprehensive at the prospect of going on an actual date with Theo Anderson?

Was it because I actually liked him?

Was it because with him was the possibility of an actual relationship? A tiny slice of normalcy that I had otherwise been missing in my life.

That to accept would be to take that first step away from Cole for good.

I hadn't dated anyone since Cole and I started sleeping

together. Sure there had been dates here and there but I had always found a reason to call it quits before it ever began.

I kissed some guys. But Cole was the only man I had been with in over two years.

Because Cole had been the only one I wanted. For all of his faults, he fulfilled this crazy need I had inside me like no one else could.

But Theo was different. Or maybe it was me that was different.

I felt something alter inside me. I was reaching a breaking point and I knew that now was my moment for change.

My cell phone dinged in my purse, as if on cue. I pulled it out and looked down at the screen and had to cover my mouth so I wouldn't laugh in Theo's ear.

Mr. Winky and I miss you…

A few seconds later another text came in and this time I had to snicker out loud at the cartoon drawing of a penis with sad eyes and a pouting mouth saying, Hurry up, I'm lonely!

My heart thudded in my chest and my stomach coiled up in anticipation. I missed him too, damn him!

I was honestly starting to question whether the man had latent psychic abilities. Even from hundreds of miles away he was screwing up my world and driving me insane.

"Vivian. I wasn't trying to be funny. I really want to know if you'll go out to lunch with me today. I'm asking you out," Theo rambled and I turned off my cell phone. Cole's Mr. Winky and his cartoon eyes would just have to wait.

I squeezed my eyes shut and did the stupidest thing I could do. I knew instantly I was a fool. But I was a fool who craved the mistake she was going to make.

"I can't make it today, Theo. Maybe another time."

GRACIE and I drove into Raleigh around midafternoon on Friday. We called Maysie and I was both disappointed and slightly relieved when she informed us that the guys were over at another radio station for some press and interviews.

The thought of seeing Cole made me jumpy. I wasn't sure

what to do with this weird new vibe between us and whether that would translate into oh-my-god-you're-fantastic or oh-my-god-I'm-going-to-rip-your-face-off when I saw him.

I was feeling guilty about Theo and my cruel flirting and casual dismissal. I liked Theo. I thought he had great potential. But I was being led around by the wayward bitch between my legs. And she only wanted Mr. Winky.

I was a girl who spent way too much time fixated on guy problems. Ugh.

We made plans to meet up with Maysie at the Chili's across the street for dinner. I used the time until then to coordinate my best rock slut outfit and to try out a dozen ways to wear my eye shadow.

Because I was feeling magnanimous, I offered to do Gracie's makeup as well. She declined.

"You're loss," I tossed out as I ran my fingers through my hair. I pursed my lips at my reflection when I was finished.

I looked good.

Damn good.

Cole was going to be eating out of the palm of my hand. He wouldn't be able to look at anyone but me.

He was mine.

I ran my hands down my sides, pulling my teeny-tiny leather skirt higher up on my thighs. My bodice top showed off my navel piercing and tiny heart tattoo on my hipbone. My hair hung to the middle of my back and my eyes were done up dark and mysterious.

Damn, I think I wanted to have sex with me.

Gracie was dressed in her usual sweet and innocent style. This time with faded blue jeans and button up pink shirt that hit her belly, showing a little skin. Her white, blonde hair was straight around her shoulders and her makeup was subtle and understated.

We got a booth by the bar at Chili's and I ordered a beer and nachos while Gracie got herself water and wings. And while we waited for Maysie, I enjoyed turning some heads. In the twenty minutes since we had sat down we had been hit on twice and had a round of shots bought for us by the old dudes in the corner.

Gracie pushed the shots towards me and I noticed the slight tremor in her hands as she did so.

"Do we need to go somewhere else?" I asked her, feeling stupid for suggesting we sit next to the bar to wait for Maysie. It wasn't the best place for someone to sit when they struggled not to drink.

"I'm fine," Gracie scoffed, looking insulted at the suggestion that she was anything but okay. Despite her assurance, I returned the shots and quickly downed my beer.

Finally Maysie arrived and I knew instantly that something was wrong. Her face was pinched and there were dark circles under her eyes. She looked as if she hadn't slept properly in days.

Though I was sure sleeping on a tour bus with a gaggle of men had something to do with it, I knew it was more than that. Call it friend telepathy.

"What's up, hun? You look stressy," I said, ruffling Maysie's hair in the way I knew she hated. She didn't react in the slightest. Something was definitely up.

"This living on the road stuff isn't as great as I thought it would be," she admitted on a sigh and sagged down into the seat. I looked at Gracie who seemed as concerned as I was.

"Talk about it," I urged, putting my arm around her shoulders.

"Everyone's on edge. And I think this new manager is stirring up the tension. I don't like him. He's shady as hell."

Cole had mentioned Jose Suarez a few times but it had always been with a respect and reverence reserved for Sierra Nevada IPA and Papa John's cheesesticks. In other words, for Cole at least, Jose walked on water.

So it was a surprise to hear that from Maysie.

"Why do you think that?" I asked picking apart my loaded nachos.

"He's always off talking to Cole and Cole's being different, I guess. I mean he's still an obnoxious prick but he's pulling away some. The other guys are feeling it too. Jordan is ready to lose it."

"Jordan is always ready to lose it on Cole though," I interrupted.

Maysie shook her head. "No, this is nearing blood bath levels. It's exhausting trying to keep him from knocking Cole's head off."

I bristled a bit, feeling unusually protective over the one person who most likely didn't need or deserve it.

"Well Jordan's always been less than patient when it comes to Cole. Maybe you need to remind him to worry about his own bullshit before he goes and starts in on someone else," I snipped, making Gracie's eyes widened.

Maysie narrowed her eyes. "Since when are you defending Cole?"

"I'm not. I'm just pointing out that Jordan is anything but perfect. Do we need to talk about Olivia?" I asked, wishing instantly I hadn't gone there. I had mentioned she who shall not be named! I was entering bitch slap territory.

Maysie recoiled as if I had hit her.

"Viv, seriously. What the hell?" Gracie reprimanded and I instantly felt bad.

"Sorry, Mays. Forget I said that. It sucks you're getting pulled into boy drama," I said quickly, trying to remedy my bad case of jerk mouth.

Maysie still seemed prickly but appeared to accept my apology. "Yeah, it does suck. I'm actually thinking of coming back to Bakersville for a while. So I can plan the wedding and get my head together," she said, causing Gracie and I to gape at her.

"What?" we both asked at the same time.

Maysie shrugged. "I'm just not sure if this tour is the place for me to be. It's just so draining."

"You'd leave Jordan? For weeks, maybe even months at a time? I find that hard to believe. You two are joined at the genitals," I countered.

Maysie rolled her eyes.

"He'd understand. I need to figure out what I'm going to do with my life outside of being his fiancé. I can't follow him around on the road forever. Or however long this ride lasts. It seemed so romantic when I threw everything in to go with the guys on tour. But here we are over a year later and even though there have been breaks and times when we're not doing the band thing, it's taken over every facet of my life. I can't even plan my wedding because of all the craziness going on. I don't resent it, but I'm getting tired of it."

I couldn't have been more shocked then if she had told me she had decided to start a one-woman circus act involving chickens and flame-throwers.

"Wow, Mays. . .just. . .wow," was all I could say.

"So, do you have space for another roomie?" Maysie asked sadly, giving us a half-hearted smile.

"Of course we do," Gracie said as I opened my mouth to say, "Not really."

But that would have been a shitty thing to say. Not to mention completely unsupportive. But I was just thinking of all the extra mess and estrogen fueled drama.

My drama was enough for our two-bedroom apartment.

"Thanks guys. It probably won't be for a few weeks. I have to talk to Jordan about it first. I know it's the right thing for me. I know he's struggling with everything with the band and making me happy at the same time. I just want him to be able to focus on himself for a little while. He'll understand, right?" she asked. Why the hell was she asking us?

But I knew she just needed the reassurance. I patted her back in an affectionate gesture. "Of course he will, Mays. Jordan loves you. You guys are solid."

Maysie gave me a shaky smile that reminded me so much of the insecure girl I had known during our Chi Delta days. I hated seeing her like this. Unsure and unhappy.

While it was great that the guys were finally getting the recognition that we all felt they deserved, it seemed to be coming at a hefty price.

For everyone.

Maysie's less than exuberant mood put a damper on what I had hoped to be a great weekend.

What a downer. And I was looking so cute too! I fluffed my hair and tried to resurrect our dwindling good time.

"Let's tailgate, ladies!" I announced, slapping some cash down on the table and jumping to my feet. I wiggled my hips in time to the music blasting from the jukebox in the corner and grinned a siren smile, as I became the immediate center of attention.

"But we don't have a tailgate," Maysie pointed out. I shrugged. "Then let's go borrow one!"

Chapter 9
VIVIAN

THERE was to be no tailgating during our evening festivities, much to my disappointment.

By the time the three of arrived at the Pour House Music Hall, where Primal Terror and our boys were playing, it was already packed. The Rejects weren't due to hit the stage for another hour, but people were already lined up around the block.

Pour House Music Hall was a lot smaller then some of the venues where the bands had been performing over the last few months, but Primal Terror had insisted on several "smaller" gigs. They had risen up through the more intimate clubs and bars and apparently wanted to get back to their roots.

"We don't have to wait in line, do we? Because I'll start flashing boob to get to the front if I have to," I complained. Though I meant it. I wasn't above using some flesh just so I didn't have to wait around.

"Of course not, we're going straight in," Maysie said and I was relieved to see that the doom and gloom had disappeared. It was hard to be pissy when you were going to see your man play to an adoring crowd. There was no greater aphrodisiac out there.

Unless your guy was an attention-seeking slut bag.

As soon as we entered the darkly lit bar, I caught sight of the guys setting up their gear on the small stage. All of them, but Cole that is. He was too busy sitting on the edge of the stage, his legs hanging off the side with some girl stood between his knees.

He was leaning back on his hands. So there was no groping or kissing going on. But that didn't stop me from wanting to run over there and rip skankarilla's hair out.

My rage ignited instantly.

Damn, it was going to be a long night.

I couldn't help but notice the crusty looks the other guys tossed their lead singer's way. And how he purposefully kept his back to them.

It was sad to see an end to their easy camaraderie. I really hoped this was only a phase and they'd get back to normal soon. Because no band could withstand the obvious resentment and bitterness that swirled around between them.

I turned my attention back to erstwhile fellow and noticed that the girl now had her hands on his knees.

I felt my fingers curling into a fist.

Gracie grabbed my arm and gave it a tight squeeze, her nails digging into my skin painfully. "Don't, Viv. Just don't," she warned.

I yanked my arm away and resolutely turned my back on Cole and his bimbo of the moment. I pushed my way through the crowd and slammed my hand down on the bar. The two guys on either side of me looked down and gave me identical leering smiles.

"Let me buy you a drink, baby." I turned my most seductive smirk on a guy with a bright red Mohawk and a tattoo running along one side of his face.

"I've never been one to turn down free alcohol." I looked up at him through my eyelashes, laying it on as thick as possible. I had no interest in Mohawked and Scary but free booze was the way to this girl's heart.

"I'll be buying your drinks tonight," a hard voice said from behind me. I let out a sigh but didn't turn around. I put my hand on Mohawk's arm.

104

"I want my drinks from you though," I simpered.

"God damn it, Vivian! Don't start this shit already! You just got here!" Cole yelled over the dull roar of the crowd.

Mohawk looked from me to Cole and held his hands up. "I'm not lookin' to get in the middle of a domestic," he stated, backing away.

I turned around and gave Cole the look of death, hoping it would put him ten feet under.

"Were you planning to fuck that guy?" he asked, nodding his head in the direction of retreating Mohawk. He was angry. His eyes flashed in the dull light.

I leaned my elbows on the bar and pushed my chest out. Cole's gaze slid from my face to the part of my body he could never resist. And so did several other men around us. I shook my hair out behind me and gave him a bored look.

"No, I didn't plan on fucking him." I affected a yawn as though I were already tired of the conversation. I made eyes at the preppy guy stood on the other side of Cole. I licked my lips slowly and almost laughed at his eager expression.

Cole looked over his shoulder at preppy and snarled. "Get the hell out of here. She's off limits, dude!" Poor preppy scurried off so fast it was as though his butt were on fire.

I stood up straight and took a menacing step toward the object of my unbridled lust. "Holy double standards, Cole! Where's the little blonde?" I asked looking pointedly around the teeming group of people.

Cole scrunched up his face in confusion. "Who?"

I laughed humorlessly. "The bitch that was showing you her boob job when I came in," I spat out.

Cole frowned, as though trying to figure out what I was talking about. And then he started laughing. The urge to kick him between the legs was overwhelming.

Then the asshole pinched the tip of my nose and rustled my hair like a damn dog. "Is Vivvie jealous?" he cooed and this time I lost it.

I picked up the closest beer bottle and dumped the contents on his shoes.

Cole leapt backwards, howling in outrage. "What the fuck, Vivian?" he screamed. The noise in the bar became noticeably quieter.

I pressed myself up against Cole, my face an inch from his. My heart was thumping wildly, my blood was buzzing with fury.

"I am sick of your bullshit, Cole. You better walk the line tonight or you'll be sorry. Do I make myself clear? I didn't come all this way to be humiliated by you. If you want me here, then fucking act like it," I hissed.

Cole's eyes snapped and sizzled, his chest heaving up and down. He was flushed and just as furious as I was.

Then he grabbed the back of my head, his fingers curling into my hair and smashed his mouth down on mine.

The kiss was bruising and forceful. This wasn't about romance. This was about domination. I bit down on his bottom lip and could taste his blood.

He pulled away, his lips swollen and bleeding. "I'm happy you're here. Is that what you want me to say? Is that what you want to hear?" He grabbed my upper arms and pushed me back against the wall, his pelvis thrusting against mine.

"Does that make you happy?" he demanded.

I couldn't take my eyes away from him. He was gorgeous. And he made me feel completely and totally alive. I craved this manic insanity that I only seemed to experience when I was with him.

Why couldn't I be content with nice and normal? Why did I crawl over broken glass for this madness?

Why did I allow Cole to degrade me and humiliate me over and over again? Why did I scream at him and make a scene just so I could get this reaction from him?

What the hell was wrong with me?

What the hell was wrong with us?

I was so turned on I could barely stand. I wanted him to take me then and there. I didn't give a crap about the people openly gawking at us. I thrived on it.

I wanted the hard press of his body against mine. I wanted the chaos.

"Yes! It makes me happy," I bit out, giving him that tiny victory.

"Good," he said, leaning in and kissing me tenderly on the nose. His thumbs caressed the side of my face. A remarkably gentle act from such a volatile man.

"Stand in front. I want to see you when I sing," Cole murmured, leaning in to kiss me on the mouth. And this one wasn't hateful or angry. It was soft and almost loving. And it shook me to my core.

Then he was gone and I stood there, my back against the wall, trying to catch my breath, not sure what the hell had just happened.

Maysie stood off to the side, her arms crossed, shaking her head. I straightened my spine and walked back to the bar, ordering myself a Lemon Drop and tossed it back. Then I ordered another. And another.

If I were going to make it through the night I'd need help. And my good friend, vodka, would do the trick.

"You always put on a good show, I'll give you that," Gracie said dryly, sitting beside me at the bar, watching the people around us. It was hard to ignore the increasing number of girls who were coming into the venue. All decked out in their best metal slut gear. Most of them hoping a flash of skin would get them a night with one of the guys on stage.

I watched as a group of girls tried to make conversation with Garrett and Jordan. Both were polite but obviously uninterested. Maysie was in a corner talking to some people I recognized as the roadie crew. She didn't seem remotely bothered by the women chatting up her fiancé. And I knew Riley wouldn't care if she were here either.

Because they didn't have anything to worry about. Jordan and Garrett were loyal to the women they loved.

The girls finally got the hint and turned their attentions from Garrett and Jordan to Mitch and Cole. When Mitch was too absorbed in tuning his bass to give them what they were looking for, their entire focus honed in on the man I had come to see.

The man who would never truly been mine.

And he smiled and flirted and laughed when they rubbed his arm. He gave them exactly what they wanted. He teased and seduced with only a look and a grin. The girls ate it up. And he loved it. I could see it from here.

My chest started to ache and an unfamiliar thickness squeezed my throat.

"Come on Viv, they're about to start," Gracie said, tugging on my arm. I was being uncharacteristically maudlin. I felt like hanging in the back and sulking. But instead I tossed my hair around my shoulders and straightened my shirt to hang low over my breasts. I ran my finger around the edge of my lips, getting rid of any smudges.

Then we pushed and shoved our way to the front where I knew Cole could see me.

Their music started low and languid. Cole's deep, throaty growl into the mic echoed around the room. The crowd went instantly quiet, the light of a hundred cellphones lighting up.

I knew they were going to be amazing as always, though I couldn't help but pick up on a very significant difference. It wasn't anything anyone in the crowd would notice. It was only something close to those on stage would be aware of.

Cole stood out front, his hands clasped around the mic, his eyes closed. Garrett and Mitch stood behind him, their faces turned down to their instruments. Jordan sat at his drums, his mouth set in a firm line as he beat in time to the strains of the music.

They looked like a rock band.

But they each looked miserable. They were musicians that fed off each other. They were always looking and communicating with one another before, during and after every show.

Tonight it was like watching four separate individuals up there rather than one cohesive unit.

There was a major rift going on. And for the first time I truly worried for the fate of my favorite band. Because this didn't seem like something they'd easily fix.

But then Cole opened his mouth and I stopped worrying about the boys' drama and allowed myself to get lost in the show.

"I'm here to own you, bitches!" Cole purred, his voice a dark promise. He growled again, Jordan picking up the beat on his drums. Garrett slid his fingers along the strings, making them scream.

"And you're going to let me. . .because you fucking want it! You'll fucking love it!" The girls started going crazy and I was getting jostled from behind as a wave of arms and hair and perfume pressed forward, trying to get closer to the man who had us enthralled.

"Can I have you?" he screamed into the crowd and in one voice we all screamed back.

"YES!"

Then the music erupted and I forgot how much the man standing above me infuriated and confused me. I simply became like everyone else. I worshipped him. I desired him.

I wanted him to own me.

Cole curled his hands around the microphone and leaned out toward the writhing mass. Garrett's head was down, his blonde hair covering his face. His arms taut as he played like he had just made a deal with the devil. Mitch's face was now tilted toward the ceiling, his eyes closed as if lost. And Jordan was a machine, pounding the drums in an exhausting rhythm.

But we were all waiting for the magic. For Cole to start singing. And when he did I knew, without a doubt, it was something special. I understood why the record label was pushing him forward. Why they were trying to market him above the other guys. Mitch, Garrett, and Jordan were amazing. They were talented and without them, the band wouldn't exist.

But Cole was something else entirely. He was sex. He was destruction. He was raw and desperate.

My god, he was fantastic!

Festering and bleeding I'm dying in vain
Spoiled and lost, my soul black and stained
You despise, you destroy, you maim, you control,
I hate you for the life you claimed and you stole.

109

Seductive Chaos

Filth and defile
Loathe and revile
You dig inside and
Kiss my rotten smile.

I murder your memory,
slash it away
I rip your face from my mind,
Whatever it takes.

The blurred lines of the past,
Eat away at the truth,
Chase me, claim me,
Tighten the noose.

Filth and defile,
Hate without guile,
You pull out my insides,
And break my broken smile.

I want your death,
I want your pain,
I want to be bound
I want your chains.

Filth and defile,
I drown in denial,
You rip me apart
You kill me with a smile.

Kill me with a smile. . .

Cole ended on a long, tortured wail that made my insides shiver. This was one of Garrett's more morbid songs. Thank god he was with Riley now. His new stuff was a lot less scary.

Being at a Generation Rejects show was an experience unlike any other. And despite the tension that seemed to echo from the

110

stage, it was electric. It was frantic. It could be consuming.

And I wanted to enjoy it. And I would have if not for the sea of screaming, and sometimes shirtless women just waiting to become the object of my annoyance and desire's new plaything.

I stared up at the man making love to the crowd from the stage and wished I could stop craving him. Stop wanting him with every fiber of my being. But it was like asking me to stop watching The Real Housewives of Atlanta. There were some things out of my control.

Then Cole looked down at me, his eyes meeting mine and he winked. His smile lighting up his face in self-satisfied glory. When he looked at me like that, it was as though he were seeing only me. And that I was the girl he wanted out of anyone he could be with.

I was enough.

I hated him for these glimmers of tenderness that made keeping emotional distance downright impossible. It was hard to hate the man when you loved the heart.

Shit, what was I thinking?

I winked back; shaking my hips a bit in the way I knew drove Cole wild and he widened his eyes and pointed at me, singling me out.

It felt good. It made me feel special.

The girl beside me started to squeal loudly in my ear. As if Cole's sex-drenched smile, as if his attention, were for her.

Sad, delusional girl.

My face started to redden and my fingers turned into claws. The rage-fueled she-beast was waking from her slumber. The possessive, territorial dragon was ready to take this chick out.

I leaned back and elbowed the twit sharply in the gut, digging my bone in with enough strength to make her gasp. Then I body checked her out of my way, using my ample ass as leverage.

She fell on her butt with a loud screech. I looked down at her with a smile, just as self-satisfied as Cole's had ever been. I wiggled my fingers in her direction and she glared at me, though with no retaliation.

Maysie looped her arm around my waist and pulled me

farther to the side and away from the throng of people.

"I'm not wearing the proper clothing for a bar brawl. So watch it," she warned. I shrugged, turning my attention back to the boys on stage.

The rest of the show passed without further incident. As soon as The Rejects were finished, the house music came on while they quickly broke down their equipment. I drank a few more beers, enjoying the nice alcoholic haze that had descended.

Cole was at my side soon enough.

"You ready to get out of here?" he whispered in my ear, brushing my hair off my neck and putting his lips over my steady pulse.

"You don't want to stay and watch Primal Terror?" I asked, swaying slightly from the booze and from Cole's touch. I wanted to ask him about the odd tension I sensed between him and his bandmates. I wanted to know why even now as he pawed at me desperately, there seemed to be sadness just below the surface.

But I was mildly drunk and incredibly horny.

I looked over Cole's shoulder and smirked at the disappointed groupies hanging around hoping to swoop in and steal him away.

Not tonight, ladies.

This time, he was all mine.

I forgot about my questions and concerns. I forgot about all the reasons I shouldn't be doing this at all. I caved to the hedonistic rush that only Cole could provide.

He ran his tongue along the base of my throat, tasting me. I was still high from his performance and my body buzzed in anticipation.

This is, after all, what I came down here for, right?

"I want you, now," he breathed hard and heavy.

"Then let's go," I murmured, consequences and lingering emotions be damned.

Chapter 10
COLE

"I CAN'T open my eyes! Oh my god! What did you put on my face?" Vivian screamed, wiping at her skin.

Shit. This was not going how I planned.

Okay, so when I found out Vivian was coming down to Raleigh, I got a little excited. Believe it or not, the most action I had experienced since we were last together in Texas was with my hand.

And my palm desperately needed a break.

I had all sorts of debauchery planned. My sex-drive was going thermal nuclear. So maybe I took it a step too far. Maybe I got a little too creative.

"Why can't I open my eyes, Cole?" Vivian asked, panicking.

I started trying to scoop heavy, warm, slowly solidifying liquid off her face but the sticky stuff wouldn't budge.

"What is this shit?" Vivian demanded, swatting my hands away.

I was still in my boxers and Vivian was only in a hot pair of black lace panties. My erection, which had been large and in charge only moments before, was losing its steam.

And things had been going so well too.

We'd barely gotten out of the bar without mauling each other. Vivian practically deep throated my tongue on the cab ride back to the hotel. The elevator ride up to my room had been just this side of indecent. The elderly couple sharing the lift had gotten more than an eyeful of her fantastic tits.

It was awesome!

When we got to the room we had slowed it down a notch and taken our time, which was unusual for us.

We didn't take our time. We didn't linger. We were all about going full throttle to the finish line.

Not tonight.

Tonight I wanted it to be special. I wanted to share things with her. I wanted to indulge in some fantasies, goddamn it!

Unfortunately for me, I had learned one very important lesson...Google was not my friend.

"It's honey," I admitted, watching her flail about, thick stringy globs rolling down her face and smearing the pillow.

"Honey? Are you kidding me?" Vivian yelled. And I didn't blame her. The whole thing was seriously stupid.

But it had seemed like such a great idea at the time.

"It's supposed to be an aphrodisiac," I muttered, trying to help her again. I grabbed the end of the blanket and started wiping her face. Her eyelids appeared to be fused together.

"If you eat it dumbass! Not wear it! What the hell were you thinking? You put this shit on. My. Face!" Vivian rolled off the bed and landed with a thud on the ground. She got unsteadily to her feet and started waving her hands in front of her, shuffling about hesitantly.

"Watch out for the. . ." I began just as she rammed her knees into the bedside table.

Vivian snarled at me.

"Do you want any help?" I asked, making sure to stay out of kicking range.

"No! You've done enough for one night!" she huffed, walking into a coat rack and knocking it to the floor.

"Are you sure?" I called out, knowing I should probably help her anyway. But she looked like some sort of sludge monster. And her snarling and growling was freaking me out. I figured if I had any sort of attachment to my appendages, I should stay the hell out of her way.

My poor dick had deflated anti-climatically. I nudged it through my boxers, where it flopped pathetically.

So much for my night of pussy-filled fun. It seemed the gods were against me. I had become the king of masturbation during the last few weeks, forgoing any and all female attention that wasn't Vivian-scary-honey-monster-Baily.

And when I finally had the only woman my poor, neglected penis seemed to want in my arms, I fucked it up by literally blinding her with condiments.

I licked the stickiness from my fingers and wondered what the likelihood would be for me getting some action if I went into the bathroom with her.

"You fucking asshole!" Vivian hollered from behind the closed door.

Hmm, I'm thinking slim to none.

I pulled the ruined sheets off the bed and called housekeeping to have them bring up some more.

I tugged on my jeans and sat down on the couch, putting my feet up on the small coffee table. Housekeeping showed a few minutes later and remade the bed. I gave the young, Hispanic girl my sexiest grin and she was too flustered to take note of the strange, sticky substance covering the sheets.

I could hear the shower going and I started to get impatient. After housekeeping had left, I pulled on the elastic waistband of my boxers and looked down at my dismally limp cock.

"Sorry, buddy," I intoned sadly.

I had officially given up on any plans for a night of no-holds-barred monkey lovin' and decided to make do with some porn. Because Deep Inside Misty Rain never let me down.

I was mid-wank when a pillow bounced off the side of my head, ruining my flow.

"I'm in danger of losing my eyesight and all you can do is rub one out? Are you kidding me?" Vivian stood over me wrapped in a robe, her hair wet and tangled around her shoulders, her face scrubbed red. And her eyes were open. Frighteningly so.

"What else was I supposed to do?" I shrugged and turned my attention back to good ole Misty.

Vivian threw another pillow and this time I had to accept defeat. I tucked my junk away and promised the poor fellow extra care and attention some other time.

"I'm glad you take me so seriously," she fumed and I knew some careful maneuvering was going to be required here.

Or I could just rile her up even more.

"It was fucking funny, Viv. Stop throwing such a bitch fit about it," I said, getting to my feet and grabbing a T-shirt off the floor and pulled it down over my head.

I was getting a tad cranky. And the screaming and aggressive pillow throwing wasn't helping matters. I rubbed at my temples feeling a headache coming on. I needed a drink.

I went to the mini-fridge and pulled out the so tiny it should be illegal bottle of whisky and quickly unscrewed the cap. I tossed it back and coughed. I was vaguely aware that Vivian was still yelling at me.

Her face was flushed and I could still see some honey stuck in hair. I probably shouldn't mention that. If I had any sense of self-preservation I really shouldn't poke the snarling bear.

"You've still got shit in your hair," I pointed out.

Vivian's eyes went wide as if she couldn't believe what just came from my mouth. I smirked at her and shrugged again.

"I could have helped you get that out, you know," I told her, wiggling my eyebrows.

Vivian let out what could only be described as a She-Ra battle cry and launched herself at me.

Hell yeah!

She wrapped her legs around my waist and her hands went for my throat. She knocked me backwards and we went tumbling. I bumped into the coffee table, pushing it over. The back of my knees hit the couch and I fell to the floor, Vivian on top of me.

I started to laugh, rocking my now happy groin against her, until I saw the look of pure murder on her face. Crap!

Was she honestly trying to strangle me?

"Vivian!" I choked out, shoving her off me. She rolled to her side and sat up, covering her face with her hands.

She went from raging pissed to sobbing mess in less than two seconds. And I didn't know what I was supposed to do.

When did this go from entertaining to cry me a river? Did I miss something? It was just fucking honey!

"What the hell is wrong with you?" I barked less than kindly. I was quickly losing my patience with this song and dance.

Vivian wasn't the easiest chick to be around. She was volatile and moody. I never knew whether to expect a kiss or a kick the stomach. She was up and down, left and right. But that's what I dug about her. She kept me on my toes. We fought. We made up. She screamed, I yelled, and then we'd hump like rabbits.

So the sudden tear-fest made no sense.

Vivian furiously wiped her face and got to her feet. She shook her head when I tried to reach out for her. I wrapped my arms around her waist, trying to make her stop.

I nuzzled the back of her neck, hoping to move us past the ready to kill each other stage to the let's rip our clothes off and forget this bullshit phase.

"Just stop it, Cole. Just let me go," she begged, not really struggling, but not leaning back into me either.

Okay, so I really wasn't getting what the big deal was. Maybe it was the fact that it was almost one in the morning. Or maybe it had to do with the whiskey I had just downed. Maybe it was the serious case of blue balls that had my nuts in a vice. Whatever the reason, I was having a seriously hard time figuring out what was going on.

"Are you really that mad at me?" I scoffed, hardly able to believe that my moronic screw up could upset her that badly. Vivian was made of harder stuff than that. Which is why she was such a cool chick.

Vivian pulled away and I was left standing there, grasping at air. I felt a shift in her demeanor. The vibe in the room was anything but happy, happy, good times. It sucked.

"I'm just sick and tired of feeling like a joke to you! You fuck other girls and I scream and make an idiot of myself. You decide you want my company and I jump at the chance to be there. You feel the need to try your crazy sex shenanigans and I'm your happy little guinea pig. I'm over it, Cole! Freaking over it!" she said firmly, her voice rising.

I laughed. Bad response, I know. But I couldn't help it.

"Is this for real? You seriously think that?" I asked incredulously. How could I listen to this shit with a straight face when it was so damn ridiculous?

Vivian threw her hands in the air and groaned. "See! This is exactly what I'm talking about!"

Enough was enough!

I pulled the back of her robe and pressed her flush against my front. "Stop it, okay? This is stupid! We're not here for this shit. We're here for this," I murmured in her ear, tracing the round curve with my tongue. I moaned low and deep as I released the tie of her robe and reached my hand inside to find her boob.

I gave it a proper squeeze, followed by a stinging slap for good measure. Vivian gasped and looked at me over her shoulder, her eyes hooded. She was turned on. But she didn't want to be turned on. I loved it when she challenged me like that.

"Fuck me, Viv. You know you want to," I whispered, my lips a breath from hers. My hand released her tit and traveled down to the mound between her legs. I tiptoed my fingers to the warm wetness I knew was waiting for me.

"You want me to touch you. You want me to fuck you with my fingers. You want me to make you come all. Night. Long." I moaned again as I slowly pushed my finger inside her.

Her knees started to quiver and I knew I had her. I closed my eyes as I started to bite down on the still wet skin of her shoulder, while I rubbed my raging hard on up and down her ass crack.

And then she was pulling away again. My eyes snapped open to find her tightening the belt around her waist. Denied again.

And this time, I couldn't help it. I got pissed. Really, really pissed.

"Since when are you a fucking cock tease?" I demanded, running my fingers that still smelled like her through my hair. I was so aroused it was painful. And no amount of jerking off was going to help.

I wanted sex. With Vivian. Now!

"You are such an insensitive ass!" she hissed and I was officially done with this conversation.

I advanced on her and watched in satisfaction as she retreated until her back was pressed against the wall. I leaned in, my face dangerously close to hers.

"Do you know how many women would kill to be here with me right now? Do you get how special you should feel because I chose you?" I shouted into her face that was almost at level with mine.

It was a dickish and egotistical thing to say. I should have probably chosen my words a bit more wisely. Particularly if I ever hoped to have this woman in my bed again. And telling her she was one of many wasn't the way to do it.

But I was so fucking angry I couldn't see straight. She had led me around by my balls all night and I was sick and tired of it.

I loved the roller coaster. I loved the highs and lows of being around Vivian. But right now, with her indignant fury staring up at me, I wanted to throw something.

So I did.

I picked the lamp up off the bedside table and threw it across the room. It smashed with a satisfying bang on the opposite wall. Vivian didn't even flinch.

"Happy now?" I growled, curling my hand into a fist and punching it into the wall by her head. Not hard enough to dent or to scare her. But with enough force to make myself clear.

She was sick and tired? Well I was sick and tired.

"I'm outta here," I said suddenly, pushing myself off the wall and away from Vivian who hadn't moved an inch.

"Where are you going?" she demanded, still clutching that stupid robe tight to her body like a damn shield.

I yanked on my jeans. I grabbed my wallet and room key and threw open the door.

I looked back at Vivian, to where she stood in the middle of the room, looking a mixture of angry, hurt, and confused.

She wasn't the only one.

I was feeling all of those things and worse. I felt defeated.

Vivian had defeated me. She had worn me down and run me over.

I needed to get drunk.

And laid.

And not particularly in that order.

"Don't worry about it," I tossed over my shoulder before slamming the door behind me.

Of course I'd come back. And when I did I'd fuck her into an apology. We'd make up and all would be like it was before. We both just needed to cool down. And I needed to blow off some steam.

Then everything would be fine.

Chapter 11
COLE

I THOUGHT long and hard about going out and finding someone else to take the edge off the ache in my pants. Something needed to be done before I lost my damn mind. There was only so long I could go without sex and not become certifiable and I was reaching the end of my very short shelf life.

Then I thought about Vivian, who was up in my hotel room, with honey still in her hair and probably thinking of all the ways she wanted to hurt and maim me.

Honestly, what did I owe her? She wasn't my girlfriend. We weren't dating. Hell, she barely tolerated me most days. Why she cared whether I was boning some other girl had always been beyond me. Just because we swapped bodily fluids didn't give us any sort of ownership over each other.

Hunting for some strange shouldn't bother her in the least.

Hell, she may very well be getting it on with all sorts of dudes back in Bakersville.

Hold up! I had never thought about that possibility before.

I hadn't spent any time thinking about what Vivian's life was like when she wasn't with me. What if she was with someone else?

My gut twisted and lurched at the thought.

What was this emotion churning in my stomach? I felt almost nauseous.

Vivian and the faceless douche started to bounce around in my head, fading in and out like a bad acid trip.

I stood in the hallway, chewing on my thumbnail, a bad habit left over from a shitty childhood. And I obsessed. I let my mind do cartwheels around the guy I just knew Vivian was screwing during her Cole-free hours.

He was probably some stereotypical jock. Most likely a reformed frat freak with a nine to five and a great parking spot in front of his office.

I wanted to kill this unknown jerk off. His face became an amalgamation of everyone I hated. My dad, the guy who cooked meth out of his apartment three doors down from me back in Bakersville. Maybe he looked like Stu, the mailman, who always conveniently lost my new editions of Guitar World.

ITOOK the elevator straight to the lobby and headed for the bar. It was closed of course, but I could see through the glass door that the bartender, a hot little number with bright red hair, was still inside, cleaning up.

I knocked on the glass and waved to get her attention. She made her way over and unlocked the door.

"Can I help you?" she asked, a small smile on her face. She gave me the typical once over and I knew instantly that she liked what she saw.

I thought about Vivian, who was most likely still up in my room sulking and making a voodoo doll out of my dirty socks and knew this is exactly what I needed to get my head on straight.

"I know you're closed, but what can I do to convince you to pour me a drink or two?" I asked, leaning my hip against the jam and hooking my thumbs in my jeans pocket.

The bartender ran her hand through her hair and opened the door wider, letting me in. She closed and locked it behind me.

"Let me join you?" she asked, chewing on her plump bottom

lip. I ran my hand along the back of my neck, feeling strange all of a sudden.

I hesitated inside the bar, watching as the girl went back behind the bar and pulled out a bottle of vodka and poured us a couple of shots.

She lifted her eyebrows at me, obviously wondering why I was still lingering just inside the door.

"You were the one that wanted to drink. Are you gonna sit down?" she asked, her voice was low and raspy and made me think of all sorts of naughty things.

She wore a tight black shirt and low cut jeans. She ran her tongue along her lip and watched me as I slowly approached the bar.

I sat down on a stool, grabbed the shot glass and tossed the contents back. The slight burn making me shudder. The bartender quickly refilled my glass and I just as quickly drank it.

She chuckled, a purposefully sexy sound and leaned over the bar, pressing her chest up and out for my enjoyment.

"I'm Breanne. And you're Cole Brandt."

I blinked in surprise. Yeah, the band was getting bigger but I had yet to experience recognition outside of our concerts and interviews.

"Uh yeah," I said, running my thumb along my lip. Breanne poured each of us another shot.

"I saw your show last month in St. Louis. It was incredible," she enthused, running her fingers along the back of my hand.

"I love that song you guys do. Perfect Regret. It's amazing! And your voice is unlike anything I've ever heard." She was getting her fan girl all over me.

I grinned, liking the adoration. I cocked my head to the side as I regarded her. "Thanks, that's cool of you to say."

"Are you here for a show? Are the other guys staying here?" Breanne asked, swallowing the vodka in one long gulp. She picked up a cloth and wiped down the bar, never taking her eyes off me.

"Yeah, we played at a bar in town tonight. It was a great show," I told her, trying to find my comfort level in this interaction.

Normally I didn't have any trouble talking up people. Girls in particular.

But tonight I was struggling.

I had a good idea of why, or more particularly who, had my brain short-circuiting.

Breanne pouted. "I wish I had known. I would totally have come to your show. What a bummer," she said, her fingers resuming their slow, lazy trek up and down my arm.

"Yeah," I said lamely.

After a few awkward seconds where any pretense of chitchat dwindled and died, I cleared my throat. "Can I get another shot?" I asked.

"Sure. Anything you want," Breanne said with a grin that let me know when she said anything, she meant anything.

"We're playing another bar on Tuesday in Charlotte," I said, not knowing why I told her that. I didn't want this girl thinking I wanted her to come. I didn't give a shit one way or another about her. But I was uncomfortably trying to fill the void.

I had come here wanting one thing and now I was pussing out.

Breanne looked as though I had offered her a round trip ticket to Paris. Her dull, brown eyes lit up. "I'd love to come! Oh my god! Maybe we could hang out afterwards," she suggested and I shrugged.

"Sure," I found myself saying. I really needed to shut the hell up.

"You want something else to drink. Or are your cool with the vodka?" she asked, her excited smile making me feel like a worthless dick. I should never have told this random girl to come to a show.

Something was seriously wrong with my head. My game wasn't just off, it was non-existent.

Breanne's rhythmic fingers became more purposeful as she wove her hand into my hair. It bugged the shit out of me. I hated when girls messed with my hair. Except when Viv pulled it, but that was a different story.

I shook my head, trying to dissuade her but Breanne the

Bartender was one persistent lady.

This would be so easy. I knew I could have this chick on her back in less than five minutes. Part of me really wanted to. I missed the easy effortlessness of banging girls I never had to talk to again.

Breanne came around from behind the bar and perched up on the stool beside me, turning her body so that her knees fell between mine. We were close enough I could smell stale beer and bar on her clothes.

Her makeup was thick. I could see a line around the outside of her face. Her hair color was obviously as fake as her nose. As a rule I didn't bother paying attention to this stuff.

What was wrong with me?

She wanted to fuck. That's what I came in here to do. Right?

But when I looked at Breanne, I didn't see her. My mind saw strawberry-blonde hair, angry green eyes, flushed skin, and perfectly pursed lips.

I smelled sex and vanilla and Vivian's perfumey shampoo stuff that got stuck in my nose but I liked it anyway.

What was I doing down here instead of upstairs where I wouldn't be swilling crappy rail liquor and contemplating the stupidity of sticking it in a girl who I had a feeling would go stalker when we were finished?

"So what brings you down here this time of night?" she asked, tapping her knees against my inner thigh.

"Just needed a drink," I said nonchalantly.

"Were you alone?" she asked and I caught an edge to her voice.

Simmer down girl, you don't even know me.

I downed another shot and wiped my mouth with the back of my hand.

"Nope," I told her, thinking that maybe it was about time I went back up to my room. I thought of Vivian waiting for me to come back and the appeal of being anywhere near this girl in front of me, or any other girl for that matter, was lost.

Breanne took the shot glass from my limp fingers and put it on the bar. She hopped down and stood between my legs, her hands running up my thighs as she leaned in.

I tried to back up but I almost fell off the stool.

"Whoa, sweetheart, don't you think we should talk some first," I laughed nervously.

If I weren't feeling so off balance this entire situation would be hella funny.

Breanne grabbed my hand and pressed it against her tit as she started to palm me through my jeans.

"I don't think you came in here wanting to talk, Cole," she said with a grin. I didn't like the sound of my name on her lips. It sounded all wrong.

She rubbed my crotch furiously, trying to get a reaction. My hand sat, unmoving on her boob, the alcohol buzzing in my system making me a little dizzy.

Breanne made a noise of frustration when she realized I wasn't responding the way she wanted me to. She looked out toward the very visible hotel lobby. If anyone chanced a look in here, they'd see exactly what was going on.

Ordinarily I enjoyed some good ole public indecency as much as the next self-centered bastard, but this whole exchange was bugging the shit out of me. Between my less than clear head and Breanne's over eager hands, I was ready to call it a night and head back up to share my bed with the only woman on my mind.

While I was going through a dozen different ways to get out of this situation, Breanne gave me a coy smile and pulled off her shirt, letting it fall to the floor. Before I could register what was going on, she quickly unsnapped her bra and let it join her shirt.

What the hell?

My eyes instantly went to her chest. I'm only human after all. And it was a very nice chest.

But it left me cold.

"Come on," she urged, wiggling her boobs so they jiggled.

If I hadn't been ready to bail before now, this awkward titty show was the final nail in this unsuccessful bag and bang.

I leaned down and picked up her black bra and shirt and handed them to her. She frowned as I pressed them into her naked chest. I pulled out my wallet and tossed some cash on the counter.

"Thanks for the drinks. I appreciate it. Keep the change. I'd better get going," I said, hopping down from the stool.

Breanne didn't put her shirt back on. She stood there, her eyes wide and completely bewildered.

"Are you serious? You're leaving?" she asked, her voice rising in a shriek.

I've had my fill of over dramatic females for one night. And only one of them would I even contemplate putting up with. And it definitely wasn't this one.

"Yep, I'm leaving. Thanks," I said shortly, walking away from her.

"You're an asshole!" Breanne yelled as I unlocked the door and let myself out.

"Yeah, I know," I said over my shoulder before the glass shut behind me.

THE ride up to my room in the elevator was the longest of my life. I was feeling restless with pent up energy. When the doors finally opened, I practically ran down the hallway.

I didn't know what I'd say to Vivian. But I had a good idea what I would do.

I would kiss her and hold her and touch her. I wasn't good with apologies. I could count on one hand the number of times I had uttered the words, I'm sorry.

My father had drilled in my head early on that to apologize was to show weakness. And even though I knew he had been full of shit, it was ingrained in me to avoid those words at all costs.

Even when I knew I was wrong. Even when I knew to say it would go a long way in smoothing over a situation that had gotten ridiculously out of hand.

But I could show her in other ways.

Ways I knew she'd like.

And I'd definitely enjoy.

I stumbled, getting the key card out of my pocket and when I finally got the door open, I swung it open with enough force to send it bouncing back in my face.

"Vivian!" I called out, kicking my shoes off and heading to the bed, where I expected to find her.

Except she wasn't there.

I looked around but the room appeared empty.

I turned on the light in the bathroom and went inside. Nothing.

Vivian was gone.

"Damn it!" I yelled, sweeping my arm across the vanity, knocking my toothpaste and deodorant onto the floor.

I pulled my cellphone out of my pocket and dialed Vivian's number. I honestly expected her to still be here when I came back. It hadn't entered my head that she'd leave.

We fought all the time. She or I had stormed out more than once. But she had never left before.

And when she didn't answer her phone, I could only stand there in shock.

I think I had underestimated just how angry she was. I hadn't been wrong when my instincts told me this fight; this argument, was different.

I'd been on this ride with Viv for years. I thought I knew her. I thought I could predict how she would react.

I was an idiot.

I re-dialed her number again.

And again.

And again.

And it went to voicemail each and every time.

I gripped my hair with my hands and wondered what I should do.

Should I give up and go to bed? It was late. We had to be on the bus early in the morning to head to Wilmington.

I stared down at my phone, willing it to ring.

I had seriously fucked up this time.

I shoved my phone back in my pocket and left my hotel room again, not bothering to put my shoes back on. This time I headed back down the hallway and knocked on the door by the elevator.

No one answered so I pounded on the door with my fist. "Open up you cunt rag!" I bellowed, beating my palms against the wood.

"What the hell, man?" Mitch muttered after answering the door. He looked like he had just woken up. I looked over his shoulder and saw that someone was in his bed. I couldn't tell who. And I didn't really give a shit. I was just glad he hadn't answered the door naked. I'd had enough trauma for one night.

"Which room is Gracie in?" I asked. Mitch's expression was strange and he looked over his shoulder nervously. I didn't have time to think about what weird shit he had going on.

"Uh, room 321. Two floors down," he said, his voice pitched low.

"Thanks," I said in a rush.

"Wait, Cole!" Mitch called out as I turned to go. He came out in the hallway, closing the door behind him.

"Why are you going to Gracie's room?" he asked, folding his arms over his chest.

"What's it to you?" I narrowed my eyes, not wanting to share my personal bullshit with him right now. I wasn't up for a touchy feely, let's talk it out conversation.

"I know you're looking for Vivian."

I frowned. "What the fuck do you know, Mitch?" I asked, losing my patience.

"Uh, she called Gracie, needing a place to crash. She was pretty upset," Mitch said and cocked my eyebrow.

"So is Gracie the one playing sleepover?" I asked, not surprised in the least but not caring at all.

Mitch flushed and shrugged. "I'm just saying, don't go in there acting like a big dick. Vivian may be loud and bitchy but Gracie says she's really hurt right now. So whatever you did must have been a doozy."

I sneered at my friend who seemed to be trying his hand at some Dear Abby advice.

"I think the estrogen out here needs to simmer down a bit," I replied.

Mitch rolled his eyes. "That's cool, be the asshole. It's what she'll expect you to do anyway," he said and turned around, going back into his room where apparently he had finally fucked

Gracie Cook. And he left me feeling a bit like a douchebag.

I took the elevator down to the third floor and made my way to room 321. I knocked on the door and waited. And waited.

Finally Vivian answered and stood there in her pajamas, her face splotchy and I knew she had been crying. All of my patented remarks died in my mouth.

I had nothing to say. Not seeing her like this.

Had I caused her to be this upset?

"Viv," I began but she held up her hand, stopping me.

"We have nothing more to say to each other. I told you I was done. I meant it." She sounded tired but I knew she hadn't been sleeping.

"Can I come in?" I asked, sliding my bare foot into the doorway, edging my body closer.

She shook her head. "No, you can't."

"Why not? What the fuck is going on?" I asked, feeling familiar frustration settling in.

And to think I had rushed back up here for this! Why had I deluded myself into thinking I wanted this drama in my life?

"Because I'm tired. I need to go to sleep. And I'm tired of talking in circles with you. I'm tired of arguing. So, can I just see you in the morning?"

She started to close the door and I braced it open with my hand.

"Not until you explain how we went from having a perfectly good night to this bullshit. Look, I get that you overreact. I get that you fly off the handle. Hell, I like that about you. It's hot. But trying to be a mind reader ain't my thing. I don't do head games."

Vivian snorted. "You don't? Really? Then what have we been doing for the past two years, Cole, if it hasn't been one giant head game?"

I frowned. "We fight. We get pissed off at each other. And then we make up. It's what we do, baby," I said softly, reaching out to cup her face. I hated seeing her sad. I preferred every other emotion to that one.

It made me feel entirely too much.

Vivian closed her eyes but didn't pull away. I considered that progress. "Aren't you sick of it?" she whispered.

My thumb caressed the apple of her cheek. "I could never get tired of you," I told her honestly. Because it was the truth. No matter how many times I had her, I always wanted more.

She was the only woman I had ever met who could handle me. Who put up with me. Who didn't expect more than I could give her. And to me, that made her pretty damn special.

So I didn't understand what the problem was all of a sudden.

"Cole, I know you're with other women. You don't bother to hide it. But I can't deal with that anymore. I can't play the scorned woman in some elaborate fuck fantasy you have. This is destructive. It's messed up. And it's over."

My heart thudded painfully. I calmly continued to rub her cheek.

"You don't mean that, Viv. I know you," I said, bowing my head down so I could kiss her lips. But she pulled back before I could.

"No, Cole, you don't. You don't know me at all. You've never bothered to know me," she said fiercely.

I dropped my hand and took a step back.

"I ask you about your job. You tell me about stuff," I supplied feebly.

Vivian crossed her arms over her chest and glared at me. "Then what's my middle name?"

"Um. . .uh," I stuttered. Crap!

"Okay, how many siblings do I have?"

"Wait! I know this," I started but she kept going.

"How did I get this scar?" she asked, pulling her shirt down to reveal a thin, long sliver of puckered skin along her breast bone that I had licked a thousand times before. I had never thought to ask about it. It had never entered my mind.

I stayed quiet. What could I say? I had never cared to know those details about her life. That wasn't what we were to each other. I wasn't the guy to know about her family vacations or to go home with her at Thanksgiving. I had never pretended to be boyfriend material. So why was I being punished for it now?

I started to get mad. Really, really mad.

"I cut it on barbed wire when I was climbing a fence into a cow field when I was eleven. I had to have twelve stitches and a tetanus shot," Vivian continued.

"That's great, but. . ." I began but she just kept going.

"What's my favorite food, Cole? How about the movie that makes me cry every time I watch it? No? Well, it's Old Yeller. That damn dog gets to me. But you didn't know that, did you? Let me try something else. Maybe something a little easier. What panties am I wearing right now?"

All right, this I could answer.

"Purple satin. The ones with the bows on the side," I said without pausing. I grinned, proud of myself for getting something right.

Vivian sighed and started to close the door.

I pushed it open again.

"Wait, I got that one right!"

Vivian shook her head. "Yeah, you did. And you just proved my point."

"Which is?" I prompted.

"That you don't give a shit about who I am. You don't care about the things I like or the stuff I've done. You don't even really care about why I got upset earlier. You just care about the fact that I spread my legs whenever you want me to. You care about the color of my underwear and whether my skirt is short enough for you to get your hand up where you want it." She placed her hand on her chest, palm flat.

"Who I am in here, doesn't matter. I thought it didn't bother me. But it does. I can't keep doing this. I can't keep pretending that I can have sex with you and be okay with you using me. Because I tried to convince myself that I was using you too. But that's not true."

My mouth was hanging open unattractively but I was knocked stupid.

"I have never used you. Because every time we've been together, it has meant something to me. And I can't continue allowing this to happen when you have no intention of this becoming something deeper. You'll never do that. And I can't keep pretending that's okay."

"Vivian," I started to say. I didn't know what would come out of my mouth next. I had no idea whether it would be to tell her she was wrong or right. I didn't know if I would let her walk away or fight for her to stay.

But she took the choice from me.

"Goodbye, Cole," she said and firmly shut the door.

Not goodnight but goodbye.

Oh hell no!

I pounded on the closed door. "Vivian! Open the fucking door! We're not done!" I yelled. There was nothing but silence. I pulled my phone out of my pocket and dialed her number.

I heard it ringing in Gracie's room but she never answered it. I started alternating between banging on her door and obsessively calling her.

"Fucking hell, Vivian! Just open the goddamn door!" I screamed at the top of my lungs, kicking the wall with my foot.

"Sir, you are being a disturbance. I need to ask you to leave this floor." A pimply faced, middle-aged twat that I recognized from the front desk put his hand on my arm. I hadn't noticed him come off the elevator.

"Get your fucking hands off me!" I roared, knocking his hand away as I started pounding on Vivian's door again.

"Vivian!" I yelled.

Pimply-faced dude pulled out a walkie-talkie and started talking into it. I didn't pay much attention; I was too focused on taking Vivian's door down.

Then two guys Pimply dude said were hotel security were dragging me into the elevator.

I gave up fighting after that.

Garrett came down to the lobby to talk to the night manager on duty and took me back to his room, because according to him I couldn't be trusted on my own.

"Just let it go, man. You'll get us all kicked out," Garrett warned, obviously pissed at being woken up in the middle of the night.

I tried calling Vivian again and when she didn't answer, I

threw my phone against the wall where it smashed into pieces.

"What the hell, Cole?" Garrett asked, looking as worked up as he ever had.

I shook my head and lay down on the couch in his room. I flung an arm over my eyes.

"It's nothing. It's done with," I muttered, not wanting to talk about it anymore.

Fuck Vivian and her bullshit.

I didn't need the head-trip.

And she said I was the mind fuck? Whatever!

There were plenty of girls to take her place. I'd make sure to find a couple after the show tomorrow night. Hell, I might not even wait that long.

I'd get over it and move on. Not that there was anything to move on from.

Vivian Baily didn't mean shit to me.

I repeated that over and over again even as her face danced across closed eyelids.

And I swore I didn't care even as I thought about the look in her eyes when she said we were done.

And I ignored the pang in my chest when I realized she was right.

Chapter 12
VIVIAN

HAD done it. I had severed the proverbial cord. I had cut ties. I had put a fork in it, we were done. I was every crappy break up metaphor out there.

Because I had officially ended things with Cole. Our hormone driven, lust-fueled, so-much-angst-it-might-kill-me relationship was finished once and for all.

And I was relieved.

Wasn't I?

I mean, I didn't feel good per se, but I felt okay about it.

Okay was fine, right?

Of course it was fine! It was great! I was Vivian Baily, woman able to resist the sexual allure of Cole Brandt! That deserved its own brand of commendation.

Yep, I felt okay.

So maybe I had slept like crap in Gracie's bed. I had tossed and turned and thought about going back to Cole's room with my tail tucked between my legs. That look on his face when I told him it was over had been stuck on replay in my head. It was on an endless loop.

What did that look even mean?

Because he didn't look happy. He didn't look angry either. He looked...devastated?

Well that certainly couldn't be right. I didn't matter enough to be a blip on his radar, let alone devastate him. Psh.

But that didn't stop me from wanting to run back to him. The familiar chaos was even more tempting now that I had made the decision to let it go. Then I chastised myself for being such a loser.

My internal battle had left me exhausted and irritable. I wanted to talk to Gracie. I wanted my friend's affirmation that I hadn't overreacted. That the honey fiasco had just been the tipping point in our dysfunctional coupling.

But she didn't show up until the next morning. I had bitten my nails to the quick and gone through the entire contents of her mini-bar. I was hung-over and pissed off. Though I hadn't been sure if I was pissed at Cole for being an asshole or pissed at myself for wanting the asshole so damn much.

I was so caught up in my boy troubles I never thought to wonder about where my wayward friend had been for the entire night. It wasn't unlike her to shack up with someone, though it was unusual for her not to talk about it afterwards. Gracie believed whole-heartedly in kissing and telling.

She had been entirely too discreet. But she was in luck, because I wasn't in the mind frame to care much where she had parked her v-jay for the night.

After Gracie had returned to the room, we packed up our stuff and checked out of the hotel like we were on the run. I sent a quick text to Maysie, making a lame excuse about our neighbor needing us to watch her cat and then we hightailed it back to Virginia.

Gracie listened to me bitch and moan the entire way. She offered little in the way of advice, because honestly I wouldn't have wanted to hear it anyway. But she agreed I had made the right choice.

So I was feeling better by the time we pulled up out front of our apartment. I was feeling down right euphoric about my supreme act of girl power. Cole would not bring me down. He could keep his hunky rock god body far away from me.

And then my phone chirped in my purse. I made the mistake of looking at it.

You forgot to say goodbye. :(I thought we had some making up to do.

And my heart had fallen straight into my adorable kitten heels.

Had Cole really just used a frowny emoticon? And why was he texting me from Maysie's phone? Did she know he had hijacked it?

My finger hovered over the screen as I thought of some snarky response. Before this weekend I would have called him a wank nugget. He would have retaliated with some sort of sexual-laced innuendo. Then the door would have opened to phone sex and plans to screw at a later date.

Not this time. I was a new woman full of awesome!

So I erased his text rather than give into the urge to write him back. And I thought that would have been the end of it. I had little doubt that Cole would move on to the next warm body with a pulse in no time.

I hated the twinge of disappointment when I was proven right.

I hadn't heard from him since.

I arrived at work on Monday morning in a not so cheerful mood. It was virtually impossible for me to pretend I was hunky-dory when I wasn't. I wore my emotions all over me like baby vomit.

When I arrived at The Claremont Center to find Theo waiting for me with coffee in hand, I wanted to turn back to my car and leave. Not that I didn't want to see him, I just wasn't sure I could affect a professional demeanor in the state I was in.

Not with my humiliation and minor heartache fresh and raw.

"White with sugar. I figured you had a sweet tooth," Theo said, handing me the Styrofoam cup. I took a sip and couldn't help but be pleased that he had read my coffee choice so perfectly.

I had been ready to swear off men. But when they come baring coffee and smiles that pretty, a girl could be tempted to re-think her stance on the subject.

"Thanks, Theo. Please don't tell me I forgot another meeting," I said, walking through the glass doors and heading to my office.

"No, nothing like that. I just, well, I felt like I should come by and apologize in person for how inappropriate I was the last time we spoke."

My mind jogged backwards in time, trying to identify exactly what he was talking about. My head was still a soggy mess from my weekend spectacle. There wasn't room in my grey matter for much else.

I must have looked perplexed because Theo's lips quirked into a shy smile.

"When I asked you out."

Oh that.

I set my free coffee (the absolute best kind of coffee) on my desk and held up my hand. "You really don't need to. It's fine," I assured him. I wasn't entirely sure whether I wanted him to repeat the offer, though I wasn't repulsed by the idea.

It was nice to know that walking away from Cole hadn't turned me into a nun.

One thing I was sure of, however. Scoring dates on the clock had to be frowned upon.

Theo looked relieved and I stood there appreciating how adorable he was. He was the complete opposite of Cole in every possible way.

He was fair and buff. I could make out the defined lines of his muscles under the expensive cut of his suit.

He young enough that his obvious success and responsibility were impressive. He seemed to want to spend time with me. And not in the naked and sweaty kind of way. And he brought me coffee.

The only thing Cole ever bought me was a box of condoms and a hard time.

It would be so easy to fall into something with Theo. I liked being with someone. I know that wasn't very feminist friendly. Riley would have smacked me across the face right before she took my girl card away and shredded it.

But it was the truth. I couldn't remember a time in my life

when I hadn't been involved in some way with a guy. Sure, my relationship with Cole was questionable at best, but he was still someone I had devoted spending time with. He provided regular sex and even conversation when it suited him.

I enjoyed feeling wanted and desired. I liked knowing I had someone I could call when I was feeling lonely. I liked knowing that there was someone out there who wanted to spend time with me. For whatever the reason.

I was social and I enjoyed attention. And I knew, subconsciously, that perhaps that said quite a bit about the state of my self-esteem. Though I knew I was pretty. I liked my body and I thought that I was intelligent. I had friends and family that loved me. But there was still something inside me that craved what a relationship could give me.

I wanted to be happy. I wanted to be cared for. I wanted my fairy tale happily ever after. I blamed Titanic and every 80's power ballad ever released. Though how I had allowed myself to think Cole could offer me anything I was looking for was beyond me. Call it two-year insanity.

I was by no means some depressing ingénue who cried over the state of her love life and wrote bad poetry. I wasn't deep. I didn't think about world hunger or how to end the conflict in the Gaza strip. I liked to watch bad reality television and I was unashamed to admit that I enjoyed pop music beyond acceptable levels.

I was a drama queen. I was a bitch if you crossed me. If I didn't like you, I wasn't one to hide it. You'd know it. And I was addicted to infatuation. The anticipation I felt when I knew I was going to see the guy I wanted.

So there.

However, call it a growing maturity or maybe a lingering lack of closure where Cole was concerned, but I didn't jump at the chance to let this beautiful, strapping male buy me dinner.

I could flirt with him, let him adore me with his eyes, but I wasn't ready to make it more than that.

Not right now.

But this girl wasn't dead yet. And I knew the day would come when I was ready to climb back on that horse and give it a ride again.

And perhaps Theo could be the horse.

Except he wasn't a horse and the thought of riding him like one made me flush to the roots of my hair.

I cleared my throat and banished all thoughts of Theo riding out of my mind. I was determined to not let my need for attention, or my fear of being alone to dictate things. I would do things right.

For once.

So I didn't comment with the tried and true Vivian Baily response meant to elicit another invitation.

Instead I gave Theo my best professional smile. Genuine if a little cool and shook my head.

"Honestly, we don't have to talk about that." I opened my drawer and pulled out the plans for the gala and handed them to him. "Since you're here, why don't we discuss the final ideas for the fundraiser so I can start getting orders put through."

And just like that I became grown-up Vivian.

And I think I liked her.

MY phone had remained quiet for the rest of the day. After Theo and I hammered out the final details for the gala, I had taken an early lunch. Gracie and I had made plans to meet at Barton's.

Pulling into the parking lot, it felt strange to be here for anything other than drinking like a fish or watching the guys play a show. I wasn't sure I had ever even bothered to eat the food.

I walked inside and was hit with a wave of grease and stale beer. It was pretty busy with the normal mix of businessmen on lunch break and college kids getting an early start on drunk-thirty.

Gracie was sat at the bar talking to Dina, who had been the main bartender for as long as I had been coming to Barton's.

I slid into the stool beside my friend and crossed my legs.

It was still strange not seeing Jordan behind the bar or Maysie waiting tables. This was where they had met all those years ago. They had found love amongst the fatty burgers and cheap beer. Lucky bastards.

"Hey, Vivian. What can I get ya? Your normal?" I cringed and shook my head. I couldn't stomach a round of buttery nipples at noon on a workday.

"I'll have an iced tea and a Caesar salad, please," I said, glancing at the menu.

"When did you become a teetotaler?" Dina smirked and I flicked my hair back.

"When I became a proud member of the gainfully employed," I quipped. Dina handed me my drink and nodded.

"Good for you, girl. Gracie was just telling me about the show this past weekend. It sounds like our boys are doing pretty good for themselves."

"Yeah, they are," I agreed with a strained smile.

"I heard Garrett's song on the radio the other day. The Perfect Regret one. I almost wrecked my car I got so excited," Dina enthused.

"Wow, really?" Gracie piped up.

"Yeah, it was on that college station, KT102. I had almost forgotten how sexy Cole's voice was. It made me want to strip off my panties there and then," Dina laughed and I didn't feel the jealousy or bristling irritation if that comment had come out of anyone else's mouth.

Dina had never been competition for Cole's attention given that she played for the other team and all. I was more her type than Cole was.

Not that that mattered anymore because who Cole chose to focus his attention on was no longer my concern.

Nope, I didn't care in the slightest. I was done. Finished. Dunzo. Over it.

I sipped my drink and looked around the restaurant. I recognized a few people from Rinard College. Jaz, a waitress who had been at Barton's forever was wiping down tables in her section.

My eyes skimmed over people eating their lunch until a movement caught my attention. Someone was waving at me.

I grinned. I couldn't help it.

Because Theo was walking purposefully towards me. He had chucked his grey jacket and was wearing only a cotton shirt, rolled up at the sleeves. We had only parted ways an hour ago but I couldn't deny that it was good to see him again.

"Are you following me?" I asked coyly, putting my iced tea down on the bar and swinging my legs out so that I was facing him.

Theo held his hands up. "No, I swear. No stalking. I was supposed to meet Tina from our finance department for lunch but she just called to say she couldn't make it. I was getting ready to leave when I saw you. I think it's fate, wouldn't you say? Someone out there in the universe must want us to share a meal together," Theo chuckled and sat down on my other side.

Gracie, who had been talking with Dina, was now looking at me questioningly. She widened her eyes as she took in the sight of Theo. He did make one hell of a first impression. Luckily he was looking over the menu and didn't notice her blatant staring.

"Who is that?" she whispered less than subtly.

I rolled my eyes and put my hand on Theo's arm. I felt his muscles clench beneath my fingers and my stomach fluttered.

"Theo, this is my roommate, Gracie Cook. Gracie, this is Theo Anderson. His company is the one sponsoring the gala I'm coordinating," I explained, introducing the two.

Theo held out his hand for Gracie to shake, which she did politely.

"So this is Theo. I've heard so much about you," Gracie simpered. I could have smacked her. And I may just have to when we left.

Theo laughed and glanced at me, his blue eyes amused. "Oh really? And what have you heard? I'm dying to know what Vivian says about me when I'm not around."

I surreptitiously pinched Gracie's arm in warning. If she mentioned how cute I thought he was I'd never forgive her.

She glared at me before turning back to Theo who had missed

the silent exchange.

"She's just told me about your plans for the gala. Sounds amazing," she said and when Theo turned to Dina to give her his order she stuck out her tongue at me.

With his order given, Theo looked back at Gracie, though I could feel his awareness of my space beside him. The attention whore in me soaked it up. The emerging mature Vivian scolded the tramp and told her to settle down.

"Vivian has done such a fantastic job. She really is wonderful," he enthused and Gracie coughed.

"Yeah, she is something all right." I pinched her again, just because she deserved it.

Theo's eyes rested on my face and his look of appreciation made me feel warm and fuzzy. "And she's someone I really want to get to know better."

Gracie made a choking noise behind me but I didn't acknowledge her in the slightest.

"Why?" I asked, before I could censor myself.

"Why what?" Theo asked, furrowing his brows.

"Why do you want to get to know me so badly? What's your angle?" I asked suspiciously, not able to help myself. I knew what men meant when they said they wanted to get to know me better.

That was the oldest euphemism for sex there was. I found myself bristling at the thought of yet another man only wanting to know me for what lay between my legs. My hopes at being taken seriously, of a man desiring me for me suddenly seemed ridiculous and foolhardy.

Theo's hot palm enveloped my hand, his fingers squeezing mine.

"There's no angle, Vivian. I want to get to know you because you intrigue me. You're smart. You have amazing ideas. You're funny. You're insightful. I know that probably isn't appropriate given that currently I'm your client. But one day soon I won't be your client. I'm patient."

"Well, thanks," I said, not sure what else I should say.

Theo's smile grew wider. "And you're someone who is worth taking the time to get to know. So what do you say? Will you let me learn all of your dirty secrets?" he teased shyly.

"I. . .uh. . ." I stuttered, trying to think of a response.

"Oh my god, Vivian, Gracie, check it out!" Dina called out from the other side of the bar. Theo slid his hand away from where it rested on top of mine and turned his attention to the direction of the television mounted on the wall.

I swallowed thickly, feeling dazed from Theo's comments and still not sure how I was supposed to answer him. I was coming out of a two-year physical relationship with someone who had never much cared for the person I was beneath my pretty skin. And here was a guy who wanted to "know me." The emotional implications of that weren't lost on me.

Theo was appealing to me in a way Cole never had. No matter how much I wanted him to, no matter how I craved for him to miraculously become the entire package, he wasn't.

Cole was a raging, hot fire. Theo was a calming river. Which was fine with me because I had been burned once and I wasn't looking to repeat my past mistakes anytime soon.

I was determined to be on my own for a while. I owed it to myself to not jump into anything with anyone. But that didn't mean I couldn't sample the waters.

What would a date here and there hurt? After he wasn't my client anymore of course.

"Look! It's Cole!" Dina pointed at the television screen and my stomach plummeted into my feet.

My eyes, against their own volition zeroed in on the man who I had only said goodbye to several days before. And even though he wasn't here in the flesh, seeing him, even on television was too raw. Too real.

Too soon.

"Turn it up!" Gracie said, clapping her hands in excitement.

"Who is that guy?" Theo asked.

I didn't answer right away. I couldn't. My entire focus on was on Cole Brandt.

What else was new?

A reporter from some entertainment show was standing beneath an umbrella with Cole. A huge stage stood behind them

144

and I could see that wherever they were, it was pouring down rain.

Cole's dark hair was matted down over his forehead and I could see that his torn T-shirt was plastered to his chest from the moisture. The ring in his lip gleamed and the guy liner he was wearing had smeared down his face.

He looked like a fallen angel.

Dina had cranked the volume and the sound of Cole's husky voice filled Barton's as though he were in the same room.

"We're lucky to be on this tour with Primal Terror. It was the break of a lifetime," Cole said, running his hands through his hair, standing it on edge.

"You're getting a lot of good press out of this tour. A lot of magazines and blogs are calling you guys the band to watch this year. You have an album set to drop in the spring and with only a month left of the tour, you seem poised to take on the world. What's next for Generation Rejects? Or more specifically, Cole Brandt?"

Cole chuckled in that lazy, self-assured way of his. You would think he had been giving interviews his whole life.

"We're just looking at all the possibilities right now. As for me, I'm enjoying the ride," Cole said, flashing a smile at the camera. His grin pierced my heart. Jerk.

"Thanks for talking to me, man. And we can't wait to see the show. If it ever stops raining. Coming live from Primal Terror's Wicked and Ugly tour, here with Cole Brandt, lead singer of Generation Rejects, I'm Callum Ward."

And then the program switched to some commentary on the newest celebrity sex tape scandal.

"Can you believe that? Cole was on TV!" Dina said, turning the volume back down.

Gracie pulled out her phone and started texting, most likely either Maysie or Mitch. The smile on my face was fake and thin and I realized I had never answered Theo's question.

He was looking at me now, with an unreadable expression.

"You know that guy, I take it," he deduced.

I swirled the melting ice in my drink with my straw to try to distract him from my discomfort.

"Uh yeah, that's Cole. He's the lead singer for Generation Rejects. They're a local band. Have you heard of them?" I asked, wishing we could change the subject.

"Can't say that I have," Theo said and there was a note in his voice that could only be construed as confused.

"They play at Barton's a lot. Well, they did before they went on the road. This is where they got their start. Gracie and I are friends with Maysie, the drummer's fiancée." I was rambling. Why was I rambling?

"I take it you don't like their music much," Theo said, surprising me.

"Why would you say that? I like their music," I argued.

Theo ate a fry from his plate and shrugged. "You just looked like you had sucked a lemon when that Cole guy was giving his interview. I guessed it was because you thought they sucked or something."

I laughed lamely. "No, they're fine."

I had nothing to say after that. The earlier easy rapport that had been steadily building between us had flickered and died.

I hated how much power I allowed Cole to have, even when he was thousands of miles away and had no place in my world.

Why couldn't I stop thinking about what he was doing? Wondering what show they were playing tonight. I wanted to ask him about his interview and I wanted to know how he was holding up.

I quickly pulled money out of my purse and laid it on the bar. "I've got to get back to the office," I said suddenly, getting to my feet.

Gracie and Dina, who were still discussing the finer points of Cole's interview looked up as I made my excuses to leave.

"Okay. See you at home," Gracie responded.

I turned to Theo and wished I didn't feel so strange.

"I'll see you later. I'll call you to touch base later this week," I said and I knew I was being distant. I didn't want to be. But I felt I just needed to get out of there and deal with this lump in my chest.

Theo reached out and took my phone that I gripped tightly in my hand. He tapped on the screen for a minute and then handed it back to me.

I looked down at the screen and saw his name and cell phone number.

"That's my cell. Not my office number. Call it when you want to take me up on dinner. I'm just going to put it out there, Vivian. I want to take you out. I want you to go on a date with me. So call me, please." Theo was earnest and sincere and I wanted to say yes.

I really did.

But I couldn't.

Not yet.

I gave him a small smile and nodded, not able to think of any adequate way to respond.

Chapter 13
COLE

WAS living the life. I had everything I wanted. I was the king of the fucking castle.

At least that's what I was trying to tell myself each and every day.

Because sometimes it was hard to remember that this is what I always wanted.

In the weeks since Raleigh, everything had been kicked into overdrive. Our shows were selling out faster and faster. And we were starting to get almost as much press coverage as the band we were opening for.

Last week, Jose had told me that I had been asked to do an interview for Spin magazine. I was stoked, until I registered what he said. I had been asked. Not the band. When I had said so to Jose, he said it wasn't going to be a huge piece. Just a few questions. And they had specifically asked for me.

Then we had gotten the cover art of our new album. We had been excited to see it. Jordan had ripped open the box and pulled out a CD. He flipped it over and then promptly threw it in my lap, stalking off to the back of the bus.

Garrett and Mitch had grabbed one to see what Jordan's

problem was.

The picture of the band on the back was his problem. Because I was standing in the front. My body had been enlarged due to the perspective of the shot. Jordan, Garrett, and Mitch were shadowed behind me. You could barely see their faces.

I thought the picture was pretty awesome. The guys did not agree.

"We didn't agree on this picture. We chose another one," Garrett pointed out to Jose.

"I can put in a call to the label, but they have final say over the design and layout. I think it's great," was our manager's response.

"Yeah, that's because it's not your nose stuck up Cole's asshole," Mitch muttered, tossing the CD back in the box.

"Stop your bitching, boys. It's a great cover. They used Garrett's artwork, which we wanted. What does it matter if they didn't use the picture we wanted? This is our first album. That's what's important," I reasoned. I was pretty proud of myself. I hadn't gotten pissed; I had been calm and understanding.

Paging Oprah!

Mitch and Garrett mumbled their agreement but I knew that Generation Reject's armor had some major chinks.

I took the CD back to my bunk, where I was beginning to feel I spent most of time. I stared at the picture that had caused such a problem.

I looked good. I grinned. This is what we had been working toward for the last five years.

My smile started to slip. I really didn't see what the big deal was. Yeah, so the other guys were more in the background. So maybe you couldn't see their faces clearly.

It was still a great freaking picture.

I pulled my phone out of my pocket and automatically started to dial Vivian's number. When it started to ring, I realized what I was doing and hung up.

I had just done it out of habit. Not a big deal. So what if I hadn't spoken with her since Raleigh. The fact that I still haven't hooked up with anyone else had absolutely nothing to do with her and everything to do with the fact that I had been so damn busy.

I ran my hands through my hair and sighed. Despite my arguments to the contrary, I couldn't deny that I wanted to tell her about the CD. I wanted to talk to her about all this stuff going on with the band.

I didn't realize how much I liked having someone to listen to my shit until I didn't have that certain someone anymore.

What would it hurt to call her? It's not like I was asking her to fly out and fuck me.

Though if she wanted to, I'd fly her out in an instant.

I had to rearrange my junk. My pants had gotten uncomfortably tight all of a sudden.

No, I just wanted to check in and make sure she hadn't gone off the deep end. I bet she was depressed. Eating her weight in ice cream and watching chick flicks. It was only right that I make sure she didn't do something stupid in her misery over losing me.

I mean, we may not be screwing anymore, but I still cared about what happened to her. And I was convinced that she was probably wallowing in bed.

I dialed Vivian's number again and listened to it ring. Yeah, this was just me being a nice guy.

"Hello."

My chest twisted and my gut knotted up.

"Vivian! Hey! I was just calling-"

"You've reached my voicemail. Leave me a message and I'll get back to you as soon as I can." Beep!

I turned off my phone and dropped it onto the bed beside me. I looked at the Generation Rejects CD again. Where was the pride? The excitement? The over the moon fucking joy?

I was king of the castle but the crown was proving to be pretty damn heavy.

JORDAN and the other guys weren't really talking to me. I felt like the invisible man. Personally I thought I wasn't the only one that could be accused of a big ego.

I had done the Spin interview and then Primal Terror had asked me to sing a song with them a couple of shows ago and now it had become part of their set. The crowd had eaten it up.

Then I had done some press for the label. But it's not like the rest of the band weren't there. But I had answered most of the questions. It had just seemed to be the natural thing to do.

And last night, a local newspaper in De Moines had interviewed us and the reporter had called us "Cole Brandt and the Generation Rejects." Mitch had jumped all over that one.

"We're just the Generation Rejects," he had said angrily. I rolled my eyes, annoyed by his attitude.

And when Jose suggested I start writing some songs for the band, Garrett had put down his guitar and walked off.

"How's it going?" Jose asked, sitting down beside me. I was hanging out on the loading dock while the roadies set up our equipment for tonight's gig. We were due to go on stage in three hours.

"It's going," I said. I wish I smoked. I could use something to do with my hands. I was feeling antsy and jittery. And not remotely pumped like I normally was before a show.

"I spoke with the other guys a few minutes ago. They mentioned you wouldn't come to sound check."

Of course they'd make me out to be a fucking diva. Like I was the one with the bad attitude. I felt myself getting angry all over again.

"They didn't like my suggestion to try out the new song. They told me to take a hike. So I did. I don't need that shit," I defended. All I had done was say we should try out the song Garrett and I had written a couple of weeks ago with an added vocal run at the end. I thought it would go over well with the audience. Jordan and Mitch had said it was just another excuse to make the set all about me.

There had been some yelling. I may or may not have told them to go fuck themselves. And yeah, I had left. Needing some space wasn't a crime. And it definitely didn't make me the bad guy.

"Understood. But you need to be a professional and get your ass back in there. If they want to act like children, so be it. But that doesn't mean you have to. I want to see you succeed, Cole. And sometimes that means rising above the bullshit," Jose said, clasping me on the back.

Lately it seemed Jose Suarez was the only one who had my back. My friends had turned on me. Vivian had left me. Despite how popular I was becoming, I was really fucking lonely.

"Thanks, man," I said. Jose nodded and left me to go talk to the roadies.

I stared down at my phone, scrolling through my contacts. I had no one to call. Everyone I would have normally talked to weren't currently speaking to me.

I shoved my phone back in my pocket and went around to the front of the venue where a small crowd of people had already congregated.

I was recognized pretty quickly and the sound of female squeals did a lot to alleviate my sour mood.

A girl caught my eye instantly. I startled at the sight of her from behind. Her long, strawberry-blonde hair hung down her back and I could have sworn it was Vivian.

My heart started beating frantically and I headed towards her quickly. What was Vivian doing here? My joy was immediate and overwhelming.

I put my hand on her shoulder and turned her around so that I could look down into her brown eyes.

Wait a minute. Brown?

The face that looked up at me in surprise wasn't Vivian's. The disappointment sank in quickly.

"Hey," the girl said, her voice high pitched and grating.

Now that I was looking at her, she didn't resemble Vivian at all. The fact that I wished she did infuriated me.

I let my hand slide down until I was holding her hand lightly. "Come with me," I said, cocking my head toward a door that led backstage.

The girl looked at her friends, who were staring at me with their mouths hanging open.

"Okay," she squeaked and I slung my arm around her shoulders. I didn't ask for her name. I didn't want it. It didn't matter. I hadn't been with anyone but Vivian in way too long.

Time for that to change.

Twenty minutes later and I wanted to growl in frustration. Because things weren't going so well.

I had my eyes squeezed shut and was imagining that the breasts barely filling my palms were large and full and the hand down my pants belonged to someone who wasn't there.

"That's it, Viv, just like that," I groaned, lost in my fantasy, as the hand squeezed my cock. I kept my eyes closed and thought of Vivian's face when I made her come. Ah yeah, that's what I needed. I was almost there.

"My name isn't Viv!" a voice huffed, bringing me out of my detailed daydream and deflating my erection instantly.

I opened my eyes and looked down at the woman laid out beneath me on a couch in an empty dressing room. Her shirt was open, her boobs nothing like the girl I had been picturing in my head.

I sat up and scrubbed my hands over my face. The girl scrambled to sit upright beside me and started to button her shirt.

"My name is Andrea," she said indignantly.

"I really don't care," I said tiredly, not caring how bad it sounded.

The girl huffed again. "I'm leaving," she announced, as if it would bother me. It didn't. I wasn't into it. Not even a little bit.

I didn't say anything when the girl who wasn't Vivian slammed out of the room. I leaned back on the couch, feeling oddly empty.

I was pissed. I was edgy.

I stormed out of the dressing room and headed to where I knew the other guys would be. Garrett was eating a sub and Mitch was texting on his phone. Maysie and Jordan were all cuddled up on the couch.

"Hey," I said to the room at large. Jordan lifted his hand in a barely civil greeting. Mitch ignored me completely and Garrett nodded his head.

I threw myself into a chair and started tapping my hands on my knees. My lack of orgasm was messing with my head.

I had been so damn close too. Why did chicks have to be so touchy?

"So I was thinking we really should play that new song," I said, knowing I was walking into a landmind.

Garrett put his sandwich down and wiped his mouth. "It's not ready. We had this conversation two hours ago. We still have to bridge the last chorus," he argued.

"Well I think that last chorus should be the end of the song. Why won't you listen to me when I tell you that I think it sounds better like that?" I asked angrily.

"And why is it such a fucking big deal to you? You've never gotten this damn worked up over a song arrangement before. In fact, you don't usually have anything to do with it at all," Jordan called out.

I tapped my knees harder, feeling my anger rise. "Because I'm sick of not having a say about our songs. I think as the lead singer, my input would be important. That what I think should carry some weight," I said.

"Here we go again," Mitch muttered.

"Do you have something to say, Mitch?" I shot out, getting to my feet.

"Yeah, you're the lead singer. That doesn't mean you have any more of a say than the rest of us," Mitch stated, putting his phone down.

"No, I just want a say in the first place!" My voice started to rise. I shoved my hands into my pockets and stood my ground. "I want to play the song. I think it's ready."

I didn't really know why I was pressing the point. Except that I felt this was a test to see how much they valued and respected my opinion when it came to the meat and guts of our music. And given the way they were dismissing me, I think I had my answer.

"No, we aren't," Garrett ground out.

He and I stared at each other and I never thought I'd see the day when we couldn't talk about something and figure it out.

I remembered standing with him at his parents' funeral. I had seen him at his worst. And he had seen me at mine.

But now I looked at him and I didn't see my friend. I saw

someone who didn't take my role in our band seriously. Someone who was standing in my way and holding me back. I hadn't wanted to agree with Jose when he told me I was better off without these guys. But, standing there, I knew he was right.

"You have five minutes," a stagehand said, interrupting our tense showdown. Garrett threw away his trash and gave me a level look.

"We're not playing that song. End of fucking discussion."

I stood there seething, feeling like a child who had been put in his place.

Well, we'd see about that.

THE concert was proving to be a disaster. We were off. It was obvious to everyone. Our music lacked the energy we were known for.

It didn't help that not one of my bandmates would look at me.

Their resentment was all over our set. It tainted everything. And when I sang it was full of the anger I felt towards the jackasses behind me. I couldn't even look at them.

So being who I am, during a lull, I went to the side of the stage and asked one of the stage hands to bring me an acoustic guitar. I walked back to my mic, looping the guitar strap around my neck.

Jordan and the others had stopped playing completely, the silence behind me was deafening. I knew they were wondering what the hell I was doing.

If they were going to fuck up the vibe of our show, then I was going to bring it back. By doing what the hell I wanted to do!

"Hey guys! I know this show is sucking serious balls. I don't know about you, but I think it's time to change things up a bit. Do you guys want to hear a new song?" I asked.

The answering roar was deafening.

"Well, here you go," I said and launched into the chords Garrett and I had written. I sang the lyrics and played the entire song by myself and the audience loved it. I was the center of the world. They fed me and I ate it up.

This is why I loved to perform.

But when I was done and I turned back to the guys to say, "See, they loved it, I was right the whole time," I realized they didn't see it quite the same way. Mitch and Jordan were furious. Jordan tossed his drumsticks to the ground, got to his feet and walked off stage.

Mitch dropped his bass and followed Jordan.

Garrett didn't look pissed, but he looked hurt. Why wasn't he glad that the audience loved our song so much?

He shook his head and unplugged his guitar. "The stage is all yours," he said, dropping the cable and leaving me alone.

I stood there, the spotlight trained on me, staring out at the sea of confused and increasingly angry faces.

Do I continue to play? Do I quit like a pansy, just as my bandmates had done?

I leaned into the mic and plastered a smile on my face. "Thank you Chicago! It's been real!" I yelled, gripping the neck of the guitar and walked off the stage, when what I really wanted to do was run.

I could hear the wave of boos that followed me overlapping with the chant, "You suck!"

And they weren't wrong. We had sucked big time.

I came off the stage and handed the guitar to a frantic stagehand.

The guys in Primal Terror stood to the side looking both furious and bewildered.

"What the hell, man?" Geoff, the lead singer asked.

I ignored him completely. I couldn't explain to him or myself what the hell had just gone down out there.

It was time to find my so-called friends.

They hadn't had a chance to go far. They were in our assigned dressing room, loading up their belongings when I burst into the room.

"What was that?" I roared, picking up a chair folded against the wall and throwing it. It clattered noisily to the floor.

"Why would you do that?" I screamed, losing my shit on the three guys who I had always considered to be family.

But family didn't bail on you like that. They didn't humiliate you in a stadium of 5,000 people. They didn't begrudge you the spotlight because they weren't getting the attention they thought they deserved.

Mitch was closest when I decided to start throwing fists. He took a punch to the jaw and then before I knew it Jordan had his arm around my throat.

Maysie came running into the room and started yelling at us to stop.

Garrett tried to pull Jordan off me but it didn't work. We ended up on the ground, his gut meeting my fist.

I was certain we would have kept going until one of us was unconscious if Jose hadn't come in and dumped ice cold water on both of us. He hauled Jordan up to his feet and slammed him against the wall. Maysie grabbed my arm and pulled me back.

"Enough! All of you!" Jose yelled, pinning Jordan with his forearm across his chest. Jose was a beefy guy and even though Jordan was strong, he was no match for our manager

Jose was furious. "What the fuck was that?" he screamed to the four of us. None of us said anything. What could we say? We were all guilty of letting our egos get the better of us. We had really screwed up.

Jose let go of Jordan who slumped a bit. "Go back to the hotel. I've got a hell of mess to clean up. We'll talk in the morning," he barked. We all stood there, either obstinate or afraid to move. This felt like the beginning of the end.

"Go!" he hollered and that propelled us into action.

I grabbed my jacket and exited the dressing room first. My heart was pumping; my head was fried.

And I was pretty sure I had just lost my band and my best friends all at the same time.

Why had I decided to play that song?

I knew why. I was feeling bitchy. I wanted to show them I could do whatever the hell I wanted to. That I didn't have to answer them. That was I was better than they could ever possibly be.

I had wanted to show them that they couldn't tell me what to do. Just as I had done all those years ago when I had walked out of my house and left my parents behind.

I didn't take direction well, that was obvious.

I had just never self-destructed so totally and completely before.

But I wasn't the only one to blame for this shit. And I wouldn't let the guys off easily.

What had happened to us?

Once back to my room, I peeled off my clothes and took a hot shower. I trembled under the spray, not sure what I was going to do. How do you come back from something like that?

The bond the four of us had for years felt ruined.

The thing that had made us great was destroyed.

I didn't see how we could continue on.

I got out of the shower and wrapped a towel around my waist. I grabbed my phone and sank down on the bed.

I dialed a familiar number.

"Hello. You've reached my voicemail. . ."

I listened to the recording of Vivian's voice and when the beep sounded in my ear I hung up.

"**T**HE label is pissed. They're threatening to pull the record," Jose told us the next morning. We were sitting on the tour bus, having checked out of our hotel rooms first thing. I sat by the window and the rest of the guys were gathered around the table.

It couldn't be more obvious it was them against me. I was on the outside of my own fucking band.

"Can they do that?" Jordan asked.

Jose sneered at him, barely containing his rage. "Hell yeah they can do that. They can do whatever the fuck they want to! They own Current Static, you bunch of fucking morons! And if they decide to chuck this album those songs you worked so hard on, that music you bled your souls out for, will never see the light of day. It will sit in a fucking vault while you fade away into nothing."

"It was one show. How can it be that big of a deal?" Mitch

asked, tapping his fingers on the table, a sure sign of his agitation.

He should be agitated. We were fucked.

"It's a big deal because immature children with massive egos don't sell albums. This isn't the eighties, fellas. Trashing hotel rooms and storming off stage is frowned upon. And you aren't some big name that can get away with that shit! I hate to be the one to remind you, but Generation Rejects isn't anybody. You are a blip on the fucking radar. And if you aren't here tomorrow, no one will miss you. Some other band will slide in and fill the gap," Jose yelled.

Ouch, that hurt.

"You have problems with your lead singer. Woo fucking hoo. Join the club with every other band out there. But he is your selling power," Jose pointed at me. "He is what gets you interviews. Like it or fucking lump it."

Jordan's face turned red. "What about our music? Doesn't that have something to do with it? Cole's fucking face isn't what got us here!"

Jose laughed but it wasn't from amusement.

"Grow the fuck up Levitt. You're in an industry where sex fucking sells. And Cole is your sex up for sale. Your music is fine and dandy. Your lyrics are deep and meaningful. Whatever. You are being marketed as a band that is fronted by Cole Brandt. That is what the label sees as your strength," Jose nodded in my direction and I couldn't help but feel validated.

Mitch, Garrett, and Jordan however looked as though they had just swallowed glass.

"The label wants to meet with you in a week to discuss the future of your band and your album. I suggest you take the time to figure out what you're going to do. Whether you can put your ego trips on hold and do what's best for all of you or not. Because I'm not going to waste my time and you can bet your asses the label won't either. We aren't going to wait around on a bunch of pussies to figure their shit out. You're playing with the big boys now."

I was thoroughly embarrassed by the whole thing. And I could tell by looking at my band members that they were as well.

Maysie was rubbing Jordan's back but even she seemed worried. And she should be.

"Primal Terror has asked that you be replaced."

We all recoiled at that. For the first time I made eye contact with the others and we all wore the same horrified expression.

"What?" I hissed.

Jose shrugged, raising his hands in a what did you expect gesture.

"This is their first nationwide tour. The last thing they want is to be sidelined by your drama. Because that's what the press will pick up on and it will overshadow them completely. So way to burn your bridges guys," Jose said sarcastically.

"Maybe we could apologize-" Garrett began but Jose cut him off.

"An apology ain't gonna cut it, son. You and this tour are parting ways. Now, you have seven days until you have to be in New York to meet with the label. I suggest you pack your shit and you go home to wherever it is you fucking came from and get yourselves sorted. Take a break. Regroup. Do some yoga or something. And come to the table next week either with your heads in the game or with an understanding that this shit ain't gonna work. But this petty bullshit is at an end."

Jose slammed his hands down on the table, knocking over his empty coffee mug.

"I suggest you not making me regret taking you on. I don't like to be made a fool of. And last night, you made me look like the biggest idiot on the fucking planet."

None of us said anything else.

What was there to say?

It looked like we were going home.

Chapter 14
VIVIAN

LOVED Sunday mornings. They were my favorite part of the week. Gracie usually slept in and I was able to monopolize the television for hours.

We had gone out last night, though I had refrained from getting wasted for Gracie's sake. I knew how hard it was for her to hang out and not drink. We had gone to a small club downtown and listened to some live music. It was a local punk band called Shake and Shiver.

They sucked.

The Rejects would be able to show them how it's done. It had been weeks since I had seen Cole. And he was still in every corner of my mind.

I had thought our relationship had lacked substance. That it was about nothing more than two people sharing a bed.

Then why did everything make me think of him? I went into a convenience store and found myself picking up Reese's Peanut Butter Cups out of habit because they were Cole's favorite after show snack. He particularly liked to eat them off my bare stomach.

I was driving past the movie theater and saw an advertisement for their science fiction Saturday. And that inevitably reminded me of the time Cole and I stayed in bed for an entire day watching a marathon of Star Trek movies.

Other times I would hear a joke and pick up my phone to text him, because I knew he would appreciate it.

How had he, without my realizing it, invaded every facet of my life?

Gracie and I had come home early, neither of us in the best of moods to be out socializing.

The reasons for my funk were well known. But Gracie had been in a horrible mood for almost a week now. When I asked her what was wrong, she attempted to reassure me that she was fine.

But I had heard her talking on the phone until the wee hours of the morning several nights in a row. I had recognized the angry cadence of her voice through the thin walls. And I knew that whoever was on the other end of the phone was the source of her crappy attitude.

I stretched out on the couch and blew on the top of my piping hot coffee. I had gotten my first paycheck from The Claremont Center on Friday. And while I wasn't thrilled with how much my good friend Uncle Sam took for his pockets, it was still a heck of a lot more than I had ever earned on my own in the past.

To celebrate I went out and bought myself a fancy gourmet coffee machine. Complete with a mixed assortment of flavored drinks. I was currently indulging in a caramel macchiato.

I flipped through the channels until settling on my all time favorite movie, Dirty Dancing, for the thirtieth time. It was the perfect way to prepare myself for another week of work. Though I couldn't complain. I had a dream job. And even though it had picked up to crazy levels in preparation of the Kimble Project Gala in two weeks, I was having a blast.

And then there was Mr. Theo Anderson and his refusal to relent in his persistent wooing.

And woo he did.

He made sure to bring me coffee several days a week and he called me throughout the day under the pretense of an asinine piece of information he needed to relay.

I always called him on his miserable excuses.

And then we'd flirt and tease but I was always conscious to pull back before it became too serious. Theo hadn't brought up the subject of going out on a date again since our lunch at Barton's but I knew he was waiting.

He thought it was because he was my client.

He had no idea that I was waiting for reasons not related to my job.

I was waiting to forget about a certain lead singer.

I knew that it would only take time. Though I was beginning to worry that I would be old and grey before the Cole Brandt effect finally wore off.

I was right at the climax of the movie. Johnny Castle had just blown onto the scene and said his iconic line, "Nobody puts Baby in a corner," and there was a knock at the door.

I frowned, not knowing who could possibly be coming by for a visit at this time in the morning.

I pulled my robe tighter around me and got to my feet. Whoever was on the other side of the door was extremely impatient.

"Hang on. Where's the fire?" I grumbled, twisting the deadbolt and pulling the door open.

"Maysie?" I asked, looking down at my best friend.

She gave me a wane smile and reached out to give me a hug, which I returned, though I was still in shock at her sudden arrival.

"What the hell are you doing here? Are you moving in? Because if you are, you should have said something, bitch," I teased, though I was sort of serious. She had mentioned when we had been in Raleigh that she was thinking of coming back to Bakersville to get some needed distance from the drama of the boys on tour.

But that had been the last she had mentioned it. Gracie and I had figured she had said it in a moment of frustration and Jordan had calmed her down.

But here she was, standing on our doorstep, looking anything but happy.

"Can I come in? It's sort of cold out here," she asked, stepping around me into the living room.

"Sure, sorry. I'm just surprised to see you. The last we spoke you were on your way to Chicago," I said, closing the door behind her and following her to the couch. Maysie looked even more exhausted than she did the last time we saw her. I knew whatever reason she was here, it wasn't good.

"Yeah, well, we got to Chicago-" she began, sitting down.

"Do you want me to get Gracie? How about a coffee? I just bought this amazing machine," I broke in. It was in my nature to be a mother hen, even if I was abrasive in how I went about it.

"No, I'm fine. And don't wake up Gracie. I can fill her in later." Maysie waved away my offer.

With nothing left to do, I sank down beside her, ready to listen.

"I don't see any luggage. Am I to presume you're not moving in?" I asked.

Maysie shook her head. "No, I'm at Garrett's."

"Really?" I asked, surprised. Though I shouldn't have been. That was where Jordan had lived before going on the road.

"Yeah, with Garrett and Jordan," she added and the world stood still.

Or at least it felt like it.

"Jordan and Garrett are back in town?" My voice cracked and I reached for my coffee. I took a sip, not caring that it was now cold. Because if Jordan and Garrett were back in town, then that meant Cole was back in town.

And I wasn't sure I was ready for Cole to be back in town.

No. I knew I wasn't.

"We all got in a few hours ago. We caught a flight from O'Hare at six this morning." Maysie was twisting her fingers over and over again. She was upset. Seriously upset.

"That's a really early flight. Are you on the run or something?" I joked, even if the last thing I felt like doing was laughing.

Cole was here.

In Bakersville.

Suddenly the small town felt even smaller.

How would I ever be able to avoid him?

"Pretty much," Maysie stated, pulling me out of my Cole centered fixation.

"Just spill it, babe. Tell ole Vivvie what happened," I coaxed.

"Their show in Chicago last night was a freaking disaster. I told you that the band hadn't been getting a long. That Jordan and Cole had been at each other's throats. Well it had been getting worse. And Garrett and Mitch were becoming just as fed up with the Cole ego show. He's been monopolizing every interview. He's been given press that the rest haven't. It had been slowly building to a breaking point. I'm not saying Cole was doing any of this on purpose, but the boys were feeling slighted. Macho pride and all that."

I nodded. I had picked up on the tension in Raleigh. Cole had never mentioned anything. We hadn't had a whole lot of time to talk about band problems in between sealing my eyes shut with honey and telling him to get out of my life.

"It all seemed to center around this damn song the guys had written on the road. It's an awesome song. It really is. I just don't understand why they were fighting so much about it," Maysie agonized, foregoing her finger twisting and started chewing on a strand of her hair.

"Well, I'm sure it wasn't about the song really. If they were having problems, it was most likely the catalyst. Just the thing to push them over the edge," I supplied.

Maysie arched her eyebrow at me, her lips twisting into a wry smile.

"Since when did you get so astute?" she asked, though I knew she was teasing.

"Hey, I actually paid attention in psych class. Unlike someone else I know," I countered, swatting her knee. Maysie had been a lot more concerned with learning about Jordan Levitt than learning about Freud and Jung.

"You're probably right though. Because they started arguing about this stupid song last night before their show. Cole insisted they had to play it. Everyone else said it wasn't ready. So they got on stage and they weren't the same. Their shows have been different lately. I don't know if you picked up on that in Raleigh," Maysie said and I nodded in agreement.

"I did," I told her.

"Well, Cole took it upon himself to play the song anyway. He grabbed a guitar and sang the whole damn thing."

I gasped. "You're kidding! What did the rest of them do?"

Cole could be a self-centered bastard. He loved the limelight. But this seemed so out of character, even with his narcissistic tendencies.

"They walked off the stage. They left Cole out there by himself."

I was stunned. I couldn't imagine that the four guys I had seen play a hundred times before had degenerated to the point where they would abandon one of their own on stage.

"Shit," I breathed out.

"Yeah. Then Cole and Mitch got into it and then Jose had Jordan up against a wall. It was horrible." Maysie covered her face with her hands and I rubbed her back.

"They were kicked off the Primal Terror tour. Apparently their drama was in danger of overshadowing the actual shows. And they were told to head home. They have to meet the label execs in New York in a week to talk about where they go from here. Jose says they may pull the album and sever the contract."

Oh my god!

"Jordan is blaming himself. He's blaming Cole. He's ready to say forget the whole thing. Honestly I don't care if he never goes on the road again, but I know him. And I know that he still wants this as much as he ever did. It's his dream. And even though he's angry now, he'll hate himself for losing the possibilities."

I couldn't keep the question lying at the forefront of my brain quiet any longer. It needed to be answered.

"So is Cole back too?"

Maysie pursed her lips. But thank god she kept any negative comments to herself.

"He's here. He took a cab from the airport by himself. I'm guessing he's at his apartment. I don't really know," Maysie informed me.

Cole was here. He was most likely broken and upset. I wanted to call him. I wanted to rush over and take care of him. I wanted him to need me. I wanted to be that person he could lean on when things got crazy.

But then I remembered my firm resolve to be absolutely nothing to Cole Brandt.

I chewed on my bottom lip. "Is he okay?" I asked, knowing I couldn't go to the source to find out.

Maysie brought her knees up to her chest, wrapping her arms around them.

"I don't know. He's been different. They all have been. Even Jordan. They say fame can change you. And I think that's what was going on. Their star is rising and they start falling apart. I never thought it would happen. But it did. And truthfully, I'm thankful that Jose made them all go home. I'm glad they were kicked off that tour. The best thing for each and every one of them is to come back to Bakersville and get a little perspective."

Maysie was one smart cookie.

"I think I am thirsty. Mind if I take you up on your offer for a cup of coffee?" she asked and I shook my head.

"Not a problem, babe. Let me fix you a mocha latte."

GRACIE and I went with Maysie back to Garrett's house later in the day. My roommate had gotten up not long after I had made Maysie her cup of coffee and she had to launch into the entire story again.

Gracie was just as shocked as I had been. I was surprised that she hadn't already gotten the scoop from Mitch. Typically she was the first person he would call when anything was going on. But her obliviousness to the situation made me wonder what was going on between the two.

Pulling up outside of Garrett's home, I felt faintly sick. I wasn't sure whether Cole would be there or not. And I hated to admit that my offer to hang out with Maysie there had something to do with my desire to see him. To make sure he was okay.

I couldn't call him. I wouldn't be weak enough to go by his apartment. But Garrett's was neutral territory in a sense and I could feel less pathetic if I happened to run into him there as opposed to hunting him down.

Because despite everything that was going on his life, I had made the choice to cut ties. I'd feel like a bit ole' pile of wuss if I caved in so soon. No matter what the reasons.

The three of us walked into the house and found Jordan, Garrett, and Mitch sitting in the living room playing video games.

Finding them like this, you would think nothing was wrong. A case of beer sat opened on the coffee table. Jordan and Garrett were cussing each other out as they tried to shoot each other while playing some combat role-playing game. Mitch was strumming one of Garrett's acoustic guitars and none of them seemed overly concerned that their music career was set to implode.

But there was one major change in this familiar scenario. Cole was noticeably absent. Typically he would be right there with his best friends, shouting inappropriate commentary or getting wasted.

The void I felt by his absence was intense.

Garrett looked up when we entered and lifted a hand in greeting and then promptly let loose a string of curses when Jordan shot his character on the screen.

Maysie dropped her purse on the pool table in the corner and went to sit in Jordan's lap.

"Hey ladies. Guess you weren't expecting to see us around so soon," Jordan said wryly, kissing the side of his fiancée's neck.

I guess he was going to acknowledge the giant elephant in the room before it had a chance to trample us.

Gracie seemed oddly uncomfortable and I couldn't help but notice the way she and Mitch purposefully didn't look at each other. There was something definitely going on between the two and when I had a chance I would be finding out.

Gracie sat down on the Lazy Boy across the room and I made myself comfortable on the couch beside Garrett.

"Yeah, I was pretty stunned to find Maysie on our doorstep at ten-thirty on a Sunday morning. My first thought was she had wised up and left your sorry ass," I teased, trying to lessen the tension.

"Not a chance in hell," Jordan growled, kissing Maysie long and hard on the lips.

"Ugh, see what you've started, Viv!" Garrett complained, tossing the game controller on the coffee table and handing me a beer. I took it with a "Thanks" and gave him a pointed look.

"As if you and Riley are any different," I challenged.

"I wish Ri would let me put my tongue down her throat in public!" Garrett joked, smacking Jordan on the back of the head, interrupting him as he devoured Maysie's face.

"Maysie told us what happened," Gracie said, her eyes flitting over to Mitch who was looking stanchly at the guitar in his lap.

"Yeah. We're in deep shit right now. Even more if the label decides to not release our album," Jordan muttered, releasing Maysie who slithered off his lap.

"So if Pirate Records decides not to release your record, what will happen then?" I asked.

"We have no fucking clue. Except that the music on that album will never be heard by anyone. Ever," Mitch said bitterly.

"It's bullshit," Jordan said sharply.

"So what's the next step then?" Gracie asked, accepting a bottle of iced tea that Garrett had thoughtfully offered her with a smile.

"We just have to wait and see what the label says next week. We're flying up to New York next Tuesday. Until then we're supposed to 'sort our shit out,'" Garrett mimicked, obviously unhappy with the idea.

"And how exactly are you planning to sort your shit out?" I asked, noticing that throughout this entire conversation, not a single one of them had mentioned Cole.

Jordan shrugged. "We've got a lot to talk about. Things we have to work through. I'm not really sure where we'll end up at the end of all this." He said it lightly but I could tell he was worried. Maysie rubbed his back, leaning her head on his shoulder.

"Do some of the things you need to work through include Cole?" I asked bluntly. Sitting there in Garrett's living room without one of the main players felt strange and more than a little wrong.

I was frustrated on his behalf. Hurt and secondary betrayal

stung my veins. Not that he deserved any consideration on my part, but I couldn't help it.

Here were his best friends, his bandmates, and they existed in their group as if he were already gone.

Garrett gave me a strange look. I couldn't quite decipher his expression. Garrett was a hard guy to read. He hid his emotions behind a blasé demeanor. Until Riley came into the picture, I hadn't been entirely sure he was capable of feelings it all. He had spent most of his time numbing them with weed and booze.

"Cole is a big part of the problem, yeah," Garrett said after a beat.

"Really? Why is that?" Gracie gave me a look that clearly said I needed to shut up. It really wasn't any of my business and the glance Mitch and Jordan threw my way said as much.

But I wanted to know. I wanted to hear from them what exactly the problem was.

Garrett popped the cap off his beer and tossed it into the now empty case on the table. "Let's just say some people forget too quickly where they came from."

I felt my face get hot and an unreasonable irritation spread wildly through my insides. It wasn't right that they were sitting here gossiping like old bitches behind Cole's back. It wasn't cool that they were holding onto their anger without having the decency to talk to him about it.

I didn't know what went down except through secondhand knowledge. I had no idea what it was like on the road with Cole. But I did know that he had been friends with the three guys sat in front of me for years. They had built a band and created music together. They had started a journey together and there were always two sides to every story.

Given my recent anger towards Cole, I was surprised with how quickly my heart and mind had jumped to his defense.

"I think the same could be said for everyone. Don't you think?" I asked, chugging the rest of my beer and putting my empty bottled on the ground by my feet.

"You don't know what you're talking about, Viv. You, of all people should know exactly what we were dealing with. How you can sit there and be all morally disapproving when not two weeks ago you were telling Cole to take a hike," Jordan threw at me and I knew he was right.

But. . .

"I just think it's sort of screwed up that you're placing everything on his shoulders. Cole can be a handful but he's still a part of this band. So where is he?" I asked, giving each of the remaining members of Generation Rejects a pointed look.

"At his apartment, I guess," Mitch shrugged.

"Why isn't he here? Why aren't the four of you figuring shit out?"

"Vivian, this really isn't any of your business," Maysie remarked firmly, narrowing her eyes.

"You're right, it's totally none of my business. Maybe that's why it's easier for me to see how messed up it really is," I suggested.

Mitch snorted. "Oh please. As if you're an unbiased party."

I crossed my arms over my chest, accepting the barb but not letting it go without my own.

"And I think your heads are too far up your own asses to see anything clearly. It looks to me like Cole's wasn't the only ego that was the problem." I dropped my words like a bomb. I got to my feet and picked up my empty beer bottle and started to walk toward the kitchen.

"You got anything to drink besides beer?" I asked over my shoulder, more than aware of the looks everyone was tossing my way. But I didn't care. I said what needed to be said.

"Uh, there's some vodka I think," Jordan offered and I smirked at the befuddlement in his voice.

I could tell I had made him think. That I had made all of them think. And even though Cole would never know I had stuck up for him, I knew I had to say something.

And my feelings had nothing to do with it.

I had become really good at convincing myself of just about anything.

Chapter 15
COLE

I **THOUGHT** I was going to be sick. My stomach started to clench and my mouth began to water.

I had exactly ten seconds to make it to my bathroom before I threw up all over myself.

I stumbled out of my bed, tripping over the empty bottle of Everclear on the floor and made it to the toilet just in time.

I hated to puke. And I had been doing a lot of that for the past couple of hours. I felt like shit. Every part of my body ached. My head felt like someone was drilling a hole straight through my temples.

That's what I got for picking up a crate of liquor on the way home from the airport and proceeded to drink myself into a stupor.

The flight back from Chicago had been tense. I hadn't shared more than two words with any of my bandmates. A wall had been put up between them and me.

I was pissed. I was hurt. I was full of crazy fucking rage.

I had paid out the ass for a cab to take me all the way back to Bakersville. It was a hell of a lot better than riding back in Garrett's van.

I asked the driver to drop me off at the liquor store, where I proceeded to buy my weight in alcohol. I then went to my shitty apartment, a place I honestly had hoped to never see again, and drank my way into a coma.

It had seemed like such a good idea at the time.

Now, not so much.

My phone started to ring and I couldn't do much more than moan as the sound bounced around my cell.

"Shut up," I whispered hoarsely from my fetal position on my bathroom floor.

It listened, thank god, and the ringing stopped. I sat up and slowly got to my feet. I ran the water in the sink and filled my hands and splashed my face several times. It cleared some of the fog in my head.

I smelled like shit. That was definitely vomit on the front of my shirt. I looked at my reflection in the mirror and had to laugh. I was a long cry from being the sexed up bad boy singer everyone was used to seeing.

I looked like crap. Like a heroine addict before they overdosed in an alleyway. My cheeks were sunken and I had dark circles under my eyes. Despite feeling like asshole warmed over, I had enough residual vanity to make myself strip my clothes and jump in the shower.

Being clean helped to clear my head. I was hung-over as hell and I knew I needed to get something to eat. But the thought of leaving my apartment and going out there, out where people would know me and want to talk to me, seemed like a really bad idea.

The last thing I needed in my general state of suckitude, was to try and make conversation with anyone.

My phone started ringing again.

Obviously the person on the other end didn't understand that I was super busy wallowing in pathetic self-pity.

I picked up the source of my annoyance and went to hit ignore when I saw who it was.

Jose Suarez.

Figuring ignoring my manager wouldn't be in my best interest right now; I put the phone to my ear.

"Hello?"

"Where the fuck have you been? I've been calling you since yesterday!" Jose demanded.

"Man, lower your voice!" I croaked, rubbing my temples. I needed some ibuprophen stat!

"I don't give a shit if you've been run over by a damn bus, you answer the phone when I call you!" he ordered and I flipped him off, though he couldn't see me.

"Yeah, yeah. Okay, what's the emergency?" I yawned and even that simple movement made me feel like I was going to throw up again. I was a fucking mess.

"Are you screwing with me? What's the emergency? Well except for the fact that your career is in the shitter, nothing really," Jose bit out sarcastically.

Oh, yeah. There was that.

"Sorry, I didn't mean it like it sounded," I apologized.

"I'm getting the impression that not a lot of shit sorting is going on down in east bumblefuck, or wherever it is that you fuckers live," Jose snarled.

I really needed some ibuprophen. And I needed to stop tasting my stomach lining in the back of my throat.

"Have you spoken to the other guys?" he asked and I shook my head. Oh right, he couldn't see me.

"Nope." My mouth popped around the word for emphasis.

"You planning to talk to them?" he asked snidely.

"I guess," I said petulantly.

"You guess. Huh. Well that doesn't sound much like someone who's invested in saving his band," Jose pointed out. He didn't sound angry about it. Just thoughtful. And thoughtful Jose was kind of scary.

"I don't know if it's worth saving anymore. If they think it's okay to walk off stage and leave me like that, I'm not sure I want to play music with them anymore." And there I had said it. It was the thing that had been swirling around in my head since the entire concert fiasco.

I was bitter. I was really freaking bitter. And my feelings were hurt. I could admit that what my friends had done had cut me deep.

And maybe I was making decisions based on emotions, but I couldn't think past it. I wasn't sure we would ever be able to get to a place where we would be able to move passed our hurt pride.

There was a lot of ugliness between the four of us right now.

"I hear ya. I really do. So maybe now is a good time to talk about some news I have for you," Jose said and I figured I needed to be sitting down for whatever he had to tell me.

"News?" I asked, rooting around in my medicine cabinet for pain reliever. The throbbing in my head had started to get worse. My brains were starting to liquefy.

"Yeah, so I was talking to my man, Roberto, who works over at Deep Hill Records," he began and my ears perked up.

"Deep Hill Records? Are you shitting me? They're one of the biggest labels out there," I said, stopping my scavenger hunt in my medicine cabinet as Jose got all of my attention.

"No shit, Sherlock. Deep Hill is the big leagues. Pirate Records is great and all but they're young. They're still a starter company. They don't have a lot in the way of reach or overall capital. Deep Hill, however, could launch your name into the universe. And they're interested, Cole. Really fucking interested."

I sat down heavily on the toilet seat and tried to get a breath. I couldn't quite figure out what Jose was telling me.

"What do you mean they're interested?" I asked, feeling like a total idiot.

"It means they want to see more from you. Just you. My man is a head A&R dude. He's been in this industry since the late nineties. And he thinks you have something, Cole. He thinks you could be huge. He wants to talk to you about what Deep Hill could do for you. About working on an album."

Jose's words were going in one ear and out the other. I couldn't grasp what he was telling me. It was all a little too much for me to take in right now.

I felt like death.

My friends had abandoned me.

My band was on the edge of total ruin.

And Jose was saying that a guy at Deep Hill Records thought I could be a star.

I was going to be sick.

"I'm gonna have to call you back," I whispered, bile building up in the back of my throat.

"We need to talk about this now, Cole. My guy isn't going to wait around forever. I know you have your sit down with Pirate next week. But you need to think long and hard about what you're going to go in there and say. And if it were me, I'd say fuck it. Do what you have to do to get out of that contract. I've been reading over it and there are stipulations where you could be released without financial penalties. We need to talk about your strategy. Because I want to help you go beyond Generation Rejects. Cole, this is your chance to go all the way, man!"

I started to sweat.

The words terminate your contract and go beyond Generation Rejects buzzed in my ears. My stomach flipped over and I dropped the phone on the cold tile as I leaned over the toilet and retched.

JOSE didn't stay on the line after that. And I didn't bother to call him back. I couldn't handle his great ideas for my future right now.

I was so fucking confused.

When I thought it was safe to leave my bathroom, I headed out to my living room and sat down on my couch. I turned on the television and was annoyed to see only static.

"Fucking hell," I muttered, getting up and going over to mess with the cable behind the TV.

After a few minutes and with no success, I called the cable company. It seemed that my cable had been shut off. Seemed I had forgotten to pay the bill while I was on the road.

Oops.

I threw the remote control on the couch and went into my kitchen. Opening the refrigerator had been a mistake. Something had obviously crawled in there and died. And my stomach went into immediate revolt.

I slammed the door of the fridge closed and debated the intelligence of grabbing my keys and making a run for it.

Because right now, my life was shit.

And I had been doing so well.

I needed to talk to the guys. But I was feeling obstinate. And ornery. And a lot scorned bitch.

I thought back to the first time we played all together at Barton's. We had been awesome. We had just clicked. There was something that happened between the four of us when we played together.

It was hard to describe and even harder to understand until you experienced it.

Music is what had kept me sane. After my parents kicked me out and I started floundering, it gave me a fucking purpose. It gave me something to get invested in.

And I found in it something to be proud of. I was made to be a lead singer. I lived for being up on that stage and making people want me.

So maybe I had started letting it get to my head a bit. But you tell me one person who could do what I did every single night, who could have the women throwing themselves at them, having people tell them how amazing they were, and not start to feel like maybe they were right. That you are pretty awesome.

And what was wrong with feeling good about yourself?

I had spent most of my life feeling pretty shitty about who I was. I had never been good enough. Even when I broke the school's scoring record my junior year. Even when I was offered a scholarship. None of it mattered.

Most of the time growing up I had been pretty sure my dad had hated me. I couldn't remember a single time he had given me a compliment or had said "Good job, Cole."

That didn't mean I expected sympathy. I didn't wallow in my daddy issues and use it as an excuse to do whatever the hell I wanted.

Though it didn't take a PH.D. to dig down to the root of my psychological issues.

For someone who had never received any positive attention from the one person I had wanted it from, being inundated with it every night, in the form of the crowd, or chicks wanting in my pants, or record labels telling me I was a star in the making, it was pretty damn addictive.

So I had taken the praise and the attention and I had run with it. It had come to define me.

But that didn't mean I was a bad guy.

Right?

Then why was I sitting here. . . alone?

I was alone.

And that pissed me off. I had worked too damn hard and for too damn long to be in the same dingy apartment I had been living in since I was nineteen. I had thought when the Rejects had started to get some attention, it was my ticket out. My chance to prove everyone wrong.

So why was I still here worse off than I was when I left?

Something needed to change. And I was beginning to think I knew exactly what that thing was.

As if on cue, my phone rang again and if it was Jose again, I'd answer and tell him to make his calls.

Because if I couldn't get to where I wanted to be doing things the old way, then it was time to try something new. Garrett, Jordan, and Mitch wouldn't hold me back from anything, ever again.

So I grabbed my phone, full of self-righteous fury.

But it wasn't Jose.

It was Garrett.

"Hello?" I said, answering it before giving myself time to think about exactly what I was going to say.

"Hey, man," Garrett said, sounding as neutrally bland as he ever did. There was a long moment of silence where neither of us said a word.

I wasn't entirely sure what he expected me to say. Or what I expected him to say. But currently neither of us was saying anything at all.

I cleared my throat. My earlier anger still simmered in my

blood.

"What can I do for you?" I finally asked.

"Well, what do you think, Cole? We're back in Bakersville. We haven't heard from you. I figured you'd want to get together so we can hash shit out," Garrett retorted.

"You mean so you can sit around and tell me what an arrogant prick I am," I corrected.

"Look, dude, that's not it at all. We all have shit we need to address. So why don't you get off your sorry ass and get over here. The sooner the better."

I bristled instantly. Why did I need to jump through hoops because Garrett and the others had deemed it time to talk? I didn't appreciate the demand in his tone. I thought back to my conversation with Jose and the opportunities that were already presenting themselves.

I didn't need this bullshit. I didn't need three assholes to tell me what they thought I should change.

Fuck them!

"Yeah, well, I can't."

I could hear Garrett grinding his teeth. It was loud and it was annoying.

"What the fuck are you talking about? We need to talk. I know you're pissed. We are too. But I think-"

I cut him off, not interested in whatever psychobabble, hippie love shit was about to come spewing out of his mouth.

"I said I can't come right now," I said through clenched teeth.

Then there was silence again.

It lasted so long I started to think that Garrett had hung up.

"Hello?" I said.

"Is that how things are going to be? This is it?" Garrett asked quietly and I felt a twinge of guilt at the sound of regret in my friend's voice.

Was this how it was going to be? Was I really going to shaft my band and go out on my own?

Was I really going to leave behind everything that had made me who I am and think only of myself?

The possibility was too tempting to ignore.

But I still couldn't be the dick that they expected me to be. I still owed them something.

"Look, I've got to get my head in the right place. Give me some time. Yeah, I'm pissed, Garrett. I'm really fucking pissed. I don't want to come over and it turn into another round of the Jordan and Cole agro hour," I said, feeling really tired. I still hadn't found any ibuprophen and my headache was attacking my brain with renewed force.

"Cole, man, I don't think it'll be like that. You and Jordan just need to hear each other out. You're friends-" Garrett argued.

"No, he's your friend. He's never been my friend. I think that's fucking obvious," I said, sounding like a whiny bitch.

"Shit, are you for real? You've been playing in a band together for years. Stop being such a pussy. Your feelings are hurt. I get it. But you need to get over that shit for the sake of the band," Garrett growled. He was pissed. I could tell because he wasn't neutral anymore. He was spitting nails.

"For the sake of the band? What band, Garrett? Because where I'm standing I don't see anything resembling a group I want to be a part of."

Garrett hissed in a breath.

"Well, if that's how you feel, I won't stop you. And I'm not going to argue over the fucking phone like two high school cunts. If you want to talk about the band and about what the hell has been going on, you know where I live."

And he hung up.

I threw my phone on the couch and kicked over the trashcan.

I covered my face with my hands and screamed as loud as I could. Two seconds later there was a pounding on the other side of my wall.

"Shut up! Some people are trying to sleep!" my meth head neighbor yelled through the paper-thin partitions.

I had hoped that my life would change for the better.

How wrong I was.

Chapter 16
VIVIAN

"**Y**OU seem distracted, Vivian. What's wrong?" Theo asked as we sat in at the table in the foyer of The Claremont Center on Tuesday morning. It had only been two days since Maysie had shown up our doorstep and I was a nervous wreck.

I had skirted around town, dodging places where I was convinced I'd run into Cole. I stayed the hell away from Barton's, the liquor store, and Deanne's Diner, only because I knew how he loved their pecan pie.

But even as I tried to avoid him, I couldn't help but look for him everywhere I went. I was picking up ice cream and facial cleanser at Walmart and I couldn't help but look anxiously around for that dark head I was desperate, yet loathed to see.

I went through the drive- thru at Burger King for a vanilla milkshake and I found myself peering into the dining room, wondering if Cole was perhaps there, picking up his usual Whopper with cheese.

And when I drove down his street, because it seemed like the shortest way to get to my hairdresser, I tried to suppress the instant swarm of butterflies that unleashed their holy terror in my stomach when I caught sight of his beat up clunker sat out front of his building.

So damn straight I was distracted. I was a huge, giant, sweaty mess of distraction and it wasn't getting any better. Every hour, every minute, every goddamned second that passed, knowing that Cole and I were in breathing distance from one another felt like a ticking time bomb.

I just waited for it to go off in my face.

I wanted to clench my hands into to fists and shake them at the sky screaming, "Why God, why?" in full melodramatic glory.

But I was at work. And that sort of psychotic behavior just wouldn't do. So I plastered the fakest of fake smiles on my face and shook my head, as if to swipe all the lingering cobwebs away.

I gave Theo my best smile and even incorporated a little eyelash batting for good measure. "I'm just tired," I excused.

"You do look a little tense. Is there anything I can do? I give one heck of a massage," Theo offered, giving me a timid smile. He really was such a sweet guy. Why oh why couldn't I be hopelessly attracted to him? Why couldn't I rip his clothes off and have my wicked way with him?

I had felt I had been on the cusp of feeling something towards him. I had been feeling the tingles in all the right places. I had been indulging in the semi-regular fantasy that included him walking into my office, sweeping everything off my desk in a total alpha gesture, ripping my panties off and fucking me senseless on top of the gala budget plan.

Things had been progressing. At least in my head.

But now Cole was back in town. And all of my fantasies, all of my tingles had fizzled into non-existence.

Damn it! I felt like I was back at square freaking one!

"Thanks, Theo. I'm sure I'll be fine with a good night's sleep," I said, brushing off his shyly sexual offer.

Theo looked down at the table and I had the sense he was feeling a tad rejected. I wish he would stop making me feel so guilty. It was starting to tick me off.

"Well, I'm here. You know if you need to talk, or whatever," he stumbled.

I smiled. Not knowing what else to say. I hated dangling

precariously like this on the edge of indecision. I wish I were firm enough in my resolve to be rid of Cole that I could move forward with Theo, no questions. No doubts.

And while Cole was hundreds of miles away, it was easier to work towards that. But now that I knew he was here in Bakersville, even if I hadn't even seen him yet, I felt like he was pulling me back into his tractor beam. How could one person hold so much sway over another? It didn't' seem right. In fact it was downright cruel.

"Thanks, Theo. You're such a good friend." I patted his hand and almost cringed at my word choice.

Theo tried to play down his own wince. I had friend zoned him. Why had I done that? Did I want to do that? Why couldn't I figure out what was going on in my own damn head?

"Well, I try to be," Theo answered and I hated the look of disappointment on his face. One that I had put there.

I was such a damn fool.

MAKE it a double, Dina!" I called out, tapping my fingers on the bar. I turned in my stool and looked out at the crowded restaurant. Barton's was packed for a Tuesday night. But it was Ladies' Night and women drank half price until closing. Most of Rinard College's legal aged drinkers were crammed into the space. The girls looking to get wasted and the guys hoping to take them home.

I remembered that particular mating ritual well.

After Theo had left, I had tried to get my head into my workday. I ended up checking my email a half a dozen times and then mindlessly filing. My mind was on anything but work.

It was annoying.

So when Gracie had called and asked if I wanted to meet her at Barton's for dinner I had agreed, mostly because I couldn't take going home and drive myself crazy over thoughts of what Cole was doing.

But there was also a part of me that was much bigger than I wanted it to be that hoped to run into him there.

Though I should have known, given the state of his relationship with the rest of Generation Rejects, Barton's was the last place he'd show up.

So it was with a nagging disappointment that I joined, Gracie, Garrett, Maysie, Jordan, and Mitch for a round of beers and a mountain of hot wings while the guys watched football and us girls talked about the latest episode of Scandal.

We had moved things over to the bar after we had finished eating. It was already much later than I had meant to stay out on a work night, but I was determined to enjoy myself.

As much fun as it was to hang out with my friends, I couldn't ignore the nagging strangeness of being with this group of people without Cole. Even though he wasn't there and his name was purposefully avoided like the plague, his presence was felt intensely.

I felt it. And I know everyone else did as well.

"I friend zoned Theo today," I yelled to Gracie over the noise.

Gracie twirled her straw in her lemonade and widened her eyes.

"You did what?" she asked.

Garrett leaned in, resting his arms on the bar as he tried to hear what we were talking about.

"Who's Theo?" he asked.

"The cute man who wants in Vivian's pants," Gracie teased and I rolled my eyes.

"That's cool," Garrett said, looking like he was already regretting getting involved in our conversation.

"Well it would be if I could stop being such an idiot," I muttered, rubbing my forehead.

"How did you friend zone him?" Mitch asked from my other side, seeming genuinely perplexed.

I noticed that Gracie instantly tensed when Mitch moved in closer to stand behind us. They had carefully sat away from each other all evening. Our group was suffocating under so much unresolved tension.

I had yet to figure out exactly had changed between Mitch and Gracie. But whatever it was, it clearly was there to stay for a while.

I looked at the both of them with raised eyebrows but they ignored my silent question.

They weren't going to tell me shit.

"I said, "You're such a good friend, Theo."

Garrett and Mitch groaned in unison.

"I don't even know this dude and I feel bad for him," Mitch stated, reaching around me to grab his beer. I watched Gracie's eyes follow him, her expression hurt but tender. And I suddenly knew exactly what the problem was.

They had slept together.

Those sneaky bastards had finally screwed and no one had told me. I met Gracie's eyes and gave her a look that said I know what you did, you dirty hoe!

She flushed and quickly looked away. I was totally going to find out about this later.

But I kindly let it go for now.

"I thought you liked him," Maysie piped up, coming to join us at the bar. Jordan was talking to Moore, Barton's manager.

"I do like him. I just can't make the leap," I complained.

Gracie shook her head. "And I think we all know why," she scolded.

"God, seriously? You're still hung up on Cole?" Mitch spat out as though his name were a bad word.

"You don't understand," I responded unconvincingly. Garrett and Mitch both shook their heads as though I were the biggest idiot in the world. Gracie simply looked sad for me.

"Whatever," I muttered, tired of talking about the crappy state of my love life.

Jordan came back to the bar, his face pinched and drawn.

"What's wrong, babe?" Maysie asked, looping her arm around his waist.

"Well, nothing's wrong, really. Moore just offered to pay us a shitload of money if we'd play tonight."

Garrett sat up straight and Mitch put his beer down on the bar.

"How much is a shitload?" Mitch asked.

"Five hundred bucks," Jordan said and we all gaped.

"Why so much?" Maysie asked.

"Because apparently the band that was supposed to play tonight backed out at last minute. He's freaking out back there." Jordan jerked his thumb in the direction of the middle aged, overweight manager, who was indeed wringing his hands and looking like he might pass out.

"Well, we can't exactly call Cole," Mitch snarled and it was on the tip of my tongue to tell them all to stop being so silly. To tell them to put on their big boy pants call Cole.

But before I could say anything, Maysie jumped in with a surprising suggestion.

"What about Paco? He's an amazing singer. And he knows all of your songs."

"Paco? The dishwasher?" Gracie asked, frowning.

Maysie nodded. "Yeah. I know it's weird. But it's five hundred bucks and given the way everything's in limbo right now, you can't turn down that kind of money. And it's only one gig. And it's Barton's. Who will ever know?" she asked, and the guys started to nod.

"We'll need to run back to the house and grab our gear. But yeah, I say let's do it. I think we could all use this," Garrett agreed.

I couldn't believe that they were going to put someone else up on that stage with them and let him sing. I couldn't understand their willingness to replace Cole so quickly.

Garrett must have seen the look on my face because he leaned in and lowered his voice.

"This is Cole's choice, Viv. Don't look at us like we're the bad guys here," he said and then he and Mitch were up and out the door. Off to get their equipment while Jordan went into the kitchen to talk to the dishwasher turned singer.

"I can't believe you suggested that," I told Maysie, feeling depressed by the whole thing.

Maysie shrugged. "Cole's not coming back to the band, Viv. What else are they supposed to do? They've got to move on."

"How do you know he's not coming back?" I demanded.

"Because Garrett talked to him this morning. And they got into it. And it was left that Cole was looking into other opportunities. Generation Rejects is going to have to start looking for another singer."

It annoyed me that Maysie didn't seem bothered by it. That the fact that Cole, who had been with the band for years, was suddenly leaving and no one seemed upset by the news.

Was I the only one who couldn't believe Cole would leave his band like that?

"That just doesn't sound like Cole. Maybe Garrett misunderstood," I suggested.

Maysie looked at me as though I were speaking tongues.

"I don't think you know Cole as well as you think you do, Viv," Maysie said shortly, clearly annoyed that I was defending the former lead singer at all.

Jordan came out of the back with a very excited looking Paco.

"Maysie, my love, thank you!" Paco tried to hug Maysie, who put her hands out stopping him with a laugh.

You needed to keep your distance from Paco. He was bit on the touchy feely side. The middle aged, paunchy, and balding dishwasher looked nothing like lead singer material. But he was enthusiastic; I'd give him that.

Moore and the other wait staff started to clear tables, making room for the amps. I had seen them do this a thousand times before. I had always loved watching the guys set up for a show.

There had always been an air of excitement when I knew Generation Rejects were going to play.

Not this time.

This time I felt like crying.

An hour later, the guys were plugged in and ready to go. The normal ring of Barton's customers fanned out around them, seeming as confused as I had been to see Paco at the front, microphone in hand.

Jordan, before sitting down at his drum kit, took the mic from Paco and spoke into it.

"It's awesome to be back at Barton's!" He pumped his fist into the air and everyone cheered.

"We sure have missed you guys!"

Another round of cheering. Paco stood awkwardly off to the side. His Barton's shirt grease stained and torn.

"I'm sure you're wondering why Paco is up here with us tonight," Jordan grinned, though from here I could see that it was strained.

He held his hand out to indicate the dishwasher. "Well, I don't know if you've ever heard this guy sing, but he's incredible. So we asked him to join us tonight."

"Where's Cole?" someone yelled out from the crowd. I saw Jordan, Mitch, and Garrett exchange glances.

Jordan cleared his throat and forced another smile.

"Well, there are going to be some changes with the line up of Generation Rejects. I'm not sure exactly what's going to happen. But tonight, with Paco's help, we're gonna rock your faces off!" he yelled into the mic and the crowd, though hardly convinced, seemed to accept the excuse, for now.

Paco took the mic and screamed loud and shrill, making me flinch. The guys looked at each other again and the same look was on their face that had to have been on mine.

Oh shit.

But luckily for them, after Paco got over his nerves, he settled in. He was a pretty good rock singer and Maysie was right, he knew all the lyrics to the songs. And while the crowd wasn't as energetic as they normally were, they seemed to be enjoying it enough.

I turned back to the bar to order myself another beer when I caught a movement outside the front window of the restaurant. I looked more closely and saw a recognizable shock of dark hair and the glint of light from a lip ring I knew all too well.

It was Cole.

He didn't come inside. He stood out in the cold, looking in through the window, a pained expression on his face.

I didn't move for the longest time. I could only watch him as he watched his band perform without him.

And then I was on my feet.

I pushed through the crowd and hurried outside just as Cole was turning to leave.

"Cole!" I called out.

He looked up and I was shocked to see the gleaming wetness in his eyes. I had never seen Cole cry. Ever. But right then, I knew he was about to.

This was a man whose heart was breaking.

And mine broke for him.

He shoved his hands into his pockets and started to walk past me. I reached out and grabbed his arm, my fingers digging through the worn leather of his jacket tightly. Not letting go.

"Don't go," I said, pleading with him. For what I didn't know.

He shook his head, his hair falling into his face. Looking at him under the glow of Barton's neon sign, he looked older than the last time I saw him. He looked haggard and tired.

"I can't stay here, Viv. I just can't." His voice broke and his words twisted in anguish.

He was killing me.

This wasn't a Cole I had ever seen before. And I didn't know what to say or do. I was speechless.

"They've replaced me," he said quietly.

I shook my head. "It's just Paco-" I started but he cut me off.

"They don't need me anymore."

He bit down on his lip, his eyes trained to the ground.

"I thought that's what I wanted. I thought I didn't need them. I was wrong. I was so fucking wrong. But now it's too late."

Then he looked up, his eyes meeting mine and they ripped a hole through my chest.

Slowly, he reached out, his ice-cold fingers softly touching my cheek. They lingered there as if he couldn't help himself.

"I'm always too late. And now I've lost everything."

And then he dropped his hand. I felt the absence of his touch instantly. He shoved his hands back into his pockets and walked away, his feet hurried as though he couldn't get away fast enough.

Chapter 17
VIVIAN

AFTER Cole had left, I went back into Barton's and didn't mention a thing. I didn't tell anyone that I had seen him.

I was unwilling to share with his friends or mine about my run-in with an obviously devastated Cole.

I'm always too late. And now I've lost everything.

The way he had touched my face and looked into my eyes unsettled me in the worst possible way.

I tried to convince myself that he was talking about his band when he uttered those cryptic words.

What else could he mean?

But from the way he gazed at me with such longing, it almost had me imagining those words were meant for me as well.

I was ridiculous.

Here I was, still holding onto the unrealistic hope that the man I had casually slept with for the past two years would wake up one day and realize I was the only one for him.

My romantic delusions would be my undoing.

The rest of Generation Rejects 2.0's performance wasn't half-bad. Paco did a decent job covering the songs we all knew and loved and eventually the crowd seemed to forgive him for not being the man we all wanted him to be.

When they were finished and the bar closed down, I didn't feel up for sticking around for the after show drinks. I couldn't laugh and joke around with my friends when I knew somewhere not far away, a certain someone was home alone and grieving the loss of something that meant so much to him.

I got into my car and headed home but somehow I ended up on a dead end street staring at Cole's old clunker sitting in front of his rundown apartment building in the worst part of town.

My car idled in the middle of the road as I looked up at the second story window where a light was on and the curtains drawn.

Should I go up?

Should I call him?

And now I've lost everything.

His words were haunting me.

The look in his eyes was destroying me.

But I did the only thing anyone would do when they were desperately trying to protect their heart and soul.

I put my car into gear and drove home.

I slept like crap, spending most of the night tossing and turning in my bed. I woke up for work the next morning exhausted and angry with myself.

Why was I letting Cole get to me like this? Why was I letting him dominate my every thought?

So what! He had shown me a sliver of vulnerability! That didn't mean that he had changed. That didn't mean that he wasn't still the same self-serving dick he had always been.

I couldn't let three days with him back in town detonate my entire life. I needed to remember that self-respect was essential for the Vivian New World Order that I was instituting.

And self-respect did not mean crawling back to the man who had used me for years just because he seemed sad!

I was so focused on my internal pep talk I startled when I found Gracie awake, dressed, and making breakfast.

She too was all dolled up and looked ready to head to work.

"What's with all the pretty?" I asked, indicating her outfit.

She looked down at her adorable skirt and button up shirt ensemble and shrugged.

"Interview."

"Really?" I grinned and then I frowned, annoyed she hadn't told me about this sooner.

Gracie hadn't had an easy time of things since she had gone to rehab last year. The normally smart and focused girl with hopes of starting her own fashion magazine had settled on becoming a barista at the local coffee bar downtown

I knew she was disappointed in herself. She had been in the same journalism program as Riley in college. And now Riley was in grad school and working as a freelance reporter for a local newspaper.

Gracie had decided her aspirations needed to sidelined in place of getting herself together. And more power to her. That was where her head needed to be.

"Where?" I asked, getting out the bread and popping a slice into the toaster.

"Nothing major, just at the Southern Gardens magazine. They're hiring a part-time columnist to write about festivals and events in the area."

Well it wasn't the New York Times, but it was a start. I gave her a huge smile and reached out to hug her. Gracie rolled her eyes and accepted my hug and I knew she was excited even if she was unsure whether she should be or not.

"You'll nail it. I have no doubt," I said with confidence. Gracie sipped on her tomato juice.

"I hope you're right. I need to do something more than sling coffee before I lose my mind."

We carried our breakfast into the living room and I turned on the news, as was my normal routine.

"So what did you think of the impromptu show last night?" Gracie asked, nibbling on her bagel.

"Honestly? I thought it sucked. Paco wasn't bad, but it wasn't Generation Rejects we were watching. It's sad that we may never see them play together again," I noted a tad despondently.

Gracie nodded. "Yeah, I just can't understand why they're

letting such petty crap get in the way of their dream. Guys are worse than girls sometimes."

"Hasn't Mitch mentioned what he's thinking about all of this?" I asked her, knowing my mention of the Rejects' bassist would get a reaction.

Gracie stiffened instantly, as I knew she would, and dabbed her mouth daintily with a napkin. She took her time answering me.

"I haven't really spoken to him about it," she said after a while.

"And why is that?" I dug. I hadn't had a chance to talk to her about what was going on with her and Mitch. And it helped to focus on someone else's floundering personal life than fixate too long on my own.

"We just haven't really talked," Gracie responded, as if it were no big deal.

"You act as if that's not major, G. You and Mitch used to talk every day, even when he was on the road. What changed?" I interrogated her further.

Gracie was starting to look increasingly uncomfortable. She fidgeted a bit and started to pick at her bagel.

"Well. . .um. . ." she began.

"Well, um, what?" I pushed.

"We had sex," she said, dropping the bomb I had been expecting but was no less shocked to hear.

"Are you flipping serious?" I squealed, my voice reaching a piercing volume.

Gracie winced and nodded.

"When was this?" I asked, trying to be considerate of the fact that my roommate looked less than thrilled to be talking about this particular subject. But I wanted to know what happened. Because even though this seemed like a good thing, obviously it hadn't turned out all sunshine and roses. Something had gone wrong afterwards.

"When we were in Raleigh," Gracie admitted and it all clicked into place. I had wondered at the time where she was all night while I lay in her hotel room crying my eyes out. But I had been too mired in my own drama with Cole to put too much thought into it.

"So. . ." I prompted, wanting her to continue.

Gracie glared at me, clearly annoyed that I was pressing the issue.

"So, Mitch told me he loved me. I told him I couldn't be with him. He got pissed. I got pissed. We fought. Now he's dating some girl named Sophie he went to high school with."

Wow, that was a lot of information for first thing in the morning.

"He's dating someone? So soon?" I asked, still trying to process my friend's angst filled story.

Gracie nodded, her jaw clenching. "Yeah. Apparently they had talked on and off for years. They dated for a while when they were seniors. He had mentioned her to me before, but whatever. It's not like I have any say in what he does or who he sees," she spat out defensively.

"Are you jealous?" I couldn't help but asking.

Gracie glared at me again, but this time with a hell of a lot more venom.

"Why in the world would I be jealous? I just told you I turned him down. I told him that I couldn't be with him. Mitch is my friend. That's all he'll ever be," she argued.

"Except you're not even really friends anymore," I pointed out.

Gracie sighed. "Well, yeah, there is that."

"But you slept with him," I said slowly, trying to piece together the things Gracie wasn't saying.

Gracie sighed again. "Yes, I did. I was drunk. Mitch was drunk. I was lonely and at the time I was feeling things, never mind, it doesn't matter. I ruined an amazing friendship because I couldn't keep my legs closed. I just had no idea Mitch felt that way."

"Are you blind?" I laughed incredulously.

Gracie frowned. "I just didn't think, I don't know. I just can't focus on a guy right now. No matter what I thought I felt at the time. Not with me only now starting to get my life back together."

She was insistent.

I had been worried something like this would happen eventually. The day had finally come when Mitch was tired of waiting around. And Gracie's heart had gotten smooshed in the process. I just wish she wasn't so damn stubborn.

She set her plate down on the coffee table and absently picked at a piece of fuzz on her skirt. "He's with someone else now, so it doesn't matter what I think about any of it anyway. It's all a moot point."

"That doesn't explain why you aren't talking," I said.

Gracie gnawed on her bottom lip. "It's too weird now. Stuff was said that can't be unsaid. Some things you can't come back from." She got to her feet in a sudden, fluid movement.

"It sucks. I miss him. I really do. But he doesn't seem to want to hear anything I have to say. And I have to accept that. I hurt him. I didn't mean to, but I did. And if this Sophie girl can make him happy, then I'm happy."

She was such a horrible liar.

But I didn't call her on it.

We were quiet for a moment. We were both such a mess. Our love lives were in tatters at our feet. Both of us held prisoner by feelings we'd rather not have.

"I've got to get going. Wish me luck," Gracie said after a while, giving me a forced smile.

I stood up and hugged her again.

"Good luck, G." I rubbed her back and squeezed her hand.

As she walked out the door, I knew it was time we got up, dusted ourselves off, and stopped letting the men of Generation Rejects run over our hearts.

"I HAVE something to ask you but I'm worried you'll turn me down again," Theo's rich voice filled my ear as I leaned back in my desk chair.

We were only fifteen minutes into our now usual morning check-in. This morning had begun with the typical rundown of gala specifics that I was finalizing. The fundraiser was next weekend and I was up to my eyeballs in details. But I was excited. I had even been able to snag some extra tickets for Gracie, Riley, who would be down for the weekend, and Maysie. We were all planning to get dressed up and go together. I appreciated my friends' support. Lord knows I'd need it.

If I didn't expire from stress before then.

Marion had recently given me a new assignment. It was a concert series coming up in May. She seemed impressed with how I had taken charge of the Kimble event. She didn't hesitate to pay me the compliments I needed to hear. She was a good boss. Efficient but not overbearing. And I liked being able to do well and prove she hadn't made a mistake in hiring me.

If I were honest with myself, part of me would be slightly relieved once the gala was over. I loved that Theo and I had become friends but I was also aware of how precariously we were tiptoeing along the edge of dating. And I also knew that my less than subtle avoidance wouldn't hold him off forever.

He had been considerate in not pushing me. But from the tone of his voice, I knew that he was through waiting.

"Okay," I said, clicking my pen in an anxious gesture.

"I know you wanted to wait until the gala was over, but considering it's only a little over a week away, I don't think we would be doing anything wrong by having dinner together. There's this great French place that just opened in Granton. It's getting amazing reviews. I'd really like to take you there tonight if you'll agree." Theo's offer was given with a mixture of barely concealed impatience and eagerness.

I sat up a little straighter in my seat, running through excuses in my head. Saying I have to wash my hair seemed like too much of a burn and I have a doctor's appointment was totally ridiculous.

Did I want to go out with him?

This was the question of the moment and one I flip-flopped on several times a day. Without being able to stop myself, Cole's face as I had seen it last night danced across my mind.

This was all his fault, the bastard.

So in a moment of defiance towards Cole and his unnatural

hold over me, I clenched my fists and gave Theo the answer he wanted.

"Sure, I'd love to."

"Really? Am I hearing things?" Theo joked.

I couldn't help but chuckle. I really had put this poor guy through the ringer. It was time to reward him for his persistence. Being pursued by such an amazing guy was flattering. And who knows, this may be exactly what I needed to move on once and for all.

"No need for a hearing aid, I want to go," I assured him.

"Thank god! I was beginning to think I would be entering senility before you agreed to a date with me," Theo admonished good-naturedly.

I forcefully banished all thoughts of Cole from my mind. I couldn't let him have anything to do with my decisions. He could have no bearing on my love life anymore. Not that he ever should have to begin with.

"Well, what time should I be ready?" I asked brightly.

"Text me your address and I'll be by around seven thirty?"

"Sounds great," I said, feeling determined.

I would enjoy myself, or die trying.

That evening I dressed in my nicest red dress. Nothing low cut or overly revealing. I styled my hair into soft curls down my back and my makeup was understated yet flattering.

I did a little twirl in front of my mirror and gave myself a low whistle. I looked hot. Damn hot. I knew Theo would approve.

So why was I thinking of Cole's reaction while I got ready?

Gracie was out to dinner with Jordan and Maysie. She was still in a funk when I had gotten home. She wouldn't say how her interview had gone so I hadn't pushed it. Truthfully I needed to be in the right frame of mind for my evening ahead and Gracie's depressive personality wouldn't help.

My doorbell chimed as I slid my strappy black heels on my feet. I spritzed my wrists and cleavage with some vanilla perfume and grabbed my tiny clutch.

I opened the door to find Theo holding the most obscenely large bouquet of flowers I had ever seen. His shy smile lit up his face as he took me in.

"Oh my god, you're gorgeous," he said, his mouth gaping slightly as he started with my feet and made his way up my body.

I preened at the compliment and took the bunch of flowers from his hands.

"Thank you, come inside while I put these in some water," I said, waving him into the apartment. I pressed my face into the blossoms and breathed in their smell.

And then sneezed.

And not a delicate, dainty sneeze. This was a nose-full-of-snot-sprayed-five-feet-away sneeze.

And I couldn't stop. I kept freaking sneezing.

I dropped the flowers onto the counter and rushed around, trying to find a tissue. I attempted to pinch the bridge of my nose in an effort to stave off the flow of mucus that had already started to drip disgustingly.

"Crap, are you okay?" Theo asked, following behind me.

"Achoo!" I sneezed violently and held my hand up for him to leave me be.

I wiped my nose, once I had located the tissues and eyed the flowers warily. "Are those Gerbera daisies?" I asked.

Theo looked confused and picked up the bunch of flowers that had set off my sneezing attack.

"I really don't know. I just picked these up because I thought you would like them."

My nose started to tickle again and I pressed the tissue to my nose again.

"I'm horribly allergic to daisies. I'm sorry." I was now stuffed up and my eyes were watering like crazy. I was in danger of going into a full-blown allergic reaction if he didn't get the flowers out of my apartment.

"No, I'm the one who's sorry! I swear I didn't know!" Theo looked stricken and I felt horrible. What a crappy start to our date. I hated the niggling feeling that this didn't bode well for any sort of dating experience between the two of us.

"You had no idea, Theo. It's fine. But you're going to have to take them out of here. It's the pollen. It causes my hay fever to go nuts."

Theo opened the front door and tossed the offending bouquet out onto the sidewalk.

"Is that better?" he asked.

I continued to cover my nose and nodded. "Just give me a minute to get myself together," I said, my words muffled by the Kleenex. "Make yourself at home. I'll only be a second."

I hurried into the bathroom and cringed when I looked at myself in the mirror. My eyes were bloodshot and puffy. My nose was as red as fucking Rudolph the Red Nosed Reindeer's. I blew my nose and found some antihistamines in the medicine cabinet.

I tried to fix my makeup but there wasn't a whole lot I could do. I thought briefly about calling the night a wash but I knew I had already given Theo enough of a runaround.

I came out of the bathroom, a smile plastered to my face. "Okay, I'm ready."

Theo jumped up from the couch and like the gentleman he was, he didn't make any comment about my red face and swollen eyes.

"Are you sure?" he asked, peering at me.

I nodded. "I've taken something so this," I indicated my messed up face, "should be fine in no time."

"If you're okay, we should get going. I made us reservations for eight."

I followed Theo out to his Hummer, making sure to hold my breath as we walked past the discarded flowers.

Theo and I had always enjoyed an easy banter. However, tonight was different. Maybe it was my psychotic sneezing fit or perhaps it had to do with the fact that this was an official date, but conversation was a lot more stilted than usual.

We ended up talking shop for most of the ride to the restaurant, which I found to be incredibly boring. The last thing I really wanted to talk about on a date was my job. But it was the only thing that truly connected us.

The restaurant Theo had picked was called Bistro Margot and it was packed. It was a good thing that Theo had made reservations. We were seated right away at a dimly lit booth near the back. It was private and intimate, with a candle that flickered madly. The atmosphere was very romantic if not a little try too hard.

I opened the menu and my eyes bulged as I took in the prices of the meals. Holy cow! $30 for an entrée?

"The food looks fantastic," Theo enthused, smiling at me. I wish I could share his excitement. Because nothing seemed remotely appetizing. My experience with French food was limited. Okay, it was non-existent. But I didn't want to look like an ignoramus so I pretended to study the menu seriously. I could pretend that I knew what Porc a la Dijonnaise meant. But even the descriptions weren't very helpful.

When the waitress came to take our order I pointed to the only word I recognized. Steak Tartar. Theo looked surprised by my selection.

"You like Steak Tartar?" he asked. I waved my hand indifferently.

"I love it," I responded as though it was something I ate all the time.

"Wow, you're hardcore, Viv," he said and I wondered what the hell I had just ordered.

We sipped on our wine and smiled at each other with a strained stretching of lips.

"So, tell me about yourself," Theo said.

"That's a pretty general question, Theo," I teased, drinking my wine a little faster.

Why was I feeling so lightheaded all of a sudden? I was by no means a cheap drunk. And I should definitely not be feeling the effects of wine after one glass.

But I stupidly decided to pour myself another glass.

"Well, how about your family? Tell me what growing up as Vivian Baily was like," Theo prompted, eating some of the hors d'oeuvres he had ordered. Something called Assiette de Fruits et Fondue de Brie, which was only fruit and baked cheese with crackers. Sounded a lot fancier than it actually was.

"Not much to tell, really. I had a very stereotypical childhood. My parents are great. My mom is a veterinarian and my dad is a lawyer. I have an older sister, Sarah, who is physical therapist and an older brother who is a counselor. I get along really well with my siblings and my parents love me. Not much else to say," I answered blandly. I was bored. Really, really bored. And my head was becoming cloudier by the minute.

Which made keeping my eyes open really difficult. Particularly with all of this riveting conversation.

I drank the rest of my glass of wine and began to pour myself another but my hand knocked over the bottle. Wine spilled all over the crisp, white table linens and dripped onto Theo's lap.

He jumped to his feet and started to pat the wet spot on his crotch. I snickered and pointed at his pants.

"It looks like you pissed yourself," I slurred.

Oh shit, what was wrong with me?

"Are you okay? How much have you had to drink?" Theo asked, frowning.

I held up two fingers. "Two glasshes," I slurred, propping my head on my hand and poking at the Brie on my plate as our waitress came rushing over to mop up the spilled wine.

"That's it?" Theo asked, as if he didn't believe me.

I nodded, my head slumping.

"Did you take anything before you left the apartment?" Theo asked, shaking my arm to keep me awake.

I opened my mouth but no words came out. My tongue felt thick. Had I taken anything before I left the house?

Oh yeah. I had taken the antihistamine. And then I'd had wine. Probably not a good combination.

"I took an antihista. . .an antihistamer. . . .an antihissic. . ." I couldn't get the word out correctly.

"An antihistamine?" Theo prompted and I tried to put a finger on my nose.

"That's it! You get ten points!" I said loudly.

"Shit. You need to eat something and drink some water. And you definitely need to stop drinking this." Theo swapped my wine for a glass of water.

"Hey! I wanted that!" I pouted.

Theo scooped some fruit onto my plate. "Eat. You'll feel better

206

once you have something on your stomach," he suggested.

And I did as I was told. "Mmm, this is so good," I moaned, closing my eyes as I swallowed the melon and cheese.

Theo cleared his throat and moved around in his seat.

"I wasn't sure I wanted to go out with you," I said, proving that antihistamines and alcohol took away all of my filter.

Theo cocked his head to the side and smiled, clearly amused by me. "Oh really?" he asked.

I licked some cheese from my fingers before grabbing some more. This shit was good!

"Yeah. Because there's this guy I've been fucking for a while. The sex is unbelievable. And he's gorgeous too. The things he does with his tongue, oh god. And his cock," I held up my hands, indicating the size of Cole's well-endowed penis.

"He's hung like a horse. I'm not even kidding," I informed my date, who seemed less and less amused by my dinner talk.

I took a drink of water to wash down the crackers. "And I think I love him. Like a lot. But he's an asshole. And he's with other girls way too much. And I just couldn't put up with that anymore. But you're nothing like him. You're sweet. And even though I haven't seen your Mr. Winky, I'm sure it's nice enough."

I gave him a sloppy grin and I barely registered the fact that Theo was most definitely not smiling anymore.

Our waitress showed up and put our dinners in front of us. I stared down at the pink blob of meat on my plate and started to feel faintly nauseous.

"You really should try to eat something," Theo said shortly, digging into his own dinner and purposefully not looking at me.

I poked the meat with my fork. "What is it?" I asked, sort of scared by the pile of gross in front of me.

Theo raised his eyebrows. "It's Steak Tartar. It's what you ordered. I thought you had eaten it before."

I shook my head. "I have no idea what this shit is."

"Well, you're in for a surprise then. Because it's essentially raw hamburger," he informed me as he turned back to his more appetizing meal.

"Raw hamburger?" I squeaked.

Theo's face softened. "Just try it. Some people really like it," he suggested.

I picked up my fork and jabbed it into the mess on my plate. I put a small piece in my mouth and my throat instantly seized in revolt. My body did not want me ingesting this vile thing served as food.

Oh no, I was going to be sick.

"I have to go to the bathroom!" I jumped to my feet and hurried as fast as I could to the women's room, where I lost the contents of my stomach into the toilet.

I sagged to my knees and laid my forehead on the toilet bowl. Now that everything was out of my belly, including the alcohol, the fuzz in my head receded slightly. I was still shaky, but I wasn't feeling so out of it.

I flushed the toilet and went to the sink to rinse my mouth. This was officially the worst date in the history of worst dates.

Christ! Had I really told Theo about the size of Cole's penis?

What was wrong with me? Was I trying to make him hate me?

There was a knock on the door and Theo's voice was heard on the other side.

"Are you all right, Vivian?" he asked, concerned.

"I'm okay," I called back, feeling like the most horrible person ever.

"I had the waitress take the Steak Tartar back. She's bringing you a grilled chicken dish instead." He was so damn considerate. And I had developed an allergic reaction to his gorgeous flowers, gotten high off antihistamines, and told him all about my former fuck buddy's package all before running to the bathroom to yak.

And on top of it all I looked like death warmed over.

My god, just shoot me now and put me out of my misery.

I rinsed my mouth again, trying to rid myself of the taste of puke and bile. I opened the door and found Theo waiting for me.

"I'm so sorry, Theo," I said, bowing my head in embarrassment.

Theo put his arm around my shoulders and gave me a squeeze. "I get the feeling that nothing with you is ever boring," he stated.

"No, I guess not," I agreed.

If he only knew.

Chapter 18
VIVIAN

THE grilled chicken was much more palatable and once I had solid food in my stomach, the last of the antihistamine-induced fog disappeared and I once again had control over my mouth. And more specifically what came out of it.

"So, what I said about my ex," I started to say as we were leaving the restaurant.

Theo raised his hands. "I really don't need to hear any more about it, if it's all the same to you," he joked, even though I saw a hint of seriousness in his eyes.

"Fair enough," I commented as we waited to cross the street to the car park. I felt horrible for how badly the night had turned out and I was at a loss at how to salvage it.

And then I heard music. Loud, raw, and pretty damn awesome.

Down the road was a small bar I had been to several times. Generation Rejects had played there before and it was a really cool place to hang out. It sounded like a band was playing now.

I nodded toward the bar. "You want to grab a drink and listen to some music?" I asked.

Theo looked a little uncertain. "Isn't that a biker bar?" he asked and I wanted to laugh.

"No, Theo. It is not a biker bar. Come on. Let me buy you a drink to make up for being such a crap date," I pleaded.

I could have asked him to my apartment and made him a drink there. Given the look of irrational terror on his face at the prospect of heading over to Benny's, I should have nixed the whole idea.

But I felt uncomfortable with the idea of hanging out with him, alone, in my apartment. Expectations would be made and I wasn't sure I could deliver. I needed to keep things as public as possible.

"I'll take care of you," I teased and finally Theo relaxed.

"Come on, buy me a beer," he said, letting me pull him across the road and into the loud, smoke filled bar. I wasn't sure how the place got away with allowing people to smoke in the building, but no one seemed bothered by the thick haze hanging in the air.

A band was playing hard rock on the stage and the place was filled with your less than savory types. I wasn't sure what possessed me to want to come. Even with my rock show past, this was a bit more hardcore than I was usually comfortable with.

And I had just dragged my preppy date into a den of wasted toughs. Way to make great decisions, Vivian.

"Let's get a drink," I yelled over the din. Theo darted an anxious look around and nodded. At least he had taken off his suit jacket and rolled up his sleeves. Though the pair of us still stood out like sore thumbs. I noticed the strange looks we received as we pushed through the crowd on our way to the bar.

"Yeah, this is not really my scene, Viv," Theo remarked, leaning in close so I could hear him over the commotion.

I nodded, feeling foolish for suggesting it in the first place. "Let's just have a drink and then bounce."

I waited for the bartender to see us when I felt eyes burning a hole into my back.

I turned toward the far end of the bar and saw a pair of hooded, dark eyes regarding me.

Of all the bars in all of the world. . .

Cole had four empty shot glasses turned over in front of him. His eyes bored into mine and slowly he lifted the full shot glass in his hand and tossed back the contents.

Theo put his hand on the small of my back, breaking my staring contest with Cole.

"What do you want, Vivian?" he asked, dipping his mouth in close to my ear. I looked back at Cole and was startled by the furious expression he wore. His mouth was set into a firm line and his eyes sparked across the distance separating us.

I turned to Theo slightly, though I kept my eyes on the caged lion on the other end of the bar. I could feel his angry aggression from here.

"I'll have a Lemon Drop," I said.

A woman dressed head to toe in black leather sat down beside Cole and leaned in to speak to him. He inclined his head in her direction but his gaze never wavered. Her arm curled around his shoulders, her fingers playing with the longer strands of his hair.

She was speaking to him but he wasn't responding. He was too busy hurling nasty eye daggers my way.

Why was he so pissed to see me?

What the hell had I ever done to him?

"It's so loud in here," Theo yelled. I tried to smile but I felt like it was more effort than I was suddenly capable of.

Theo tucked my hair behind my ear, his fingers trailing down the side of my neck. "Can we go back to your place for a while? I can barely hear myself think," he asked, his eyes heated.

I sipped on my drink and my eyes, of their own volition, crawled back to Cole.

Only he wasn't there anymore. And neither was the slut who had been talking to him.

My stomach knotted up and plummeted to the floor. I knew exactly where he had gone.

I finished my drink, feeling the alcohol burn my throat and gave Theo a blinding smile. "Sure. Let's get out of here," I said.

Theo waved down the bartender so we could pay our tab and I looked around the crowd, my head bobbing in time to the beat of the music.

Someone wrapped their hand my waist, fingers clutching the silky material of my dress. And then I was being yanked around.

"What the hell?" I retorted angrily, only to stare up into the furious eyes of none other than Cole fucking Brandt.

"Cole," I breathed out. His arm was tight around my middle, my chest pressed against his, our faces dangerously close. I could smell the liquor on his breath. And from the flush of his cheeks and the wild glint in his eyes, I knew he was loaded.

"Who is that?" demanded, inclining his head towards Theo, who had his back to us.

My irritation sparked and I pulled out of Cole's retraining grip.

"None of your damn business!" I bit out.

I started to back up and knocked into Theo who turned around to give me a kind smile. His expression turned curious when he saw a very angry Cole breathing fire in his direction.

"Who the fuck are you?" Cole asked him. Theo looked over his shoulder, as though Cole were talking to someone else.

"Excuse me?" Theo asked, glancing at me.

"Why are you with my girl?" Cole demanded and my eyes widened.

His girl? Was he serious?

"I think you are mistaken. I'm on a date with this woman," Theo argued reasonably.

"You're what?" Cole roared, garnering the attention of everyone around us.

"Cole, enough! You're drunk and you're acting like an idiot," I hissed, pushing him squarely in the chest. He stumbled back a step but then steadied himself as much as he was able to, even if he was still swaying on his feet.

"You're on a date with this douchebag, Viv? Are you kidding me?" Cole started laughing maniacally, clutching his gut as he bent over in hysterics. My rage started to mount.

"Vivian, do you know this guy?" Theo asked, watching Cole with growing concern.

Cole righted himself and took a menacing step toward Theo. "Oh she knows me, man. She knows me intimately. She knows how it feels to have this dick inside her pussy." He grabbed himself crudely before taking another step forward.

"She knows how it feels when I fuck her over a table and how it feels to have my tongue between her legs. So yes, she knows me. She's known me in every position, all night long."

Cole leaned down and ran his tongue along my cheek. "Mmm. I love me a mouthful of Vivian."

That was it. I had had enough. I clocked Cole in the jaw, knocking him on his self-important ass. My hand throbbed and I hoped I hadn't broken something.

"Don't you ever talk about me like that ever again!" I screamed, standing over him, cradling my hand against my chest and glaring down at him. Cole rubbed his jaw and grinned up at me.

"You've got one hell of a right hook, baby. Now come here and let me kiss it and make it better," he leered. I kicked him in the leg. Hard. With the spike end of my shoe.

"Ouch! Why'd you do that, Viv?" Cole yelled, trying to get to his feet. But he was so drunk he could only stumble to his knees before collapsing on the floor again.

I reared back to kick him again but Theo put a hand on my arm.

"What are you doing, Vivian?" he asked, looking appalled. I looked around and realized we had a circle of people surrounding us, watching with avid interest. Once again, Cole and I had become a sideshow.

I lowered my foot to the floor. "I'm sorry, Theo," I said regretfully, hating how he had seen this very ugly side of my personality.

Theo looked absolutely repulsed by the entire situation. "Is this the guy you were talking about at dinner?" Theo deduced. Cole was still trying to get to his feet. Finally some biker dude took pity and helped him up. He swayed a bit but otherwise stayed upright.

I didn't bother to answer Theo. I figured it was obvious by this point.

"I'm sorry, Vivian. I'm so, so sorry," Cole appealed, scrubbing his hands down his face.

My anger dissipated marginally. I had never heard Cole

apologize for anything. That alone was enough to make me wonder if we had entered the Twilight Zone.

When Cole pulled his hands away from his face, his eyes were wet and red. He looked as lost as I had ever seen him.

"Don't hate me. Please," he begged, reaching for my hand. I let him take it and he curled his fingers through mine, pressing our joined hands over his heart.

"I couldn't stand it if you hated me the way the rest of them do. Not you. Never you," he whispered and I had to lean in close to hear him.

His fingers squeezed mine and I could feel the erratic beat of his heart beneath my skin.

"I don't hate you, Cole," I told him honestly and the naked relief on his face left me speechless.

We stood like that for a while, with Cole's hand clutching mine, pressed to his chest, while I looked up at this sad and broken man who had always seemed so untouchable. I had never thought I'd see the day where anything wrecked him.

But that day had come.

"Vivian. We need to go," Theo said, snapping me out of my Cole induced stupor. I pulled my hand from Cole's and backed away, all too aware of how this must look to Theo, who looked anything but happy. He was staring at Cole, who had dropped his head, his chin colliding with his chest.

I didn't want to leave Cole like this. Despite everything, I just couldn't.

"This is why you didn't want to go on a date with me. You're still hung up on this guy," Theo said, as though he couldn't understand what I was thinking.

"No. That had nothing to do with it," I lied.

"Look, I'd rather know this now then get into something with you and have my heart broken. If you're still in love with this guy, then just say so."

Whoa! Who had said anything about love?

Oh that's right. I had at dinner. Way to go, Vivian!

"It has nothing to do with me not being over him. I just can't leave him when he's like this," I countered.

Theo shook his head and reached out to take ahold of Cole's arm. Cole tried to pull back and almost lost his footing again.

"Let go of me, jackass!" Cole seethed.

"We're going to get you home. Chill out," Theo said with annoyance.

I blinked in surprise. Theo looked back at me nonplussed. "You coming?" he asked.

I nodded and followed Theo as he pulled a barely walking Cole out to his car.

The ride to Cole's apartment was tense, even after Cole had passed out and started to snore.

A few minutes later, we were parked and I was struggling with something to say.

If there was anything I could take away from this date gone wrong, is that Theo deserved more than a woman who would never be able to give him her heart. Not when it foolishly belonged to someone else. Someone who most likely would never give his in return.

"It's okay, Vivian," Theo murmured, picking up on my internal tirade.

"I don't know why I can't get over him. I mean, look at him!" I despaired, indicating Cole in the backseat, sprawled out and drooling all over the upholstery.

Theo gave me a wry smile. "We can't help who want," he responded sagely.

Truer words have never been spoken.

The two of us struggled to get Cole out of the car and up the stairs to his apartment. And while I rooted around in his pockets for his keys, I blushed when Cole stirred long enough to tell me to tug on his junk a bit.

Finally we got Cole into his apartment and deposited him on the couch. Theo stood awkwardly by the door as I pulled off Cole's shoes and covered him with a blanket.

"I should probably stay. You know, to make sure he doesn't choke on his vomit or anything," I said, following Theo out into the hallway.

"How will you get back to your place? Do you need me to stay with you?" he asked. He really was such a nice guy. I wanted to slap myself silly for not jumping at the chance to be with him. It was time to start questioning my sanity.

But Theo was right. You can't help who you want. The heart is a senseless bitch.

"That's okay, thank you though. I'll call a cab," I said, wrapping my arms around my body. It was freezing in the hallway.

Theo dug into his pocket and pulled out some cash pushing it into my hand. "For the cab," he said and I tried to give it back to him.

"I can't take this," I insisted but Theo wouldn't hear of it.

"Please, for me," he urged and I clutched the money in my hand.

"Thank you, Theo. For everything. And I'm so sorry this was such an epic failure," I said, trying to smile but finding the muscles wouldn't work. I felt like such a jerk.

"It wasn't so bad. It'll definitely prove a conversation starter down the road. The world's worst first date," he quipped and this time I found that I could smile. He was making all of this so easy.

He held out his hand for me to shake. "Friends?" he asked, though I saw it pained him to say it.

I shook his hand firmly. "Most definitely," I promised. He held my hand a beat longer than necessary.

When he finally let go, I felt a little better and thought that maybe I hadn't ruined everything after all.

Cole started moaning from the apartment and I knew I should get back inside.

"Good luck with all that. If you need anything, you know how to reach me," Theo said. I nodded and watched him walk down the hallway before going back inside.

Cole was trying to sit up but wasn't very successful. "I need to piss," he muttered, starting to unzip himself.

Oh hell no!

I hurried over to him, kicking off my heels and hoisted him to his feet.

He was practically dead weight and I sagged underneath

him, both of us careening into the couch.

"Whoopsie daisy," Cole laughed as I tried to get us upright.

"I'll whoopsie daisy your ass into the ground if you don't shut up," I warned, steering him into the bathroom.

"You gonna help?" Cole leered, using his hand to prop himself against the wall as he pulled out his dick and took aim at the toilet.

I hurried out of the bathroom, his drunken laughter following me.

When he was finished, he called my name and I helped him back to his bedroom. It was a pit. I tripped over a pile of clothes and beer bottles as I stumbled towards his bed.

I dumped him unceremoniously down on top of the covers and lifted his legs one at a time so that he was stretched out. I repositioned the pillow so that he was turned slightly onto his side, just in case he threw up in his sleep. No need for a Jimi Hendrix.

I started to stand up when Cole's hand reached out and curled around my wrist. It wasn't tight, but it was strong.

"Don't leave me," he whispered, his eyes open in slits.

"I've got to get home, Cole. I have to work in the morning," I argued.

Cole's lower lip trembled and his face started to crumple. Shit, was he going to cry? First in the bar and now here? Who was this man and what he done with the arrogant asshat I was used to dealing with?

"I need you, Viv. I really need you. Please don't leave me. I can't be alone. I'm so tired of always being alone," he begged and I crumpled.

He tugged on my arm and I scooted closer.

"Just lay with me. I miss holding you." His voice began to waver and I knew he was close to unconscious.

Making my decision, I shuffled up onto the bed beside him and curled into his side. His arm came around my body and pulled me closer so that my back was pressed against his front.

His fingers laced between mine and I tucked our joined hands beneath my cheek. I felt him nuzzle into my hair and the soft, ghost-like caress of his lips against the back of my neck.

He let out a deep breath, as if he were finally, after all this time, content. I felt his body relax and soon his breathing was deep and even and I knew he had fallen asleep.

Pinned to his familiar body, enveloped in his scent, I listened to the gentle cadence of his breaths until I was able to follow him into sleep.

Chapter 19
COLE

I **HAD** to be dreaming.

If I was, I didn't want to wake up.

Because the tantalizing smell that filled my nostrils was familiar and had my cock springing to attention. I could feel soft curves pressed against me, warm from sleep.

Her silky hair brushed my face, her hot breath on my skin.

I refused to open my eyes, worried that when I did, I'd wake up and find myself alone. And I couldn't handle that. I needed this fantasy. I needed her here, lying curled against me.

I had to be asleep. Why else would Vivian be here?

And I wasn't going to waste a perfectly good dream. I knew exactly where I needed this to go. It was my fantasy after all.

I traced my fingers along the lines of her body, taking my time as I made my way to the hem of her dress. I bunched the material in my hands and lifted it above her hips.

I ran my hand along the defined curve of her hip, slipping my finger beneath the thin string of her panties as I teased the sensitive skin.

Vivian groaned and moved restlessly as I touched her. I wanted to look at her. I wanted to see her gorgeous face flushed

219

as she took pleasure in what I was about to do to her.

But I wanted this dream to last as long as I could make it. So I kept my eyes resolutely shut.

I found the wet spot on her underwear and grinned to myself. She wanted me. She always wanted me. I moved the insignificant piece of cotton to the side and ran my thumb along her clit.

"Oh god!" she groaned, spreading her thighs so I had easier access. I was slow and purposeful as I coated my fingers with her arousal. She was dripping with it and I could hear her pants coming loud and fast.

Not able to put off feeling her from the inside for another moment, I pushed two fingers deep inside, moaning as her muscles clenched down hard.

"Fuck," I murmured, moving my fingers in and out. In and out.

"Cole," Vivian rasped and I couldn't stop myself from opening my eyes.

And I was shocked when she didn't go away. She was still there. Lying in my bed, her hair fanned out around her. Her dark, red dress bunched up at her stomach and my fingers plunging in and out of her sexy body.

Her knees were bent, her hips rising to meet my hand as I pressed in as far as I could go.

She was here. Vivian was in my bed and I was touching her. Finally. God, how I had wanted to do this for so damn long.

Her eyes were still closed, her head thrown back and I couldn't stop myself from replacing my fingers with my mouth. I had to taste her.

I covered her mound with my lips and suckled on her clit until she was bucking beneath me.

Her fingers curled into my hair and gripped painfully. I smiled against her and pushed my tongue into her pussy. I lapped and licked until I tasted her coming in my mouth.

She screamed at the top of her lungs, followed by a string of curses that had my neighbor banging on the wall.

Even after she settled down, I didn't stop. I kept licking and tasting her, not able to get enough.

I chanced a look up at her face. Her eyes were open and she was watching me between her legs. I couldn't read her expression. I couldn't tell what she was thinking.

But I knew what I was thinking. I repositioned myself and quickly got rid of my pants and boxers. I fit between her legs and grabbed her thigh, pulling her down the bed until she was lined up right where I needed her to be.

"No, Cole, stop," Vivian said, sitting up and pulling her legs together.

I ran my hands up her thighs and gripped her waist. I leaned down and kissed the base of her throat, my lips lingering over the erratic heartbeat

"What's wrong, baby? I want to make you feel good," I pleaded, running my fingers up under the skirt of her dress again.

Vivian grabbed ahold of my wrists and squeezed with all of her might.

"We are not having sex, Cole. So get your damn hands off me," she warned.

I quickly pulled my hands back as though she had burned me. I sat back on my haunches and watched in disbelief as she swung her legs off the side of the bed and got to her feet. A little bit shaky I might add, feeling a smidge of satisfaction for making her knees tremble.

"I just thought, after you came in my mouth, that you wanted to keep going. Sorry for the misunderstanding," I said sarcastically.

"I was asleep, Cole! I thought I was dreaming," she fumed.

I smirked. "Do you dream about me tongue fucking you often?" I asked.

"I should have known," Vivian muttered under her breath, sliding into her strappy sandal things with heels that looked like weapons. I didn't want her throwing them, so I decided to backpedal a bit.

"Why are you even here?" I asked, trying to think back to last night. The only thing I could recall was going to Benny's and ordering a round or ten. I didn't remember much after that.

Though there were clearly some things between then and

now that I needed to know about.

"You were wasted at Benny's. I was there with my date. . ."

"You were on a date?" I asked, frowning.

Vivian sighed. "Well, thanks to your drunken dramatics, it ended before it really began. So thanks for that," she hurled at me.

I rubbed the skin between my eyebrows, my head pounding with a dull ache. For being as drunk as I had obviously been, I wasn't that hung over.

"Did we. . .?" I made a hip thrusting motion to make my point. Because if we fucked and I couldn't remember it, I was going to be pissed. I had waited too damn long to have Vivian Baily in my bed again. I'd be livid if I had blacked out during it.

Vivian picked up a pillow and threw it at me. I caught it easily and tossed it back onto the bed. "No, we didn't have sex! Though apparently this morning is a different story." She sounded so disgusted that it gave me pause. Would sleeping with me have been that horrible?

Didn't she just enjoy herself?

"Vivian, hang on a sec. I'm sorry for misreading shit. But I just thought. . .you seemed into it. And I thought because you were here, you wanted to be with me. Am I wrong?" I hated how weak I sounded. I hated that her rejection was ripping my insides out.

With everything going on, finding her beside me this morning had seemed like a miracle.

I had missed her more than I realized. She had become an integral part of my world. A world that was slipping between my fingers.

Showing up at Barton's the other night and finding some other fucker fronting my band had been a hard blow. And the crowd seemed to be eating it up, whether I was there or not.

It hurt.

No, it had killed me.

And seeing Vivian there, I realized with a sudden realization that Generation Rejects and my friends weren't the only things I had lost.

So I had gone home and gotten drunk. And more drunk. And

when I sobered up a bit, I started drinking all over again.

Somehow I had ended up at Benny's. Apparently the body needs more than beer and liquor to sustain itself. My raging blackout was a testament to that.

My life was beyond fucked. I had messed up the only relationships I had ever counted on. And all the fame and fortune wouldn't make up for the fact that I had no one.

And then I had found Vivian in my bed and I thought, for a brief moment, that maybe not everything was lost.

Guess I was wrong.

When had I become such a sappy bastard?

Vivian's face softened. "I need to go, Cole. I'm glad you're feeling better," she grabbed her phone and made a quick phone call.

"Hello. I need a cab at 72 Park Lane. As soon as possible. Thank you." She hung up the phone and turned to me, her chin raised and a marked distance between us. "Can I use your bathroom?" she asked, not meeting my eyes.

"Sure," I mumbled.

I was in the same spot when Vivian came out. I grabbed her hand as she went to walk past me to the door.

"Wait, Vivian. I haven't talked to you in weeks. And there's so much shit going on. I've really missed you. Can I see you later? Can I come by or can we go out somewhere?"

Vivian shook her head, cutting me off.

"I don't think that's a good idea, Cole. Nothing has changed between you and me. Last night was nothing. It was just one person worried about another. I didn't want you to hurt yourself, so I stayed here. Let's not make it into something that it's not. You and I have never been the sort to read into whatever was between us. I don't want to start now."

Had I done this? Made her so damn bitter?

"And as for what's going on with the guys, I think you need to take a long hard look at what got you here. You need to stop drinking yourself into a coma and start thinking about this with a clear head. Figure out what you want and where you hope to go from here. Stop blaming everybody and everything."

Vivian slung her purse over her shoulder and opened the door. A blast of cold air blew in.

"I hope you get it together, Cole. Because you're damn close to ruining everything."

And then she was gone.

Like she had never been there.

What the fuck?

I picked up my phone, a brand new iPhone I had picked up from the airport. Jose had called half a dozen times over the last day and a half. I thought about listening to the messages I knew he had left, but I decided against it.

Vivian was right. I needed to get my head together. And listening to anything Jose had to say wouldn't help.

I went back to my bedroom and looked at the mussed sheets, still able to smell Vivian's lingering scent.

I grabbed the only clean pair of jeans I had left and a ripped T-shirt and headed for the shower. My stomach rumbled. I couldn't remember the last time I had eaten.

So after I was clean, I found my wallet and keys on the table where Vivian must have left them and I headed into Bakersville. I had been purposefully avoiding the town since I had gotten back on Sunday. I hadn't wanted to run into anyone and have to explain what I was doing back.

And I definitely hadn't wanted to run into Jordan, Mitch, or Garrett.

But I was done hiding. It was time for me to, as Vivian had said, figure what I wanted.

I got some breakfast at the only decent diner in town and then got into my car and started driving. I knew where I was headed as I started to follow curved country roads I had known my entire life.

I pulled up in front of an old Victorian. It had at one time been yellow with white shutters. At some point in the last five years, it had been painted a pale blue and the wooden shutters had been replaced with ones made of maroon vinyl.

What was I doing here? Was I actually going to go and knock on the door? What would I say?

I got out of my car and stared up at the house that had been my home for the first eighteen years of my life.

I didn't recognize the cars in the driveway. The place was a lot nicer than I remembered. The battered wooden lattice had been replaced and the shed out back looked to have been taken down and replaced with a swing set.

Wait. A swing set?

I walked up the now sturdy steps to the front door and knocked.

A few seconds later I was greeted with a petite woman with red hair that was definitely not my mother.

"Can I help you?" she asked, smiling.

"Uh, I was actually looking for Kenneth and Joan Brandt. They used to live here," I said, peering behind her into the foyer I remembered but that was now completely different.

The woman chuckled. "Oh, we bought the house from them two years ago."

I throat felt uncomfortably tight.

"Two years ago?" I clarified, my voice cracking.

The woman looked at me strangely, taking in my tattoos, lip ring, and messy hair.

"Yes," she said shortly, obviously ready to close the door in my face.

My parents had moved out of our house. They had sold it and moved and never told me.

I had no idea where they were.

"Do you know where" my voice gave out and I had to work like hell to pull myself together.

"Do you know where they went?" I asked and I hated the softening on the small woman's face. It's like she knew the pain I was feeling.

She shook her head. "I don't. I'm sorry."

My hand shook as I pushed hair out of my eyes. I needed to get out of there.

"Thanks. I'm sorry to bother you," I said quickly, hurrying off the porch and back to my car.

I threw the gear into drive and squealed my tires in my rush to get away from the house I had lived most of my life in.

My parents had moved.

They were gone.

And they had never told me.

I hastily wiped away the betraying wetness that appeared to be leaking out of my eyes.

Fuck this shit. This is why I never wanted to come back to Bakersville. There was nothing for me here.

My parents had made sure of that.

Vivian had made sure of that.

I had no friends. No band. No family.

All I had was the career Jose said I could have.

So I kept driving and driving. Hoping when I stopped I could make the decision I needed to.

"WHAT are you doing here?"

I sat in my car, outside a rundown brick building in an old industrial park on the far side of town. My head was definitely somewhere else today.

Otherwise, why would I have driven to Generation Rejects' rehearsal space?

Garrett looked down at me from my open window.

I shook my head, gripping my steering wheel. "I don't really know," was all I said.

Garrett stared at me for a long time. I was losing my shit. That's the only excuse for what I was doing there.

After a while he tapped his hand on the roof of my car and nodded his head toward the building. "Well, while you're here, come help me load up some stuff."

And then he walked off.

I should go. I sure as shit didn't want to be anywhere near Garrett fucking Bellows and his judgey condemnation.

So why did I find myself climbing out of my car and following him inside.

The place had been gutted. We had cleaned out most of our equipment when we went on the road. The only thing left was an extra drum kit, an ancient half stack and a few mic stands. Garrett had already stacked up some chairs and pushed the nasty couch off to the side.

I was relieved to see that he was alone.

"What are you doing?" I asked, watching as he started to wind up old cables and put them on top of the half stack.

"I've got a dude coming by to clear out everything and bring it back to the house. No sense paying rent for a space we never use."

I didn't say anything. After a few minutes Garrett gave me a dry look. "Don't just stand there like a limp dick, go and start breaking down the drum kit," he ordered.

Instead of bristling like I would have only a week ago, I did as he told me to. We worked in silence, packing up the remnants of our history.

"Where are Mitch and Jordan?" I asked.

"Jordan's with Maysie and Mitch is with that Sophie chick he started seeing. So I was stuck doing this myself," Garrett said.

"Well it's a good thing I came along then," I tried to joke but my words sounded flat.

Garrett didn't say anything. I twisted off the bolts and put them in a pile, carefully taking apart the cymbals and laying them off to the side.

"I went out to my parents' place," I found myself saying. Garrett looked over at me in surprise.

"You did?" he asked, twisting the mic stand and collapsing it.

I picked up the snare and put it beside the cymbals. "Yeah. Someone else lives there now."

Garrett stopped what he was doing and came over. He bent down and picked up the bolts and put them in a Tupperware container. "Wow, that's some shit. I'm guessing they didn't tell you they were moving."

I shook my head. "Fuck no. I haven't talked to those bastards in years," I said gruffly, trying to hide how much it hurt. But Garrett saw right through me.

"That sucks, man. I'm sorry," he said sincerely.

"Yeah, well what are you gonna do?" I brushed it off like it didn't matter. But it did. A lot.

"Do you know where they went?" Garrett asked, picking up the dissassembled drums and carrying them over to the half stack. I followed with the rest of the kit.

"No. And I don't care either. Fuck them!" I said with enough vehemence to be convincing.

Garrett glanced at me and smiled. "Yeah, fuck them," he agreed.

We finished breaking the leftover equipment down. "This stuff will be picked up in the morning. I say we're done here. You want to go get a beer?" Garrett asked, surprising me.

"Sure," I said.

We walked to the Appleby's down the road and sat down at the bar. Garrett ordered a pitcher of beer.

"Thanks for the help," he said after the bartender left to get our order.

"Yeah, sure. You should have called if you needed help," I said, knowing how stupid that was. Particularly with how he and I had left things.

But Garrett didn't say anything about that. He just nodded as if I was right.

"How've you been?" he asked.

I shrugged. "Been better. You?"

"'Bout the same," he answered as the bartender brought our pitcher and mugs.

We poured ourselves a beer. Garrett grabbed a handful of peanuts and threw them in his mouth, watching the television screen playing a basketball game in the corner.

"I know you think we're holding you back. And maybe you're right. I've thought a lot about shit since Sunday and I think you've got to do what you've got to do," he said suddenly.

"What the fuck are you talking about?" I asked.

Garrett shrugged, taking his eyes off the TV to look at me. "You and me, we've been friends for a long time. And I know you wouldn't purposefully fuck us over."

I laughed humorlessly. "Where was this sage wisdom when you were telling me what a dick I was?"

Garrett's mouth twisted into a sad smile. "I was pissed. You played that damn song when I didn't want you to. I wasn't thinking clearly. None of us were. But I've had a few days to calm down. And with everything going on, I think we've been pretty unfair to you."

I downed half of my beer. "And do the others agree with you?" I couldn't help but ask.

Garrett shrugged again. "I doubt it. But Jordan is a hothead, just as you are. And Mitch will go along with whatever Jordan says. That doesn't mean you weren't an asshole, because you were. What you did was wrong. But we should never have walked off that stage. And we should never have accused you of trying to push us out. It wasn't cool. We all have to take some accountability for getting to where we are."

I didn't know what to say. This didn't fix everything that had gone wrong, but I started to feel a whole lot better.

"I think it's just sad that after everything we've been through, it's going to end over something so fucking stupid. For nothing."

I couldn't argue with that. Because we had messed up big time.

"But you've got to do what you've got to do, Cole. And at the end of the day, I'll still be here if you need me."

And that was exactly what I needed to hear.

Garrett finished his beer and slid his empty mug down the bar. He wiped his mouth with the back of his hand and got to his feet.

"Thanks again for your help. I'll see you soon, all right?"

I could only nod as he tossed some cash on the bar and with a nod, walked out.

The guy with the least to say always had been the one to make me think the most.

And he had given me something I desperately needed.

Some perspective.

Chapter 20
VIVIAN

I was Saturday night and I was home. By myself.

There was something almost criminal about that.

But lately I wasn't fit for human interaction. I was moody and prone to irrational outbursts of the colorful language variety. Gracie asked innocently whether I liked her new shoes.

I adored them. They were fabulous and pink and with hot heels that made her legs go on for miles.

But I was suffering from a raging case of crotch face so instead of being the supportive friend, I told her I didn't care about her stupidly awesome footwear. I had then proceeded to tell her to leave me the fuck alone.

I had stomped off to my room, slammed the door dramatically and then promptly turned around and apologized.

Gracie inquired as to whether Aunt Flo was visiting.

It was a legit question.

But Bitch McGee (that would be me) took offense and stomped off to my room again.

The rest of my week hadn't been much better. I was short-tempered and emotional. I didn't know whether I was coming or going.

And I blamed Cole Brandt completely.

This is what happened when I spent time with him. I lost all sense of rational thinking. I became a mess of epic proportions.

I was a flipping psychopath!

It got so bad that Marion had asked, somewhat hesitantly, if I was coming down with something.

I was coming down with something all right. It was called Can't-Get-Over-A-Man-itis. The main symptoms involved spending an inordinate amount of time wallowing and feeling sorry for yourself.

I should have felt a renewed sense of power! I had put my foot down and not had sex with Cole when he was being all sweet and gorgeous-like.

I had told him what I thought and held firm.

So why was I feeling all sad and depressed with random outbursts of uncontrollable rage?

Because deep down I knew, that even though he drove me crazy, Cole was the only person who made me feel alive. With anyone else, Theo included, I was just going through the motions. With Cole, it was balls to the walls, let's set the house on fire passion.

And I was terrified with how desperately I wanted that in my life. I was scared at how willing I was to sacrifice just about anything, my pride included, to experience those tantalizing moments when every nerve in my body detonated.

Cole was my crack. And I wanted to crush him up and snort him.

When Gracie had asked me to come to a movie with her and a few of her friends from the coffee shop, I had declined. I chose to ignore the brief look of relief that flittered across her face.

I opted instead to spend my evening with my best friends Ben and Jerry.

I was grunged out in my oldest pair of sweat pants. They were a pink with the faded word "juicy" along the ass. The elastic had given out about twenty washes ago and I had them held up with safety pins. I had gone sans bra and instead wore a Generation Rejects shirt I had ganked from Cole's floor over a year ago.

And yes I had kept it. And yes I still wore it when I was lonely and depressed like I was now. And yes that made me borderline pathetic.

There was no sense bringing up the fact that I used to try to smell his scent on the cotton for months after I had "mistakenly" brought it home.

Because that would be just plain sad.

I had scrubbed my face and was without any makeup. All in all I wasn't meant for public eyes.

I was scrapping the last remnants of my icecream from the bottom of the carton with my spoon when the doorbell rang. I startled and almost screamed. Not because I was scared, but because I was in my Juicy sweatpants with no makeup on.

Who in the world would be coming by at eight-thirty on a Saturday night? I prayed it was a group of Jehovah's Witnesses or an old encyclopedia salesman I could ignore.

I quickly took my hair down and attempted to comb my fingers through it. It was a rat's nest and desperately needed a deep conditioning. I pulled up my sagging pants and walked over to the door just as the bell chimed again.

I wiped around my mouth trying to remove the evidence of my binge ice cream eating before finally opening the door.

"You've got to be shitting me," I said before I could censor myself.

"Bad time?" Cole asked, standing on my front stoop, looking gorgeous and clean and nothing at all like the last time I had seen him. He was holding two plastic bags and was wearing a pleased grin.

I thought about slamming the door in his face and hiding in my room but I figured I was capable of rising above such an immature impulse.

"Anytime you show up is a bad time," I muttered, crossing my arms over my chest, remembering that I wasn't wearing a bra and my C cups were flopping away under my T-shirt.

"Is that my shirt?" Cole asked, peering at my chest. I tightened my arms and started to back away.

"No!" I lied.

Cole lifted an eyebrow. "Actually, I think it is! I've been looking all over for it!" he accused chidingly.

"Whatever, it's mine now," I responded petulantly.

Cole chuckled. "It looks a hell of a lot better on you anyway," he conceded and I couldn't argue with the truth.

"Why are you here, Cole? I was having a perfectly good evening spending time with Leonardo DiCaprio and Baked Alaska," I said, feeling entirely too off balance by his sudden arrival.

I couldn't figure out what on earth he could be doing at my apartment. Things had been left with little opening for a renewed acquaintance. I thought I had made myself perfectly clear.

I wasn't going to sleep with him.

No matter how delicious he looked.

Or how nice he smelled.

Or the fact that he brought a bag containing all of the ingredients needed to make Lemon Drops, my favorite cocktail.

"What's this for?" I asked suspiciously. Was he planning to get me drunk so he could have sex with me? Was this his dastardly plan? If so, I saw right through it. And a horny, masochistic part of me approved.

"You were right," Cole said suddenly and without preamble.

"I usually am, but what specifically was I right about?" I asked, giving up on trying to hide my braless boobs behind my arms and opted for letting the puppies fly.

And I was also feeling extremely magnanimous so I moved aside, giving Cole silent permission to step inside.

He walked across the threshold and stopped. He looked around, taking everything in.

"This is my first time in your apartment," he said.

I nodded. "Yes it is," I agreed.

"We've known each other for over two years and I've never been here before. Why is that?" he asked as if genuinely confused.

"Because you're a self-centered jackass," I offered.

Cole smiled in that sexy, heart-melting way of his and I had to take a deep breath to calm my racing pulse.

"I think you might be on to something there," he said,

dropping the bags onto the coffee table. He took in Romeo and Juliet paused on the television and the three empty ice cream tubs on the floor.

"Shit, you weren't lying," he remarked.

"I told you I was having a hot night," I said dryly, my vanity already kicking me in the ass for choosing comfort over cuteness.

Always prepare for hot guy visits, Vivian! You know better!

Cole seemed entirely too interested in his surroundings. He took a slow perusal of the knick-knacks and framed photographs, stopping to pick up one from my senior year at Rinard. A Chi Delta sister had taken it of Maysie, Gracie and myself when we had dressed as flappers for a mixer.

"Cute," he said, putting it back. I couldn't tell if he was being serious or not. He was making me uncomfortably edgy.

"So what was I right about?" I prompted, getting back to the point of his impromptu visit.

Cole stopped circling the room and came back to stand in front of me. My entire body started to buzz with awareness. It was as though my cells were beating against my skin, demanding that I touch him.

It was so freaking annoying.

"When you said I didn't know anything about you. I think it's time I changed that," Cole said, surprising me.

What was he talking about?

Cole reached out and gently pulled down the stretched out neck of my T-shirt. I tensed up, not sure what he was going to do. He slowly and carefully traced the line of my scar that ran between my breasts.

"You told me I didn't know how you got this scar. You were right. I didn't know. And I should have. We have spent the last two years learning every inch of each other's bodies but I know nothing about who Vivian Baily is. I didn't think I even wanted to know. But I was wrong. I want to know everything."

I shivered involuntarily as he lazily traced the puckered skin.

I chuckled nervously. "That will take a while," I said a little breathlessly.

Cole dropped his finger and smiled. "I've got all night. If Leo doesn't mind, of course," he grinned.

Did I want him to stay?

I didn't know!

I was so confused!

My sagging pants slipped below my hips and I hastily pulled them up before Cole got an eyeful of my granny panties.

Oh shit, I was wearing granny panties!

Just more incentive to keep my pants on!

"Why?" I asked, not entirely trusting his motives.

Cole sighed and that vulnerability I had only just become acquainted with made itself known.

"Because it's lonely thinking and worrying only about yourself. I've missed out on a lot. One of the biggest is getting to know you. We've fucked but we've never really hung out. I've told you my shit but you've never told me yours. This has been a purely one-sided relationship for entirely too long. I know you kicked me out of your life. I know you've made it clear you want nothing to do with me. But please, Viv, just give me one night to know you. To figure out what's going on inside that beautiful head of yours. I want to show you that I'm not all bad. That I can be a nice guy. And if at the end you still want me gone, I'll leave. You'll never have to see me again."

It sounded simple enough, but nothing with Cole was ever free of conditions.

"No sex," I said firmly, pointing at him in warning.

Cole held up his hands. "No, sex. Well, not unless you ask nicely," he teased and I groaned, rolling my eyes.

"Can I put this stuff in your kitchen?" he asked, holding up the plastic bags.

"Sure, it's through there." I pointed him in the right direction. I followed him into the brightly lit room.

"This place makes mine look like a shithole," he said, taking in the soft green walls and bright white wooden cabinets.

"That's because your place is a shithole," I responded.

"True," he agreed, getting out the ingredients needed to make drinks and setting them out on the counter.

"You're making me Lemon Drops? You really are trying to

get on my good side," I stated, watching as he found the low-ball glasses and mixed my favorite drink.

"We're not having sex," I felt the need to reiterate.

Cole traced an x over his chest. "Cross my heart, I won't get in your too big for you pink sweatpants. I won't take advantage of you. But if you come on to me, I can't be sure of the consequences."

I snorted. "I think we're safe then."

Cole gave me a look screamed liar!

Because I was a liar.

If Cole knew anything about me, it was that when it came to him I had zero self-control.

With our drinks in hand, we went back out to the living room and sat down on the couch. Cole turned off the television and got out a deck of cards.

"No strip poker!" I warned.

"Seriously, Viv, you act as though I have a one-track mind," he admonished. He started to deal out several pile of cards.

"Have you ever played Spit?" he asked and I pursed my lips, still wondering if this some elaborate sex ruse.

Who was the one with a one-track mind?

"Uh, no," I said.

"Let me show you," he said and went about explaining the most complicated card game I had ever heard of.

"And when you call Spit I have to answer a question, any question about myself. And likewise if I call Spit. You have to be totally and completely honest with me."

I took a long drink of my Lemon Drop. This could get dangerous. I could feel it.

It wasn't long before Cole had beaten me soundly and was asking his first question.

He started easy enough.

"Favorite food?"

I didn't have to think about that one. "Coffee," I answered.

Cole laughed. "That's not a food, Vivian."

"Fine, pizza. Even though it makes my ass fat, I can't get enough. Slather dough in greasy cheese and tomato sauce and I'm salivating like a dog," I said.

Two minutes later I threw my hands up in the air after Cole yelled spit once again. "This isn't fair! I'll never win!" I complained.

"Stop your bitching and just answer the question. What is your most embarrassing moment?"

"Aside from having my eyes fused together with honey in some ridiculous sex act? Or the time I was handcuffed to a bed dressed as a nun and a locksmith had to set loose?" I asked and Cole actually flushed.

"Uh y...yeah, besides that," he stammered and I couldn't help but snicker.

"Okay, fine, most embarrassing moment excluding getting kinky with you, probably the time I threw up all over Tim Dalton, the boy I had a massive crush on in the fifth grade. I was mortified and even though he was totally nice about it, it ruined any chance I had of becoming Mrs. Dalton," I sighed dramatically.

"Well, all the better for me." Cole winked and I had to look away.

A few minutes later, it was my turn to yell spit and I crowed in delight.

"I won! I won!" I exclaimed, doing a dance in my seat, pumping my fists into the air.

"Yeah, yeah. Beginner's luck," Cole pouted.

I stuck my tongue out at him and put my forefinger to my chin as I thought about my question.

"Hmm. . .there are so many things I want to know! How to choose?" Cole groaned.

"Jesus, just ask something already."

I glared at him and finally thought of something.

"Why don't you like Jordan?" I asked. It had always bugged me. It was obvious Cole didn't have the relationship with Maysie's boyfriend that he had with the other guys. When I asked Maysie about it, she never really had an answer for me.

"I don't not like Jordan. Honestly. It's sort of complicated," Cole said.

"Uh, uh. That's not going to cut it. You have to tell me the truth." I wagged my finger in his face.

"It's not that I don't like him, I guess I've always been jealous of him," Cole finally admitted.

I sat back, surprised. I hadn't been expecting that.

"What? Why?"

"Because everyone likes him. He has this natural talent and he was this super big deal from the moment he started working at Barton's. He had these hot girlfriends and my friends thought he was oh so cool. It drove me nuts. I was used to being the big cheese. And then this frat dude comes along and suddenly I'm not so important anymore."

"You know that's ridiculous, right?" I reasoned. Cole gave me a look. One that wasn't entirely pleased with my less than sensitive response.

"Yes, I know it's ridiculous. But sometimes how you feel isn't exactly rational."

I got that. Probably better than most.

"But I respect him. I really do. He's a cool guy. And I honestly hate the way things are between us right now."

I dropped the cards. "What happened, Cole? Why aren't you talking to the other guys?" I asked.

Cole opened his mouth to answer me then shut it, giving me a shaky smile. "Uh-uh. You have to win to get me to answer. Now deal."

I was disappointed but determined to win some more games. There was too much I wanted to know. Too much that of the mystery that I needed to solve.

I lost the next three games. And in doing so I had to admit the age in which I lost my virginity (sixteen), who the guy was, (Samuel Davis), and my favorite movie (Dirty Dancing, of course).

"I feel like I'm giving you everything and I'm not getting anything in return. It's the story of our entire relationship I suppose," I said, only semi-bitterly. I had consumed several Lemon Drops and was feeling a pleasant, hazy glow.

It was nice having Cole in my apartment. It was cool hanging out with him in a way that I had never done before. And it was really great having him ask me things about myself that he seemed to sincerely want to know.

But I wanted to go deeper. I wanted to know Cole.

"Okay, enough of the game," Cole said, taking the cards from my hand and putting them in a pile on the coffee table.

"Hey, I was totally going to win the next hand," I complained.

"We don't need a card game to talk to each other. Let's just have a conversation like normal people," he suggested and I rolled my eyes.

"Yeah, cause we're so normal," I scoffed.

"You keep rolling your eyes, they're going to get stuck like that," he joked, smoothing the frown lines between my eyebrows with his finger.

"You said I wasn't giving you anything. Well, let's talk. What do you want from me?" he asked.

Damn. What a loaded question.

I took a deep breath and thought long and hard about how I was supposed to answer that.

"Why all the girls, Cole? Why wasn't I ever enough for you?" I asked posing the question that had tormented me for so long. I hated how weak and vulnerable I sounded, but it needed to be answered. If I was ever to move on, if I was to ever get past this thing with Cole, I had to know why he continued to hook up with other women when he had me.

What was it about me that didn't fulfill him?

"God, Viv," he murmured, cupping my cheek.

"You have always been more than enough for me. When you're around, everything else fades away. All I see, all I want is you."

"Then why, Cole? Why did you humiliate me over and over again?" I demanded, my voice cracking with emotion.

He rubbed his thumb along my skin; his eyes agonized.

"Because I'm a fucking idiot. Because I thought that being with all of those women meant that I mattered. That they wanted me. I was trying like hell to fill this ugly void inside and I ended up only feeling empty. Until I was with you. And then you made me feel alive."

My heart fluttered wildly in my chest. Hadn't I just thought the same thing about him?

"You made me look like a moron, Cole. People think I'm a total doormat for putting up with your shit. I hate the way you make me look," I whispered, feeling my eyes start to glaze over, hot with unshed tears.

"Baby, you're not a moron. I'm the moron. I'm the dumbass who didn't see what I had until it was gone. I took for granted that you were there. That you would always be there. Until you weren't anymore. And then all this stuff started going down with the band and the only person I wanted to talk to was the one person who wanted nothing to do with me."

I pulled back. His hand on my face was far too intimate.

"Growing up, all I had were my looks. The girls wanted me because I was nice to look at. And I used it to my advantage. I didn't have parents that wanted me around so I found attention where I could. And then the band happened and it was like everyone wanted me. And for the first time in my life I thought that I had something that could make me happy. But I was wrong. Because those girls, the audience, they don't want me. They want the singer. The image. There are only a handful of people on this earth that know the real Cole Brandt. And I've systematically shit on each and every one of them."

Cole leaned back on the couch and covered his face with his hands. I didn't move. I didn't comfort him. I let him be. He needed to have this realization on his own. I wouldn't coddle or console him. He needed to feel the pain and the ugly. He needed to see how his selfish behavior had impacted everyone around him.

This was Cole's come to Jesus moment.

"Jose has been telling me I'd be more successful going out on my own. He says there's a major label that wants to consider signing me, but as a solo act. Not with the Rejects," he let out in a rush.

"Why don't they want the Rejects?" I asked, not understanding.

Cole lowered his hands but wouldn't look at me.

"Jose says I'm where the money's at. I'm the one bringing the chicks in the door. I'm the image and the appeal. He's blown so much smoke up my ass I'm probably going to float the fuck away. He says he's found a clause that will get me out of my

Pirate Records contract. And then I'll be free to sign with who ever I want. I'll be able to write my own music. Do my own thing. He says the guys are holding me back."

"And what do you think?" I asked.

"I think my head is a mess and I don't know what I think."

Slowly, I reached out and took his hand, gripping it. He turned his palm up and twined his fingers with mine.

"Well, stop thinking with your head. What does your heart say?" I asked.

Cole's eyebrows rose. "What does my heart say? Are you serious?" he chuckled.

I smacked his arm. "Yes, I'm serious. Stop overanalyzing and think with that thing that beats in your chest. At the end of the day, what do you want to do?" Cole was silent as he considered my question.

"What will make you happy?" I demanded.

Cole stared at me for a long time, chewing his lip ring.

"You," he said quietly.

And then he was reaching for me and I couldn't deny him or myself any longer.

His hand curled around the back of my neck and he pulled me toward him. And just before his lips met mine, he looked deep into my eyes and I saw something shift in their depths.

"Just you," he whispered before he claimed my mouth with his.

It started softly, almost gently. But as with any time we were together, the tentative touches caught fire and we began to devour each other.

I parted my lips and he plunged his tongue inside, tasting every inch of my mouth. I reached down to the hem of his shirt, planning to rip it off him when he stopped me.

He pulled back suddenly. "You said no sex."

"Are you kidding me right now?" I practically screeched.

Cole shook his head. "You were pretty adamant, Viv. I just don't want you coming back later and saying I took advantage of you or something. That I manipulated you."

I cocked my head to the side and looked at him. "Are you

manipulating me?" I asked bluntly.

Cole recoiled. "No!" he proclaimed, grabbing my hands and kissing my knuckles. "God, no! Please believe me," he begged me.

I smiled sweetly.

Because I believed him. I really did. I knew that this time wasn't about anything but Cole wanting to be with me. For me.

This was about us.

I leaned forward. "Then fuck me, Cole," I growled, reaching for his shirt again.

And he stopped me again.

"What now?" I whined. I was three seconds away from going cavewoman and clubbing him.

"Not here," Cole said, standing up. He held out his hand and pulled me to my feet.

He wrapped his arms around me and kissed the tip of my nose. "We're doing this right. Where's your bedroom?"

My mouth went dry. Cole was hard to resist under normal circumstances. But this Cole, with his seductive tenderness, would wreck me.

"This way," I said softly and led him down the darkened hallway to my room.

I didn't turn on the lights right away and almost argued when Cole flipped on the bedside lamp.

He looked around, taking in everything, just as he had done in the living room and kitchen. Then he turned to me and slowly lifted his shirt and dropped it onto the floor. I watched as he unbuckled his jeans and lowered his pants. He kicked them off and stood before me, naked and amazing. His body wasn't overly muscular. But he was lean and defined, covered in ink.

He stared as I followed suit and took off the overly large Generation Rejects T-shirt, my bare breasts heavy with my arousal. I hooked my fingers into the edge of my sweatpants and underwear and lowered them all at once.

Since we were being all sexy and stuff, no need to kill the mood with my parachute underwear.

Why, oh why hadn't I worn a thong?

But something told me I could be decked out in full body Christmas pajamas and Cole wouldn't care.

His eyes consumed me. He licked his lips and my knees almost buckled from the intensity of his look alone.

He wanted me.

All of me.

I had never felt more beautiful.

"Come here," he commanded.

Once upon a time I would have leaped across the room and into his arms at his request.

But some things had changed.

I didn't move. I tilted my head to the side, my hair falling around my shoulders.

"No. You come here."

Cole's lips twitched into a sexy smirk.

"Is that how we're going to play this?"

I put my hand on my hip and watched in satisfaction as he crossed the room towards me. When he was less than a foot away I beckoned him closer with my finger.

"Closer," my voice was low and husky. The anticipation was killing me.

Cole took a step forward, still not touching me.

"Come on, I need you closer," I urged breathlessly.

Cole pressed himself up against me. I could feel his erection digging into my belly. He wrapped his arms around my back and lowered his mouth to mine.

"You say jump, I say how high," he promised, his eyes dancing.

Holding me, he backed up until his knees hit the bed and then he pulled me down on top of him.

"You say run, I say how far," Cole murmured, running his nose along the length of my jaw.

"You say forever, I say not long enough." He kissed a line along the column of my throat. My heart leaped into my throat and I was suddenly finding it hard to breathe.

"Just shut up and kiss me already," I chastised. The mushy, emotional stuff was threatening to undo me completely.

And kiss me he did. What had started as a gentle wooing became a violent possession. Cole rolled me onto my back and sank his teeth into the flesh of my shoulder as he dove his hand between my legs, his fingers finding my swollen clit.

I arched off the bed as his mouth suckled and licked my aching breasts.

He looked up before taking my nipple into his mouth. "What's your favorite color?"

I frowned, lost in a daze of lust. Had I heard him correctly? "Huh?"

Cole rubbed against my clit a little harder, making me groan. "Your favorite color, what is it?"

He teased my soaked folds with his fingers, not giving me enough to satisfy the sweet, almost painful ache that was steadily building.

"Please, Cole!" I yelled, ready to pull my hair out. Or his.

"Tell me your favorite color and I'll give you what you want," he promised, leaning up to kiss my lips. His fingers stopped moving altogether and I wanted to die. My body was taut and ready to explode.

"Green! My favorite color is green!" I hollered and then I screamed as Cole plunged his fingers deep inside me. His hand began a punishing rhythm as he sucked on my nipple.

I was close. Oh so close.

And then he stopped again.

"What the fuck?" I demanded.

"What's your middle name?"

I squeezed my thighs together, pushing his fingers higher up into my body. I grabbed the back of his hair and held him tightly.

"I get what you're doing. And while I appreciate it, now. Is. Not. The. Time!" I punctuated each word on a growl, wiggling my hips and pressing my legs together, encouraging him to move his hand.

Cole bit down on my bottom lip hard enough to make me yelp. "What is your middle name, Vivian?" he asked slowly and succinctly.

I sighed and flopped back on the bed. "Rose. All right? My

middle name is Rose!"

"That's my girl," he smiled down at me and then the questions were over. He removed his hand and felt around for the condom he must have laid there earlier. Sneaky son of a bitch.

He made quick work of putting it on and then he was between my legs. I was panting with need. Things weren't moving quite fast enough for me. I wanted him now! Before I lost my mind!

Cole rolled us so that I was straddling him. I looked down at him and my heart wanted to burst from my chest.

He reached up and ran his hand through my hair, pulling me down. He kissed me hard.

"Fuck me, Viv. Ride my cock and make me forget there was ever anyone but you," he snarled against my mouth.

And that's exactly what I did.

Chapter 21
COLE

WAS experiencing a major case of déjà vu. I hadn't even opened my eyes yet and already I was rock hard. And it had everything to do with the warm, female body sprawled out across me.

I knew I wasn't dreaming this time. I peeked under my lashes and couldn't help but smile. Vivian's cheek was pressed against my chest, her mouth gaping open as she snored her cute little heart out.

Was that drool?

I sincerely hoped not.

I ran my hand down her back, running my fingers along smooth skin. I had to take a piss but I wasn't in a rush to move.

I was perfectly happy just where I was.

Huh. Well lookie there.

I was happy.

Really, really fucking happy.

I hadn't been expecting this when I had made the decision to come to Vivian's place last night.

I had been in a really shitty place for the last couple of days. After talking to Garrett, I had holed up in my apartment, hiding out from the world. I had continued to avoid Jose's phone calls, though I knew he needed an answer from me. He wanted to know what I was going to do.

The problem was I was no closer to figuring that out then I was on Sunday when I came back to Bakersville. And Garrett's pep talked hadn't helped. Instead he had messed with my head even more.

But as I sat in my crappy apartment, staring at the wall because I still hadn't bothered to get the cable turned back on, I knew that I needed to fix stuff. I needed to take my life by the reins and stop waiting for everything to sort itself out.

Hiding in my apartment while the world passed me by wasn't going to solve shit. I had to stop being such a pussy.

And I needed to start making amends for all the dumb crap I've done. I had to stop being the guy who treated everyone around him like they didn't matter. I needed to take stock of where I was.

And that was alone. Miserably and completely alone.

I hated it.

But I had done this to myself.

It was time to figure out the best way to make it up to the people I had hurt.

Call it Cole Brandt's twelve-steps for recovering assholes.

And I had to start with the woman I hadn't realized was so important to me until she wasn't there anymore.

During all the crazy chaos, the only person I wanted to talk to was Vivian. She got me on some sick twisted level and you didn't turn your back on someone who understood you like that.

So I had gone to the store, an idea taking root in my head. I needed to fix my band and my relationship with my friends.

But first I needed to fix things with Vivian.

I didn't expect her to forgive me. Hell, I had a strong inkling she'd slam the door in my face. And it was no less than I deserved. But I wouldn't go away. I planned to stand outside her door all night long if I had to. Just to show her that I meant business and that no matter what, I was going to make it up to her. And I'd do it in the only way I knew how.

By being an obnoxious, unrelenting jerk.

But she hadn't slammed the door in my face. She had actually let me inside.

And now here I was, in her bed, and I felt like the luckiest man on the damn earth.

Even if her hair was tickling my nose and kept getting stuck in my mouth.

I continued to rub my hand slowly up and down her back. I loved her skin. I loved her tits. I loved her fabulous fucking ass. Shit, I loved her knees. And her toes. And the soft spot just below her ears.

My heart thudded in my chest and my hand stilled in its slow progress along her spine.

I had known this woman for two years. And for two years she had put up with my crap and given it right back to me. She never backed down but she never walked away from me either.

She never, ever left.

Until I forced her to. Until I made it impossible for her to stay.

And, whether I had recognized it at the time or not, the act of her leaving had cut me to the quick.

Because I hadn't wanted her to go.

I needed her.

I had to know that at the end of all this crazy insanity with the band, with Jose and the label, that she'd be there, waiting for me. Ready to drive me nuts and blow my mind.

I wanted to be able to pick up the phone from wherever I was and call her. Just the sound of her voice making it all better.

Goddamn it, I knew exactly what this shit was.

I loved Vivian.

I was poke my eyes out with a fork, walk over hot coals, swim in a tank full of sharks in love with her.

I didn't want her for one night. I didn't want her just for a weekend.

I wanted her for as long as she'd have me.

And if I had anything to say about it, that would be one long-ass time.

I leaned down and kissed the top of her head, closing my eyes as I wrapped my arms around the woman I loved with every damn thing inside of me.

I wanted to shout it from the rooftops. I wanted to tattoo it on my butt cheek. I wanted to shake her awake and scream it at the top of my lungs so she could hear me. And then I wanted to make love to her.

I didn't want to fuck her. I didn't want to screw her. I wanted to make sweet, sweet, Marvin Gaye style love to her.

But given the way Vivian was snoring, I didn't see her waking up anytime soon. To be fair, we had had a pretty intense night.

But I was antsy and restless. I wanted to share with her my amazing realization. Okay, okay, I also wanted to put my dick inside her. I was only human.

I was an impatient man and I didn't do waiting.

I rolled Vivian on her back and latched my mouth onto her breast.

"Ahh," she moaned, instantly awake.

"Good morning," I mumbled around a mouthful of nipple.

"What the hell?" Vivian groaned as I dipped my hand between her legs. She was ready. Shit, she was always ready.

God, I loved her.

She threaded her fingers through my hair, pulling gently. Her body moved languidly, still half asleep.

I grabbed a condom from the pile Vivian had to snag from Gracie's room last night and quickly put it on.

Vivian's eyes were heavy lidded, her lips parted as she breathed erratically. Her hair was all over the place.

And I wanted her so badly I thought I'd die from it.

I slid slowly and surely inside her. She wrapped her legs around my hips as I started to thrust.

"I love you, Viv. So fucking much," I moaned, holding onto her hips as I pounded into her.

She didn't say anything. I didn't think much of it. My entire focus was on my need to come.

I wanted her to go first though. I couldn't come without her. I reached down and pressed my thumb to her clit and started to rub. She arched up off the bed, her thighs tightening around me.

I changed the angle and continued to use my thumb to work

her over. And then she was screaming and I was screaming and we were exploding in one giant orgasm.

I collapsed on top of her, my cock still bedded deep inside her. We were breathing nosily, Vivian's arm covering her eyes.

Suddenly she shoved me. "Get off me, dickhead," she hissed. I pulled out of her, my dick cursing me for taking it away from the only place it wanted to be.

She rolled over to face the wall. I quickly took off the condom and tried to find some place to put it. I thought about going for a three pointer into the wastebasket across the room but knew, given the look on Vivian's face that would completely set her off.

In the end I wrapped it in some tissue and put it underneath her Cosmo magazine. I only hoped she found it after I had left.

"What's the problem, Viv?" I asked, frowning. I should have known nothing with this chick was ever easy. I gently rolled her onto her back and I leaned over her.

"What did you say to me?" she demanded.

My frown deepened. "I asked you what your problem was." Vivian pulled the blanket up to cover her tits and I wanted to mourn the loss of them.

She slid over to the edge of the bed and sat up. "No, before that."

I ran my hand through my hair. I really needed to get it cut.

Focus, Cole, focus! You're walking into a minefield!

"Uh, um. . ." I stammered, not sure what she was getting at. Sex fried my brain. It wouldn't be functioning at full steam for at least twenty minutes. This was a dangerous time for yours truly when confronted by an angry female of the Vivian Baily variety.

"You said you loved me, dumbass!" she yelled, her eyes narrowed and her mouth pursed.

I grinned. Oh now I remembered.

"Yeah, I did," I said, running my fingers down her face. She smacked my hand away and glared.

"How can you say something like that? During a time like that? Are you stupid as well as narcissistic?"

I was so confused. Weren't those three little words what every woman longed to hear?

I wanted to tell her so I did. I thought she'd be overjoyed. I thought it would bring us closer.

I sure as shit hadn't expected her to kick me out.

Because that's exactly what she was doing.

"You need to leave. I can't deal with you right now."

What?

"Hold up! Vivian, calm down a sec," I started but she was shaking her head furiously. And then she was getting dressed and covering the body that I had just worshipped and adored.

"No, you can't come in here being all sugary and wonderful. You can't sweet talk me and tear me down like this. And you sure as hell can't tell me you love me while fucking me! You're messing with my head, Cole! I can't let you keep doing this to me!"

She was getting seriously worked up. I jumped out of bed, not worried about the fact that I was still naked and semi-hard.

I grabbed her by her upper arms to try to stop her from walking out of the room.

"I'm not messing with your head, Viv. I meant it. Okay, so maybe it was bad timing. But I love you. I really do," I said softly, running my hand through her hair.

I didn't often do tender but I was trying. For her I'd do just about anything.

Vivian shook her head again. What was so complicated about this? Why the fucking drama?

"This is just like you, Cole! You can't use sex; you can't use me, to hide from the stuff going on in your life. This has always been our problem, can't you see that?"

"What are you talking about?" I asked. My head was starting to hurt. Vivian was giving me a headache.

"We fuck. We argue. We fuck. You do something stupid to piss me off. We fuck some more. I left you for a reason. I was fine with that. Or I was trying to be. I have a life here. And now this. Why are you doing this?" she wailed.

I got it. I really did. But just because we made things difficult didn't mean they weren't worth the effort.

"We're a mess! We suck each other dry. We should end this

now, once and for all, before there's nothing left to walk away from," Vivian appealed to me.

I shook my head, refusing to hear her. I pulled her up against me, my hand wrapping around the back of her head as I held her tight.

"If we're a mess, then I'm ready to get dirty, baby," I growled before I claimed her mouth.

She was mine.

It was time to remind her of that.

She was falling into me. I could feel it. I supported Vivian's weight as her legs buckled beneath her. And we kissed and kissed like they do in those crappy chick flicks she was so damn fond of.

It was epic. This was the beginning. This is where I started to put together all of the fucked up pieces of my life. The sun was shining, the bees were buzzing, the flowers were blooming. This was some Disney princess shit going on!

Or maybe not.

"Seriously stop it or I'm going to knee you in the nuts," she warned, pushing me away again.

Her hands were shaking. So were mine. My adrenaline was coursing and I was two seconds away from throwing her over my shoulder and tossing her down on the bed. She always listened better with my hand between her legs.

"I love you, Vivian. I want to be with you!" I started to close the distance between us but she was still shoving me.

"You said that. I get it. You think you love me. Whooptie freaking Whoo."

"No, I don't think I love you. I know I love you!" I argued. This was not going at all how I fantasized about it in my head this morning. In between mild panic of course.

Vivian rolled her eyes. "Yeah, well pardon me if I have hard time believing that sentiment when I'm so used to fending off a hundred other girls who I'm sure you feel oh so deeply about."

We were back to this. I should have expected it. I didn't blame her. But it was still frustrating.

"There are no other girls! Not anymore! I haven't fucked anyone else in over six months, Viv! No one but you!" I swore.

"Do you want a medal? How about a sticker? Because you may not have done the deed, but your tongue has still been down a lot of throats. I should know. I'm usually front and center for the entire show."

Okay, so she had me there.

I folded my hands in front of me in a pleading gesture. "Please, Viv. I don't want anyone but you. What can I do to make you believe me?"

Vivian shook her head. "It's hard to have faith in someone who has proven time and time again to not be trustworthy. Not only with me. What about your band? Cole, you're planning to step out behind their backs as well. What does that say about you? How can I ever be comfortable in a relationship with someone who doesn't honor his commitments to anyone? Not me, not your friends, not your label, not even your fans."

I opened my mouth to deny what she was saying. But she was right.

Fuck me, she was right.

"You need to make things right, Cole, if you ever want anything to happen between us. I can't let myself love someone who hasn't proven that they deserve my heart."

We stood there, staring at each other for an endless moment. I wanted to yell that she was wrong. But how could I when every single thing she uttered was the total and honest truth?

I picked up my clothes from the floor and got dressed. "I get it. I've got a lot to make up for."

I started to walk past her when she grabbed my arm. "Don't do this for me. Or because you want to prove something. Make it right because it's what you want to do. I understand if the band isn't your passion anymore. That maybe you need to go do your own thing. Whatever. You still owe it the people who have stood by you to talk to them about what's in your head."

I nodded, covering her hand briefly with mine.

"I'll be back," I promised. And I meant it. I wouldn't leave her now.

Vivian gave me a sad smile.

"I hope you will be."

WASN'T sure what I'd say when I walked up Garrett's front porch. I had no idea if this would be some sort of reconciliation or whether it would be the final severing.

But with Vivian's words swimming around in my head, I knew I couldn't put it off any longer.

I thought about knocking. I hadn't knocked in years. I could hear music from inside, the familiar strains of Fuck Me along with Jordan's voice.

I turned the doorknob and walked inside. I followed the music to the stairway off the kitchen. The light was on in the basement so I went down the steps.

Maysie was on the couch talking to a girl I recognized as Sophie McMillian from high school. Mitch, Garrett, and Jordan were playing a set I knew all too well.

I sat down on the bottom step and watched them. They didn't realize I was there until there was a break between songs and Jordan glanced toward me. He put his sticks down. Mitch and Garrett frowned at him.

"What the hell?" Mitch asked.

"Looks like we've got company," Jordan said coldly, nodding his head in my direction.

Maysie looked startled. They all did.

"If it isn't the providential son," Mitch sneered.

Garrett snorted. "It's prodigal son, dumbass."

Mitch puffed up his chest. "Whatever. What are you doing here, Cole?" he asked, setting his bass in the stand.

"I was driving by and heard some fucking amazing music. I wanted to check it out. Had no idea it was a bunch of raging douchebags," I joked, trying for humor to lessen the tension.

It didn't really work.

No one smiled. Not even a little.

Tough room.

I stood up and walked over to my mic stand that had been pushed into the corner. I kicked it with my shoe. No one said anything. They weren't going to make this easy for me.

"Seriously, man. What are you doing here? We all got the impression we wouldn't see you until Tuesday."

Tuesday. D-Day. Aka, the day we lost everything to the label.

Unless we could check our baggage at the door. But looking at the closed off faces of my friends, I wasn't sure that was possible.

"Yeah, well I figured we had shit to talk about before then."

Garrett nodded, the only friendly face in a less than friendly group.

"Uh, we'll leave you guys to talk. Come on, Piper," Maysie said hurrying up the stairs. The Sophie girl gave Mitch a quick peck on the lips and followed Maysie.

That left me alone in a room with people who weren't exactly happy to see me.

Jordan came out from behind his drum set to stand in front of me, his arms crossed over his chest. At least he wasn't trying to punch me. I considered that progress.

"So. Talk."

I wanted to tell Jordan where to shove his fucking attitude. That I wasn't the only one with the problem. But I figured I could get to that later. Right now was for saying my piece.

"I shouldn't have played the song. I'm sorry, all right. But there are more issues at hand then me playing a damn song we didn't all agree on," I reasoned, proud of how calm I was.

"I think that's obvious, Cole," Garrett piped up, putting his guitar back in the case. And then I was standing before my three bandmates. Me versus them. The way it had felt for months now.

"Why do I get the feeling that I'm gonna be jumped by the three of you?" I asked lightly.

Jordan and Mitch didn't say anything but Garrett smirked.

"Why? Are we intimidating you?" Garrett asked.

"Hardly," I snorted.

"So what issues do you see going on here?" Jordan questioned.

"You're jealous. Plain and simple," I stated. Mitch's face turned red and Jordan clenched his fists, most likely imagining he was planting them in my face.

Garrett groaned. "Why did you have to go there? Things were starting off so well too?" he complained.

"I was getting the attention. The label wanted me to do the press. The interviewers wanted to talk to me. Primal Terror asked me on stage. I get it. I would have been pissed too if one of you was stealing the spotlight. Because that's what I was doing. I was taking all the glory for myself and saying to fuck with all of you."

I looked at each of them steadily. "And Jose thinks I can do better on my own. He wants me to get out of my contract with Pirate and sign with Deep Hill Records as a solo artist," I informed them. Jordan's eyes got wide and Mitch's mouth fell open. Garrett's face was a neutral and impassive as ever, though I could see the tension around his mouth.

"Deep Hill wants to sign you as a solo artist? And Jose told you to do it? I thought he was the band's manager? Not Cole Brandt's manager," Jordan fumed.

"Yeah, well, I think Mr. Suarez has his own fucking agenda."

"Apparently," Mitch muttered.

"I've been a dick. But you guys have been dicks too," I countered.

"Excuse the fuck me?" Jordan demanded.

"Are you going to stand there and tell me my ego was the only one that needed checking? That the fact that you weren't the center of the fucking universe wasn't a huge problem? I know that you're used to being the big man on campus, Piper, but this time you weren't. And that bugged the shit out of you."

I purposefully used my old nickname for Jordan. I did it to push his buttons. I did it to test his limits. I wanted to see what he would do.

Jordan and I glared at each other for a long time, neither of us saying anything. The room was silent. I could hear the dripping from the leaking pipe in the corner.

I didn't know whether he was going to hit me or not. I could tell he was thinking about it.

And then Garrett opened up his guitar case again and plugged his battered Yamaha into the amp. He strummed it a few times, playing the opening chords of Five Knuckles Deep, one of the first songs we had written together.

Mitch followed suit, picking up his bass, and plugging it into the other Marshall amp in the corner. His rhythm mixed with Garrett's riffs.

257

Jordan and I stood there a while longer. There was a slight tick in his jaw. I was poised ready for an attack.

And then he was walking back towards his drum kit. He sat down and picked up his sticks, tapping out a steady beat in time to the music.

Garrett looked at me expectantly. "Well, I'm sure as hell not singing. Grab the mic and plug it in," he said.

I stood there for a minute, not sure what to do. Did I want this?

I grabbed the mic stand and stood in my normal spot, front and center.

And then I was singing. And screaming. And yelling.

Maysie and Sophie came down a short time later, looking relieved that we were all still standing.

But I barely noticed them.

Because I was exactly where I was supposed to be.

Chapter 22
VIVIAN

STARED at the clock, knowing that Cole and the rest of Generation Rejects were on their way to New York.

Not that I had heard that from Cole. Maysie had let me know she would be heading up with them. She and Jordan were planning to stay in New York for a few days after the meeting but she promised she'd be back in time for the gala on Saturday.

I hadn't talked to Cole since I had kicked him out of my apartment on Sunday morning.

I had been so angry. The angriest I could ever remember being towards him. It was so much worse than finding him with another woman or being handcuffed to a bed and him losing the key.

He had told me he loved me.

While we were having sex.

And then he had the audacity to act as though he didn't understand why I would have a problem with that.

It wasn't so much the timing of the words themselves; it had more to do with the fact that I couldn't trust myself once he had said them.

Because I loved him madly.

To distraction.

To my ruin.

He made it all too tempting to fall head first into my total destruction.

We were the beauty in the chaos and I wanted him to annihilate me.

But I knew that it wasn't possible for him to love me the way I loved him. Love for Cole Brandt was a pretty new toy he wanted to try out. They were words without substance. He said them without knowing what they truly meant. He didn't know how to love anyone but himself.

He didn't love me.

This became my mantra.

Because the need to touch him, to see him, to be with him every second of every day was overwhelming. And I was so damn weak when it came to Cole.

But I didn't call him. And he didn't call me. And the disappointment of that almost threw me into a moping depression.

But I held strong. I had too much on my plate to fixate on Cole and the fact that in only a few hours, his musical fate would be decided.

"Earth to Vivian!" Theo snapped his fingers in front of my face. I was standing in the middle of the large open space at the back of The Claremont Center where the gala would be held. There were people rearranging furniture and hanging colorful tapestries on the walls. Movers were starting to bring in tables and chairs. I was supposed to be directing them.

But work responsibilities became less important as I was sucked under by my Cole-centric thoughts.

Such was the danger of loving him.

I smiled, laughing. "Sorry, I was totally zoned out there, wasn't I?"

"Just a bit," Theo agreed. I hadn't really spoken with Theo since our disastrous date. He had been out of town for work during the last part of the week and I had been neck deep in the final gala preparations.

There was an element of discomfort in seeing him again. I still felt guilty and ridiculous for the entire debacle. I was still smacking myself for ruining something that had so much potential. But I would have been going into it with only half a heart.

Because a certain jerk had the part of me and wasn't giving it back anytime soon. No matter how much I wanted him to.

"This looks amazing!" Theo enthused sincerely, watching as several women started unloading the pieces of the faux ice sculptures that would be erected in the corners of the room.

"So far so good," I agreed, signing an order slip for the table linens and handing it back to the delivery person.

"I can't wait to see how it all turns out. It's one thing to imagine it in my head; it's something else entirely to see it on the actual night. I just hope everything goes smoothly," I said with an edge of panic as Theo and I walked over to the giant screen being put up on the wall.

It was the perfect space for the event. The entire back of the room was composed of windows that overlooked the river. The room was grand and expansive and would be filled with twinkling lights and swaths of blue, silver, and white. I had envisioned a classy but eye-catching event. I was scared that something would happen to screw it all up. Because lord knows, that would be my luck.

"So how was Cole after I left the other night?" Theo asked and I sucked in a breath. I hadn't expected him to ask about Cole. I sort of hoped he'd let us pretend the whole thing hadn't happened.

I forced a smile and shrugged. "He was hung over."

Theo's piercing eyes seemed to look straight through me. "And how are things with the two of you?" he queried.

Why was he asking me about this? Why in the world would he want to know?

I prayed he hadn't held out hope for us. Because that was never going to happen. Even if I wanted to make myself go there, I knew it wasn't right. I couldn't flirt and lead him on when I knew that Cole would always be there in the back of my mind.

And now that the L word had been thrown into the mix, I was even more of a lost cause.

"Couldn't really say," I said caustically, wishing he'd drop it. I was at work. I couldn't fixate on Cole. I couldn't think about how things were going for him in New York. I couldn't allow myself to wonder whether he would call when he was finished.

"Because, I was wondering if you wanted to go to the gala with me. And I didn't want to ask if the two of you were together."

"Um. . ." I began, not sure what to say.

Hadn't I stomped all over him enough for one lifetime?

Theo chuckled at my horrified expression. "As friends, Viv. I just want to escort the amazing person responsible for all of this. Just a night of fun, and dancing, and hanging out with someone I enjoy being with. Just don't get high on antihistamines beforehand and we'll be good," he teased and I couldn't help but laugh.

"Well, I'm supposed to go with my friends."

Theo shrugged. "I rented a limo. The company always springs for them. We could all go together," he offered and that seemed to take some of the pressure off.

"Sure, that sounds great," I agreed. I was relieved that Theo didn't seem to be holding my idiotic behavior against me. He was such a nice guy and I really needed more nice in my life.

"Great! I'll pick you and your friends up at your place around eight on Saturday!" Theo gave me a wave and headed over to several of his co-workers that had come in to see the progress.

My phone beeped in my pocket and I pulled it out to find a text from Cole.

In New York. Wish me luck.

Six words. That was it. But it lifted my mood instantly.

Not even hesitating I quickly typed out a response.

Good luck, Cole.

I didn't get a reply. I hadn't expected one. But my day felt a whole lot brighter.

BY the evening, however, I was on pins and needles wanting to know what had happened in the meeting with the label. After receiving the text from Cole earlier, I had honestly thought he'd call afterwards. But there had been nothing but radio silence.

I tried calling Maysie several times but her phone went straight to voicemail.

"Have you heard from Maysie?" I asked Gracie after she got home from her last day at the coffee shop. She had gotten the job with the garden magazine and was set to start on Monday.

Though, she seemed less than thrilled about it. I didn't exactly understand what her problem was. It was a hell of a lot better than making espressos every day.

"Nope, were we supposed to?" she asked, kicking off her shoes and padding into the kitchen to make herself something to eat.

I followed on her heels. "Today was the meeting with the record label," I told her.

"Oh, that's right," Gracie mused; pulling out the leftover lasagna I had made the other night.

"I just thought we'd hear something by now, but Maysie's phone is off when I tried to call her," I said, annoyed by how unbothered Gracie seemed by the situation.

"Why don't you call Cole, then," she suggested. I grit my teeth together.

"Why in the world would I call Cole?" I asked defensively.

Gracie looked over her shoulder as she put the pasta in the microwave and turned it on.

"I don't know. Maybe because he was over here the other night and I could hear exactly what you were doing through our super thin walls," she explained, giving me a wry look.

"You were here?" I squeaked, mortified that Gracie had heard us. Not that it was the first time and it wasn't as though I hadn't been subjected to all manner of noises from within her bedroom.

But I hadn't wanted anyone to know that he had been here. I wasn't ready to talk about what it meant because he had spent the night. I wasn't ready to talk about what we were to each other now.

"I do live here, you know," Gracie responded dryly, taking her pasta out of the microwave and dumping it into a bowl. She grabbed a fork and passed by me on her way into the living room.

"I didn't hear you come in. I just thought you stayed out," I excused lamely.

"I'm sure you didn't hear me. I don't think you could hear much of anything with all the racket you two were making."

"Oh whatever! Like you're any quieter," I huffed.

Gracie stirred her pasta with her fork and ate a mouthful as she regarded me.

"I was surprised when I recognized Cole's voice moaning your name. I hadn't expected to find him here. Especially not now."

"Yeah, well he showed up and we hung out and. . ."

"You decided to get naked?" Gracie supplied.

"It wasn't like that!" I maintained.

"When is it ever not like that?" Gracie asked.

"I didn't plan for us to sleep together."

"Well, from the sounds of it, there wasn't a whole lot of sleeping going on," Gracie laughed.

"I'm glad you think it's so damn funny. Should we spend some time talking about your trip on the bone train with Mitch? Maybe we can dissect that for my amusement," I snipped, irritated.

Gracie cleared her throat and covered her smile with a cough.

"Enough said. I get it. Sorry. You just made it clear you were done with all of that. And by all of that I mean Cole and his magic penis."

"It was different this time." I sounded like such a girl. Ugh!

"Of course it was." Gracie rolled her eyes and I had to wonder when she became so cynical. That was normally Riley's MO. Gracie was the peppy optimist. Something had changed in her and I found it disturbing at how hostile she sounded.

Gracie got up and looked down at me, her expression softening, her pinched mouth relaxing. "I just don't want you to get hurt, Viv. And Cole always seems to hurt you."

"I won't let him. I'm not even sure he'll have an opportunity to get close enough to hurt me."

Gracie's eyes were troubled. "He's always that close, Viv. Even when you pushed him away."

I chewed on my bottom lip stared down at my hands. "He told me he loved me," I admitted in a whisper.

Gracie sat back down heavily. "He what?" she gasped.

"He said he loved me."

"Wow." I looked up at my friend and she seemed almost as dazed as I was.

"I'm pretty sure he wants us to be together," I finished.

"You're pretty sure? What does that mean?"

"It means we didn't have a chance to really talk about it! I kicked him out!" I threw my hands into the air in frustration.

Gracie started to giggle. I looked at her sharply and she covered her mouth. But then she was laughing hysterically. And then I joined her. We were laughing like a couple of mentally unstable hyenas.

"You two are absurd!" Gracie chortled.

"I know!" I agreed.

"You seriously belong together. There's no one out there that will ever put up with either of you for very long," Gracie continued, settling down.

"Hey!" I whined, not liking the sound of that at all.

"It's the truth! Look at yourself. Look at how you are together! You're both overdramatic, narcissistic, attention seeking fools." I started to bristle at the insult, even if I got the impression she didn't mean it as one.

I wasn't narcissistic was I? I could be dramatic. But narcissistic? Really?

"You're both stubborn and unyielding. And 100% made for each other."

"But the other women. . ." I started to say.

"Yeah, there's that," she said, getting serious.

"How can I ever trust him?" I asked, my voice a plea.

Gracie shrugged. "I don't know. I'm not sure I could ever get past all that. But I'm not you. And I can't pretend to understand the crazy dynamics of your relationship. Trust is something you will obviously have to work on if you want to be together. It will take time. Do you want to be with him?"

Did I want to be with Cole?

He drove me crazy. I hated and loved him in equal measure. He lit me on fire and stoked the flame.

When we were together, I didn't want to be anywhere else.

When we were apart, I only wanted to be with him again.

Did I want to be with him? Yes I did. But at what cost to myself?

"I think I do. I just don't know if I'm up for it." I clenched my hands together in my lap.

"I guess you have your answer then. It doesn't really matter what anyone else has to say about it. I can't pretend to understand why you'd want to put yourself through that. But I'll support you anyway. It's what friends do. And if he ever touches another woman, I'll break each and every one of his fingers. . .slowly. . .one at a time. Just for you, Viv," Gracie promised, grinning.

I chuckled. "Good to know."

Chapter 23
COLE

I **WAS** back in Bakersville putting on my tuxedo. My nuts felt like they were in a vice and I was pretty sure I had picked up the wrong sized monkey suit.

I straightened the shiny silver tie and took the ring out of my lip. My hair was wild, but there wasn't much I could do about that.

I looked like a fucking waiter.

The things guys did for the chicks they loved.

I smoothed out the collar and figured it was about as good as it was going to get.

I slung my black jacket over my shoulder and headed out the door.

Time for my grand gesture.

I just hoped I didn't take a kick to the gut for the effort.

F **OUR** days ago I had been in New York. Four days ago I had finally figured out what I was going to do.

I had finally manned up and made a decision.

And it had been fucking liberating.

After playing with the guys at Garrett's, not much more was said about the upcoming meeting and what we planned to do. We left it open ended and up in the air. Not the best plan when you were sitting down with your record label to talk about the future of your music.

But we were all still little too volatile. And even though we had a moment where we came together in total synch the way we always had been able to, it didn't erase the months of bad blood that had built between us.

So I had left that day and gone home and packed for New York.

Jose met me at the airport on Tuesday around lunchtime. I had just landed and sent a quick text to Vivian. She had responded immediately. And even though the text had been short, it still made me happy.

I wasn't sure with how we left things whether she would have written back at all.

But she had. And that gave me a sliver of hope on this otherwise shitty day.

I had flown up by myself. Jose had insisted that I come in before the other guys. He had arranged for someone to collect Jordan, Mitch, and Garrett just before the meeting.

"You and I have some shit to discuss," Jose declared, steering me towards a black sedan. I threw my overnight bag in the back. I hadn't known exactly what would happen once I got to New York, so I had come prepared to stay over. If things went south, I wasn't sure I could head back to Bakersville right away.

Who knows where I'd end up?

"You are one hard asshole to get ahold of. Is there a reason you haven't returned any of my calls? I need to know what you're planning to do today. I have people on the line waiting to know what you decide, Cole. This isn't how shit is done!" Jose said tersely. He clenched his teeth as he wove through traffic.

"I get that. I just wasn't sure what I was going to tell you," I answered honestly. No sense in mentioning the fact that I had spent most of the past week drunk off my ass and feeling fucking sorry for myself.

"Then we talk it out. I need your head in the game. I want to get you to where you need to be, Cole. I thought we were getting on the same page. I thought you wanted this. I hope like hell I didn't misread you. I thought you were someone who would fight tooth and nail for the fame and the recognition. You want it. I see it every time you get on that stage. And everyone else sees it too. Which is why Deep Hill fucking wants you. They don't go after just anyone. But they're going after you."

I didn't say anything. I watched as the Manhattan skyline got closer and closer. Jose's lip service was kind of grating. This was a guy who only wanted me for what I could give him.

I could suck three ways to Sunday but if I could make him a buck or two, Jose would surgically implant his lips to my ass.

"Are you hearing me, Cole? This is your chance! You'd be a fucking idiot of you didn't do it. Do you realize how many young artists would murder their own grandma to have the chance that is sitting in your lap? Open the glove compartment," he barked, obviously irritated by my lack of response.

I thought about telling him to shove his demands straight up his nose, but didn't want to end up in the Hudson River sleeping with the fishes.

I opened the glove compartment, not sure what I was looking for.

"Get those papers out," he directed.

I pulled out a stapled stack of paperwork and saw my name and Jose's at the top.

"That's your new contract. The one that let's me work with you. Just you. There's a pen in there as well." He thought I was just going to sign it. That I was going to do whatever the hell he told me to do.

"What's the hold up? Just sign it. It's a standard contract. Nothing crazy." He was being awfully pushy.

Traffic into Manhattan was a bitch. And things inside the car were getting markedly tenser.

"I'm not signing these right now, Jose. There's a lot going on. I need to get through the next few hours, if you don't mind," I said firmly. I was sick and tired of this dick bossing me around. He was supposed to be working for me, not the other way around.

Jose seemed shocked by my new set of balls.

"Yeah, sure. I get it. I wouldn't worry about today. I've already spoken to Tate at the label and we're going to be able to dissolve the contract without a whole lot of bullshit. The label will keep the album but you'll be able to go elsewhere when all is said and done."

"You did what?" I couldn't believe Jose had taken it upon himself to do that shit! Who the hell did he think he was? I had never said that was the direction I wanted to go in! I didn't appreciate anyone, let alone Jose fucking Suarez, handling my life for me.

"It'll just be a matter of signing some papers and then it's over. I'm sure you'll get the bad little boy scolding. But who gives a fuck? You're moving on to bigger and better things, my friend," Jose was saying, but I barely heard him.

"So they want to dissolve the contract?" I clarified. Damn it! The guys were going into this blind. I had to tell them what was going on. This shit wasn't cool.

"You didn't think Pirate Records would want to keep an unknown band on after the drama you've had on the tour? Apparently Primal Terror has been pretty vocal about your infighting. And Pirate is a young company. They don't want to be attached to such an unpredictable act. But it's no skin off your nose. You'll come up smelling like roses."

"And what about Garrett, Jordan, and Mitch?" I asked, interrupting him.

"What about them?" Jose seemed confused.

"Where does that leave them?"

"I don't know. But they're not my concern. Making you bigger than Jesus is," Jose grinned and it chilled me to the bone.

I didn't say anything else. The wheels in my head were turning a million miles a minute. We finally pulled up almost an hour later, in front of the non-descript stone building that housed Pirate Records headquarters. It definitely wasn't the fancy glass skyscraper one would expect to see when going to a record label. It was squished between a hairdresser and a dry cleaner.

I got out of the car and Jose made to follow me. I held my hand out, stopping him.

"You don't need to come with me," I told him, reaching into the backseat and grabbing my bag. I rolled the new contract up in my hand and smacked my knee with it.

"I'm your fucking manager, of course I'm coming with you. I've got to make sure things go the way they're supposed to. Then afterwards we can go over that new contract."

"No, we're not," I stated, handing him the rolled up paperwork.

"What the hell are you doing, Cole?" Jose narrowed his eyes at me.

"I'm giving you your shitty contract back and I'm telling you to go fuck yourself." I grinned a little maniacally and started to open the door.

"You stupid little shit. Do you realize what you're doing? You're throwing away everything. You think you'll get anywhere without me?" he sneered.

I shrugged. "I don't really care. I just know I'd rather live in the fucking streets than sign those papers. You were supposed to be the manager for Generation Rejects. You're a backstabbing, calculating, cunt and you're definitely not the sort of person I want representing me. I'd say it was nice knowing you. But then I'd be talking out of my ass."

I didn't give Jose a chance to respond. I climbed out of his car and shut the door. I flipped him the bird and walked up the sidewalk.

Damn, that felt good.

The sound of Jose's squealing tires as he pulled away was the best thing I had heard so far today.

One down, one to go.

I had to wait for a while once I found my way to the label's reception room. The other guys weren't there yet and the longer I sat by myself, the more I started to question the sanity of my decision.

I had just fired Jose. I had just flushed my great opportunity down the fucking toilet.

I was throwing everything into the ring for guys who may not want me in the band anymore.

Whatever the risk, I couldn't have done it any other way.

Finally Jordan, Mitch, and Garrett showed up. They saw me in the corner and came over to join me.

"Where's Jose?" Mitch asked.

"Gone," I said shortly.

"Gone? What do you mean he's gone? He's supposed to be here!" Jordan demanded, sounding a little panicky.

"I fired him. We don't need him here, guys. We've got this. And we definitely don't need someone like Jose running the show. That guy's a snake."

"You made that kind of decision without talking to us about it first?" Jordan demanded and I rolled my eyes.

"Don't start this shit now, Piper. Do you trust some guy who has spent the last few months trying to break up the band to look after our best interests?" I snarled.

"You can't make decisions like that for the band, Cole. This is the fucking problem!" Jordan's voice rose and Garrett shushed him.

"He handed me a new contract on the ride over here. A contract for exclusive representation by him. Excluding the three of you! He was planning on to drop you on your ass, man. So I dropped him on his first," I shot back, glaring at him.

Jordan didn't say anything. His shoulders slumped and he sat back in his chair.

"Don't you have anything to say?" I challenged.

"He was cutting us loose?" Jordan asked, his voice surprisingly weak.

I sat down beside him. "Yeah, man. He was. He thought he had a better chance of making his big cut if I went off on my own. I told you he'd been after me to sign a contract with Deep Hill Records. I guess he went behind our back and started talking smack to the people here at Pirate. So I'm not sure exactly what they're expecting when we walk in there. It sounded like Jose filled their heads with a bunch of bullshit."

Jordan let out a heavy sigh and dug the heels of his hands into his eyes. Finally he looked at me with a pained expression.

"I think I owe you an apology," Jordan said.

Mitch and Garrett stared at our drummer in surprise.

"An apology? Is the world ending?" I crossed my arms over my chest defensively.

"I've been a dick. And I haven't given you the benefit of the doubt. You're a pain in the ass. But I get that's who you are. I should have trusted you to have our back."

Despite the barbs thrown in, it was the one thing I had really needed to hear from him.

"Thanks, man," I said.

"I don't know what's gonna happen, but we need to go in that room as a team. We need to take this on together. Because at the end of the day, this is our band. Our music," Garrett spoke up.

We all nodded.

It wasn't much longer before we were called back into a small conference room. We sat down around a table that took up most of the space. There were a couple of guys that I recognized from when we had signed our initial contract.

Danvers, the CEO, and Tate, the Vice-President of Operations. There was also a man and a woman that I didn't recognize who had a pile of papers in front of them.

"Hi guys. I wish I could say it was good to see you, but given the circumstances, I can't really say that," Danvers began, narrowing his eyes as he looked at each of us. We didn't bow our heads like naughty little school children. We kept our chins up and our backs straight.

"This is Fiona and Chet with legal. They're going to talk through the finer points of your contract. Because apparently we have pretty big problem here guys," Tate said, leaning forward and folding his hands together.

"Where's Jose?" Danvers asked.

"We fired him," I reported.

Danvers and Tate raised their eyebrows.

"Really. Well, that changes things significantly," Danvers stated.

"I know he's been talking in your ear about shit that's definitely not true," I chimed in, seeing this as my chance to set things straight.

Danvers leaned back in his chair and folded his hands over his protruding belly. "Go, on," he prompted.

"I'm not planning to jump ship for another label. I'm not looking to leave these guys and go out on my own. I'm here until the bitter end. And Jose didn't like that. So now he's gone. And here we are. And we hope like hell you don't drop us. Because we made some mistakes. We messed up big time. But we can also learn. We have a better handle now on how to navigate through some of this crazy shit. And I think, if you give us a chance, we can prove you were right to sign us in the first place," I finished, taking a deep breath.

Danvers and Tate shared a look. I wish I knew what they were thinking.

Jordan leaned forward and clasped his hand on my shoulder. "Nicely said, man."

"Thanks for that, Cole. It's nice to hear you all are taking this seriously. Because it was beginning to look like it was a big joke to you," Tate said sternly. We all shook our heads.

"We take this opportunity very seriously. And we're thankful you've given it to us, " Jordan interjected.

Tate nodded before continuing. "Look, let's get to the guts of this meeting. You've been called here because of your behavior on the Primal Terror tour. We signed you guys because we saw potential there. You have talent. That's no secret. But there's more to making it in this industry than just talent. And your unprofessional attitudes is totally unacceptable."

He turned to Jordan and the other guys. "I understand you haven't been happy with the direction of the publicity. Well that's tough tits, fellas. We plan to market this album how we think is best. What do you have to bring to the table as far as marketing experience?"

Garrett, who was normally impassive, clenched his jaw. "This is our band. We know what works and what doesn't. We have a pretty good idea of what our fans want. We just want an opportunity to talk about marketing before it's shoved down our throats. We get that Cole is a great singer. He's awesome at what he does. But this isn't a one-man show. And we want the chance to market the band as a band."

Danvers and Tate seemed to consider what Garrett had to say.

"This is the way it works, guys. You don't have any say in how things are put out in the press. It's the name of the game," Tate looked at me.

"Cole, Jose had told me that you wanted out of your contract. That's why I'm more than a bit surprised to find out that he's no longer managing you. He seemed pretty sure of the other opportunities out there for you."

My bandmates were looking at me but my attention was on Danvers and Tate. "Fuck, Jose," I spat out, not caring that my use of language perhaps wasn't appropriate for the setting.

"Like I said, I never gave him permission to talk on my behalf with you about my contract. I have no desire to terminate, nor do I plan to leave the Rejects. My priority is this album and promoting it."

I chanced a glance at Garrett and he gave me a small nod. Jordan patted my back and Mitch smiled.

It felt good to be back in the fold.

Danvers and Tate seemed pleased but still very serious. "Okay, well that's good to hear because we've already invested a lot into this release. We need to talk about where we go from here. Because what happened on the road was inexcusable. To be asked to leave a major nationwide tour does not make you look good. And it doesn't make the label look good either. We need to rethink how we're going to market you and this album in the best possible way. But you need to trust that we're going to do what we have to in order to ensure you and the album is a success. Can you put your egos aside and let us do that?" Danvers gave each of us a pointed look.

Jordan nodded. "Yeah, we can do that." The rest of us nodded.

Tate turned to Fiona and Chet. "It doesn't look like we're going to need you today. Thanks." The legal department said their goodbyes and left us to talk about all the ways Generation Rejects were going to take over the world.

After the meeting, we were all left full of the warm fuzzies. I was back with my band. We were doing this together. And even though we still had stuff to sort out, we would get there.

"Maysie and I are planning to stay in the city for a few days. Why don't you all stay too? I think it would be good for all of us to be away from the shit for awhile," Jordan suggested.

"I'm not sharing a room with you two. I've had to listen to you one too many times as it is," I replied, grimacing.

"We know you stand outside the door and listen, perv." Jordan hit me in the back of the head. But it wasn't done maliciously. It was the sort of joking reserved for friends.

"Let's do it. I could use a little Big Apple madness," Garrett said.

Mitch and I agreed.

We met up with Maysie at a tiny café across town. She was relieved when we explained how things had gone down and she had even given me a hug when Jordan told her how I had fired Jose.

"I never liked that guy," she admitted.

"So what are we going to get in to?" Mitch asked, rubbing his hands together like a lazy Bond villain.

"I don't know. There's Broadway. Or Madison Avenue! I've always wanted to go to Saks!" Maysie exclaimed. The guys and I exchanged looks.

Then we all grinned. "Let's go clubbing!" I announced, followed by a riotous cheering from my friends.

Maysie rolled her eyes.

Later that night, after we had checked into a cheap hotel on the Lower East Side, I sat with my phone in my lap, debating whether or not I should call Vivian.

I wanted to call her. I really did. I wanted to tell her everything that had happened.

But at the same time I wasn't sure I had a right to.

There was a knock on my door and I called out, "Come in!"

Maysie poked her head around the door.

"You busy?" she asked.

I waved her in. "Not at all."

"I wanted to talk to you in private for a minute without Jordan or the other guys around," she said, pulling a chair out from the desk in the corner and having a seat.

"I always knew you wanted my body, Mays. You just have to ask and I can make you a very happy woman," I teased, giving her a wink.

Maysie groaned. "Do you ever give it a rest?"

"Nope," I responded, grinning devilishly.

"Okay, I'm just going to put this out there, because I don't know when I'll ever have a chance to again," she began.

"Now I'm intrigued. Do tell." I leaned forward, resting my elbows on my knees.

"If you fuck over Viv, I'll cut you like a bitch," she warned, her eyes flashing.

Shit, I hadn't expected her to say that.

"Excuse me?" I asked.

"You heard me, Cole. I've watched you treat her like a damn yo-yo for years. I know Viv comes off tough but she's not. She's sensitive and vulnerable and you can't use her like a freaking toy you want to play with when it suits you. She cares about you. A lot. Though I'm not entirely sure why."

"Gee thanks, Maysie," I muttered.

"I'm serious. We're going out tonight on the town. And you'll do what you always do. Pick up a random girl, not thinking about the person back in Bakersville who hasn't hooked up with anyone in over two years because she's hung up on you!" Maysie was pissed. She looked ready to take my head off. But what she said shocked me.

"Viv hasn't been with anyone in two years but me?" I couldn't believe it. I had convinced myself that she had messed around. I hadn't been able to fathom a woman like her not being with someone who would treat her right. The way she deserved. The way I had never been able to treat her.

"No, asshole, she hasn't. So please remember her when you're out tonight. Think about her feelings before you take some random back to your hotel room." Maysie got to her feet and was ready to leave.

"Hold on a sec," I called out, stopping her.

277

"I haven't been with anyone but Vivian in a long time, Mays."

Maysie gave me the yeah right look.

"I'm serious. I haven't wanted to. I know I haven't been the best guy. I know I'm arrogant and full of myself. I know what you think of me. But you need to know that I don't want to hurt Vivian ever again."

I took a deep breath.

"I love her, Mays," I admitted quietly.

Maysie's eyes widened. Why was everyone so shocked when I said that? It was almost annoying.

"Well shit," she said.

"Yeah, shit indeed," I agreed.

"Then why are you here and not back there with her?" Maysie asked.

"Because I'm not sure she'll have me," I told her, admitting my biggest fear.

Maysie snorted. "Oh she'll have you. No need to worry about that."

I shook my head. "You don't understand. I told her I loved her. I laid it all out there but she doesn't believe me. She doesn't think I have it in me to commit to her."

"Do you blame her?" Maysie asked.

"Fuck no, I don't blame her! I just don't know what to do to convince her."

Maysie sat down beside me on the bed and patted my back. "You poor, lovesick idiot. Girls aren't that hard to figure out, you know," she tsked.

"Then do tell, oh wise lady!" I begged.

"You need a grand gesture. Something that will surprise her. Something Vivian won't expect. Get romantic with it. Be cliché. We love that stuff." Maysie smiled.

"Be cliché. I don't get it," I mused.

Maysie rolled her eyes. "Guys are so useless."

She pulled her wallet out of her purse and opened it up. She handed me a ticket.

"Kimble Foundation's Third Annual Fundraising Gala presents Our Fading Blue." I looked up at Maysie in confusion.

"I don't get it."

Maysie pointed to the ticket. "That's the gala Vivian has coordinated. It's fancy and a big deal. And what's more important is that Vivian will be there all dressed up and looking fabulous. You need to rent yourself a tux, get your ass to that gala and sweep her off her feet. That, Cole, is your grand gesture."

I grinned. "You are one smart cookie. Jordan is a lucky man."

Maysie grinned back. "And so are you."

I looked down at the ticket, thinking of Vivian, my smile threatening to split my face in half. "Yes I am, Maysie."

STOOD just inside the large room feeling stiff and uncomfortable. Maybe Maysie was wrong. Because this had the makings of a really bad idea.

I had no idea where Vivian even was. And I had to go to the bathroom. But hell if I was going to try to get these pants down. They looked as though they were spray painted on.

I was anxious and ready to get the romance part over with. I didn't know what the hell I was going to say. Something told me tapping Viv on the shoulder and saying "Tada!" wasn't going to cut it.

"You're looking lost," a tiny woman said from beside me. I fidgeted in my tight pants and shiny shoes.

"You could say that," I mumbled, swatting away some glittery shit that was falling from the ceiling.

The lady chuckled. "Do you work for the Kimble Foundation?" she asked.

"What? Uh, no," I said, distracted by the monstrous ice sculpture thing that looked as though it wanted to eat me. Whose idea was it to put that scary shit in the corner?

"I didn't think so. Are you here with someone?" Why was this lady bothering me? Couldn't she tell I wasn't in the mood for chitchat?

"Not exactly," I explained, trying to look around for Vivian. Though I wasn't sure how I could find anything in this huge crowd.

I thought I seen Gracie and Riley but I couldn't be sure. I knew that they had come with Vivian. Maysie had given me the rundown once we were back in Bakersville.

I hid before they could see me. I didn't want them to notify Vivian of my presence before she had a chance to see me herself.

Maybe I should have just called Vivian and gone to see her. Screw the romantic gesture. It had been days since we last spoke. She probably wanted to take my head off by now. But Maysie convinced me going grand was the only way to do this.

My pinched ball sack was cussing Maysie out right now.

"Who are you looking for, darling? Let me help you before you pass out." The little old lady seemed nice enough and she did seem concerned about my overall state at the moment. Not that I blamed her. I was sweating like a pig and fidgeting more than a whore in church.

"I'm looking for Vivian Baily," I told her.

The lady smiled and it made her look ten years younger. Hell, if she was thirty years younger and I wasn't stupidly in love with someone else, I would totally have tapped that.

"Vivian works for me! She's the one that put all this together! Didn't she do an amazing job? I'm Marion, her boss!" the lady said, holding out her hand.

I looked around the room, really taking stock of everything Vivian had done. And Marion was right. The place was incredible. I didn't take a lot of notice of fancy schmancy crap, but even I could appreciate it.

There was so much to Vivian that I didn't know. So much that I planned to spend a lot of time figuring out. I had a future to invest in. . .with Vivian.

I shook Marion's hand. "It looks bitchin'," I agreed.

Marion smirked and I realized my gutter mouth had gotten loose again.

"Shit, I'm sorry."

Marion waved me off.

"No worries. There's nothing wrong with some colorful language. I like to drop an F bomb every now then." I laughed loudly. This Marion broad was pretty cool.

She pointed across the room. "The last time I saw Vivian, she was over there."

I tried to find Vivian but still couldn't see her.

"Okay, I should go find her. Thanks, Marion," I said, granting her my best panty- melting smile.

She may be old, but even Marion wasn't immune to my charms.

"You're welcome. I hope you find her," Marion called out as I started to walk through the crowd.

"Me too," I said under my breath.

I bumped into a waiter, who spilled wine down my front. I tripped over a woman's shoe and stomped on her toe, prompting her to hit me with her purse.

I ate a couple of hors d'oeuvres and drank a few cocktails. And I still couldn't find Vivian.

And just when I was debating the futility of my plan, it was like the climax to every stupid CW drama I had ever watched when there was nothing else on TV. The lights dimmed, the music changed to a slow, romantic number, and suddenly I saw her.

She was standing in the corner, laughing with a man, letting him put his hand on her lower back.

My good mood vanished instantly and I saw murderous, gut-wrenching red.

She was beautiful in a long silver gown that slit up the thighs and plunged down the back. Her hair was pulled to the side and fell in curls over her right shoulder.

She looked down right fucking edible. I wanted to taste the skin on the back of her neck, knowing it would taste like salt and vanilla.

I wanted to hear her laugh, her eyes dancing as she looked up at me. And I wanted those same green eyes on fire when she threw her shoe at my head.

I wanted everything about her.

I slowly and purposefully walked across the expansive room towards her. I clenched my fists as I watched the guy beside her lean down and whisper something in her ear. And then he was walking away and leaving her alone.

Just how I wanted her.

I stopped several feet away and waited for her to see me. And when she did, her eyes widened and her mouth dropped open.

I grinned. "Nobody puts Viv in a corner," I said.

"Did you just quote Dirty Dancing at me?" she asked incredulously.

"Sure did, baby. It is your favorite movie." The music's slow and sexy tempo begged for me to move.

I held my hand out. "Dance with me."

She raised her eyebrows at me defiantly. "I can't. I'm here with someone else," she sniffed, turning her back to me.

I grabbed her hand and put a finger beneath her chin and raised her face so that she had no choice but for her to look at me.

"I don't care who you came with. I only care that you're here with me now. And at the end of the night, I'm going to take you home. With me. Because that's where you belong." I dared her to dispute me. I challenged her with my eyes.

She bit her bottom lip. "What is this, Cole?" she asked, her green eyes peering up at me.

I cupped her face in my hand and kissed her softly on the lips. "This is my grand romantic gesture," I answered.

I pulled her out onto the dance floor.

She sighed, though I couldn't tell if it was from irritation or surrender. But she let me put my arms around her and I wanted to shout in victory when she laid her head on my shoulder.

"You look ridiculous," she muttered.

"I'm not going to disagree with you. Theses pants may destroy my ability to have children. Just sayin'."

She peered down. "Is that a green cummerbund?" she asked.

"You like green. So, I wore green."

I was making a point. That I was paying attention to all of those tiny details. I hope she knew what I was trying to say.

We swayed together and I let myself relax and enjoy holding her.

"How did you get in here?" she asked.

"Maysie gave me her ticket," I explained, pressing her close and leaning down to smell her hair. She felt just right in my arms.

I would never get tired of how perfectly she fit against me.

"That sneak. She didn't say a word," Vivian chuckled.

"I told her not to. Don't get mad at her."

"Since when does Maysie do anything for you?" Vivian asked.

"Since she found out that I love you." I swung her around, her body moving effortlessly with mine.

"Cole. . ." Vivian began but I put my finger over her mouth. She shook her head and I dropped my hand.

"Why haven't I heard from you? I've been going crazy wondering what happened! And when I asked Maysie she said to ask you. What happened?"

"After I fired Jose, we had a great talk with the label. They're still going to put out the album. We're going back on tour but with another group on the label. They still want to promote us. But all of us. As a band."

Vivian grinned. "That's awesome! You really fired Jose?"

I nodded. "Hell yeah I did! That dude was a jerk!"

Vivian smacked my arm. "Why didn't you call me?"

"We stayed in the city for a few days. We got back to a really good place. Things aren't perfect, but I think we're headed in the right direction. I had a lot to sort through with the guys," I explained.

Vivian smacked me again. "You could have sent a text! After what happened over the weekend, after everything you said, and you left me hanging again!" Her voice rose and several people dancing beside us gave us questioning looks.

"I thought coming here would have more of an impact," I tried to tell her.

But she wasn't hearing me. "This is what I'm talking about, Cole! You throw my life into a tailspin and then take off for a few days with no word! That shit has got to stop!"

I pulled back and away from her, feeling my own anger spike to meet hers. "Well if you would stop yelling at me for a second, you'd hear me say you were right! That things are going to change! Not just with the band but with you!" I yelled. Everyone was looking at us.

And when I say everyone, I meant everyone.

Vivian covered her face.

"Why are you here, Cole? Just to ruin my night? To make me crazy all over again? Well congratulations, mission accomplished!" she seethed, squirming out of my arms and trying to push past me.

"No way, Viv. You can't leave me like this. You will hear what I have to say and stop stomping off like a spoiled brat," I hissed in her ear, pulling her back towards me.

She turned around, her face an inch from mine.

"You better make it good, Cole," she warned, her eyes flashing in rage. Just how I liked 'em.

"You and me, we ain't easy. We will never be simple. We will never be the type to sit on the same side of the booth without talking. We will never fall into the complacent boredom life becomes when you stop looking for the exciting and start to accept the mediocre. Because baby, we're anything but mediocre. We're fire. We're the explosion after the pain. You'll destroy me, Viv. And I don't care. Because I want you to. I'd rather be a pile of ashes in your aftermath then whole and complete without you."

I kissed the tip of her adorable nose.

"I've learned that your favorite color is green. That you live off coffee. That your favorite piece of clothing is your Juicy sweatpants held up with safety pins, even though I know you're embarrassed to be seen in them."

I placed my lips beside her ear. "But you still look hot in them," I whispered before pulling back slightly.

Vivian's eyes shimmered and she sniffed loudly. I kissed the wetness that fell down her cheek.

"I know that you sing in the shower and have an old Backstreet Boys CD in your car that you play over and over again. You eat pizza all the time and you also keep a bag of Skittles in your jacket pocket because your sweet tooth is seriously out of control. I also know that you're intelligent, and thoughtful, and entirely too nice to a bonehead like me. I know that you're capable of putting together something like this gala and you do it while looking drop dead gorgeous."

She was starting to ugly cry now. And that was okay. Because she was still beautiful.

"I know that there's no one in this world that I'd rather be with. No one who will put up with my shit the way you do. You put me in my place and you are most definitely not a doormat. You're the strongest person I know."

Vivian closed her eyes, the fight draining out of her.

"I just don't know if I can ever trust you, Cole. And what sort of relationship can we have if we don't have that?"

I held her tight against me, hating myself for ever giving her a single moment of doubt about my feelings for her. I had put this woman through hell and back and she deserved so much better than me.

But I was a selfish fucking bastard and I'd hold onto her with everything I had.

"I'll spend every second of every day building your trust in me, Viv. There's no one I want but you. No one will ever matter to me the way you do. This world could fall apart around me and as long as I had you, I'd be all right."

"Everything between us is drama! It's exhausting!" she argued, even as her mouth began to curl upwards into a grin.

"And you love every second of it," I murmured, leaning down to press my lips against hers.

Vivian shook her head, her eyes were sparking but not in anger. They were heated with something else entirely.

"I'm not sure we'll survive this," she laughed and I couldn't resist kissing her smiling mouth.

"You and me are a roller coaster. So buckle up and get ready for one hell of a ride, sweetheart."

Epilogue
VIVIAN

Six Months Later

"DON'T forget to stand out front. I want to see you when we play," Cole murmured against my mouth.

"I'll be there. Though I don't know how you think you'll see me with that crowd," I said, my ears already ringing from the noise just beyond the door.

We were standing backstage at The National in Richmond, Virginia. Generation Rejects had gotten on another tour. This one opening for a band called Cuban Cadillac. They were pretty cool and they seemed to get on well with the guys.

"I'd be able to find you anywhere, baby," Cole smiled before sucking my bottom lip between his teeth and biting down just hard enough to make me squirm.

"Mmm," I moaned, knowing it would drive him wild. And it did. His eyes gleamed and I had just enough time to brace myself against the wall before he pounced. His arms went around me. One hand slithered up into my hair and gripped tightly while his other grabbed ahold of my ass cheek and gave a vicious squeeze.

His tongue had just pushed its way into my mouth when we

were interrupted.

"Five minutes, Cole!" Mitch yelled and I had to laugh as my boyfriend groaned in frustration.

"That fucker sure knows how to kill the mood," he complained, resting his forehead against mine.

"You can't keep your audience waiting." I told him.

Cole gave my butt a healthy smack and I let out a squeak of alarm.

"We'll finish this later," he promised, giving me one more kiss before walking off toward the stage.

"I love you!" I called out. Cole grabbed the material of his shirt over his heart and closed his eyes, tilting his head back.

"Get's me right here, each and every time you say that, babe," he said, patting his chest. I grinned like the love-sick fool that I was.

Maysie and Jordan were making out in the corner and I laughed as Cole went up behind the drummer and started thrusting his groin against him.

Jordan elbowed Cole in the gut.

At one time that would have led to a knockdown drag-out fight.

But those two had come a long way.

Instead, Cole grabbed his stomach and punched Jordan in the arm. Then the two were smiling at each other.

Garrett and Mitch yelled for both of them and the four members of Generation Rejects ran up to the side of the stage, laughing and talking. It was hard to believe that just six months ago they almost called it quits.

It gave me a renewed sense of faith to know that their friendship had been stronger than their egos.

And sometimes good comes from the bad.

Their decision to stay on with Pirate Records had been the best thing they could have ever done.

Their debut album, Current Static, debuted in the Top 40 and it had been climbing steadily ever since. They were definitely on the rise. Their former manager, Jose, had been dead wrong. Generation Rejects weren't a mid-level band. They were set to go all the way.

"You ready to go out there and watch them?" Gracie asked, looping her arm through mine.

"Shouldn't we wait for Maysie to come with us?" I asked, looking over at our other friend who was chatting with a petite brunette with pretty eyes and a shy smile.

"She looks busy. She'll find us," Gracie said quickly, tugging on my hand. I rolled my eyes.

"You just don't want to want to talk to Sophie," I surmised. Sophie was Mitch's girlfriend and had been since two weeks after Gracie and Mitch slept together.

Sophie was a sweet girl. Cute in an unassuming way. But that didn't matter. Because she was dating the guy Gracie was secretly in love with. And for that reason alone, Gracie would never be comfortable around her.

In fact, she avoided the couple like the plague. Which was difficult when her entire social circle revolved around the band Mitch played in.

I thought it was sad. Mitch and Gracie, in my opinion, were destined to be together. But they were two people who just couldn't get it right.

And even though Mitch seemed crazy about Sophie, I still saw the way his eyes followed Gracie whenever she walked into a room. The dark, smoldering hunger obvious to anyone who chanced a look in his direction.

And I knew my roommate well enough to read the longing on her face as she watched Mitch on stage or the despair when she saw him with his girlfriend.

It was damn depressing.

"It has nothing to do with Sophie," Gracie spat out. Ouch. Touchy subject.

We handed our tickets to the ushers and pushed our way through the crowd. The place was packed, but we had prime seats right at the front. It was my favorite spot to watch a Rejects show. I loved to be part of the crowd, soaking them in as I had done the very first time.

The lights went down and the spotlight came on. Gracie and

I started screaming with the rest of the audience. Soon Garrett, Jordan, Mitch, and finally Cole jogged onto the stage. The roar was deafening.

Jordan did a run on his kit and Garrett played a few chords.

And then Cole took the mic and looked down. His eyes met mine.

I love you, he mouthed to me.

The girls behind me started yelling their heads off.

"Oh my god, did you see what he just said? He told me he loved me!" a girl screeched to her friend.

At one time I would have turned around and smacked her in the face. Or I would have "accidentally" elbowed her in the tit.

But I had grown up a lot in the last six months.

I had matured. I was secure in my relationship.

Cole loved me. He proved it time and time again.

I didn't have to doubt him.

Sure, I still felt the simmering rage of jealousy when I saw him talk to another girl.

Yeah, I had some trust issues I was continuing to work on.

But I knew he was mine. His eyes, his body, his heart was only for me.

I had become a bigger person. And I could stand in a group of women who were fawning all over my boyfriend, screaming their heads off, and saying they loved him, and not lose my mind. Because I knew at the end of the night, when the crowd was gone and the music was over, he would be with me. And only me.

Forever.

I looked over my shoulder and could only shake my head at their ridiculousness. I didn't feel the need to let them know he was mine. I had grown past such silly gestures of ownership.

"I know what'll get his attention," the skank in the barely there skirt yelled to her friend.

She lifted her shirt and showed the world, including my boyfriend, her boobs.

I said I had grown up but that didn't make me a saint. And there were some things that still pushed my buttons.

Skanks flashing Cole their body parts were definitely one of them.

I took Gracie's soda from her hands. "I need to borrow this," I told her. She looked at me confused.

Then I turned around and dumped the contents all over Miss Slutface, drenching her in cola.

"AHH!" she screamed, lowering her shirt back over her now sticky breasts.

"You bitch!" she snarled, trying to lunge at me. Her friends held her back.

I got in her face. "Keep your shirt on you stupid whore! That man up there," I turned and pointed to Cole, who was singing his ass off, his eyes on me, a smile on his face.

"That man is mine. So keep your cheap, inflatable boobs to yourself, or I'll make you choke on them," I threatened.

The girl didn't say anything. She backed down instantly, fixing her shirt so that it covered her more modestly.

I turned back around and Gracie snickered.

"You're insane," she laughed.

I shrugged and looked back to the stage. Cole's eyes were laughing. He had seen the whole thing.

You're mine, I mouthed to him.

The song ended and before the band launched into the next one, Cole leaned down, the mic in his hand and cupped the back of my head from where he stood. I had to go up on my tiptoes to reach him. He kissed me quick and hard. Just how I liked it.

When he stood back up he pointed at me. "That woman right there is my girlfriend. I'm one lucky bastard, right?" he yelled. The audience roared their agreement and I loved it. I ate it up.

I looked over my shoulder and smirked at the still dripping girl behind me. She glared back.

Yep, Cole Brandt was mine.

And even though we were nothing but drama, I wouldn't have it any other way.

There was no alternative.

We were extreme.

We were insatiable.

We were madness.

But we loved each other.
In the end, that was the only thing that mattered.
And if I had to smack a bitch for looking at him, then so be it.
Because that's how we rolled.
One piece of crazy at a time.

The End

Acknowledgments

This goes out to the usual suspects.

For Ian and Gwyn. You are my rock stars.

To my family and friends. I love each and every one of you. You are my biggest fans! And I couldn't do this without you.

Kristy Louise, you know I adore you, I'm running out of ways to tell you!

To my Bad Ass CP ladies, Amy, Stacey, Kelsie, Claire, Brittainy, Tonya. I love you guys hard! I'm so thankful to have such a group of strong, talented and amazing women that I can call my friends! You make this wacky writing world easier to handle!

To my Maniacs, thank you for your enthusiasm and endless support!

To all of the bloggers who have loved and supported me through this insane journey! You are why I'm here! Thank you from the bottom of my heart!

To the readers who read what I write. You guys rock my socks! Thank you for making this dream possible!

And for Matt. Every book from here on out is for you. You were my first champion. The first person to tell me I could do this crazy writing thing. You were my cheerleader, my platonic soul mate, and most importantly my very best friend. And not a day goes by that I don't think about you. You said the A. was for awesome...I'll try to prove you right.

About the Author

A.Meredith Walters is the New York Times and USA Today bestselling Author of Bad Rep, Perfect Regret, Seductive Chaos, the Find You in the Dark series, Reclaiming the Sand, and the upcoming New Adult book, Lead Me Not, to be released by Gallery Books in August, 2014.

Before becoming a full-time writer, she worked as a counselor for troubled and abused children and teens. She currently lives in England with her husband and daughter.

This paperback interior was designed and formatted by

E.M.
TIPPETTS
BOOK DESIGNS

www.emtippettsbookdesigns.com

Artisan interiors for discerning authors and publishers.

Made in the USA
Lexington, KY
28 September 2017